THE
PARA-PSYCHOLOGIST

Ghosts Were People Too

Dr. Eric O'Dierno

Dr. Eric O'Dierno

The Para-Psychologist: Ghosts Were People Too
© 2019 by Eric O'Dierno, PhD -Parapsychology
© 2023, Second Edition by Eric O'Dierno, PhD -Parapsychology

ISBN (9798863386867)

To Jaimie Engle and our brief, poignant, and hilarious conversation about what exactly a *parapsychologist* might do.

PROLOGUE

The moon was full in the night sky, which made it far more difficult to go undetected in the park across from the historic mansion. Nick and his grandfather crouched in the shadows.

The wind blew gently through the Spanish moss that hung down from the branches of the large oak trees around them. Nick's heart was pounding with adrenaline. His mind raced through the plan, preparing him for the battle that would soon be upon them.

Grandpa Joe had leveraged almost all his connections until he found his old army buddy to track down the inhuman creature and this time they had him cornered. Nick could feel the moment upon him. It was now or never.

Soon, Sarah came running over from around the back side of the building that housed the fiend. She huddled down next to them, "The whole building is encircled with holy oil, I even hit the windowsills that I could reach, if anything; it should keep the monster contained… for a while."

Nick turned to his grandfather, "Grandpa Joe, you better stay behind. You'll have to make sure that if that creature gets by us, we can track him down."

Grandpa Joe nodded, "He won't get by me, Nicholas. You have everything you need?"

Nick looked in his satchel and did a quick inventory. "Notebook... check. Two more vials of holy oil... check. Blessed Cross... check." Nick's eyes saw something else, "An old silver... dollar." He looked up at his grandfather and smiled.

"I figured that we needed all the help we could get," Grandpa Joe winked.

Nick smiled at the sentiment.

The three waited for an approaching car to pass and then Nick and Sarah headed toward the back entrance of the mansion. Nick reached over the top of the gate and unlatched the hook. He opened it as slowly as he could, desperately trying to avoid as much noise as possible but the rusty hinges weren't completely cooperating with him.

The beast inside the mansion was a creature of supernatural power, legendary in fact, and as such was stronger, could move faster than they ever could, and even had the power to possess people; an ability that the phantasm had honed over the centuries. It would take everything they knew, every weapon they had, *plus* the element of surprise to defeat him.

They made their way through the back-garden

area and up the staircase to the wrought iron landing outside the door of the servant's kitchen. Nick carefully opened it... clearly, the fiend was not concerned with corporeal enemies, as he hadn't bothered with locking the doors.

They went inside. The air was still, damp and musty in the old mansion. Nick couldn't help but think of all the cliché horror movie scenes he had watched that had settings just like this.

The moonlight was their ally now as it brightly lit the way for them through the windows. They did not need to use their flashlights to make their way toward the large door of the decaying parlor where the beast was residing.

Nick stood on the hinged side of the door, while Sarah stepped across to the handled side.

Their hearts pounded. If this thing escaped tonight, not only would they most likely be killed in the process, but it was certain that it would go on killing unchecked for what could be centuries or eons more.

Nick opened his notebook as he leaned on the wall. A bead of sweat trailed down his forehead. He looked up at Sarah.

She was holding the Blessed Cross in her right hand, which, if the stories were true, would momentarily paralyze the creature once presented to it.

"Timing on this is everything, one mistake..." whispered.

"I know, Nick... I know," she whispered back, pulling out the vial of holy oil from the pocket of her jacket with her left hand.

He had never seen her so determined. She looked at him with fire in her eyes. "Let's finish this." She flicked her thumb upward to open the vial and handed it to Nick.

Nick found the passage from the Necronomicon that he had transcribed into his leather notebook. Then, he quickly and quietly went over the order. "You open the door. I will throw the vial of holy oil down in front of us. I will go in and you enter behind me. You need to hold the mirror over my shoulder facing the demon. That should stun it long enough for us to open the portal. You *must* stay behind me. I'll finish reading the incantation... and we will send this son of a bitch back to his dimension forever."

She nodded.

They were ready.

Nick closed his eyes. He could hear his pulse rushing in his ears over the sounds that the creature was making inside the room.

It was now or never.

Nick turned his head and gave a sharp nod to Sarah.

As planned, Sarah swiftly turned the handle of the door and pushed it.

Nick kicked the door open the rest of the way

and threw down a semi-circle of holy oil across the floor between them and the demon, forming a mystical barrier that blocked the door.

Sarah followed immediately behind, holding the cross over Nick's shoulder as he began to read the passage from his notebook.

The black visage of the beast writhed in agony as Sarah held the cross toward it. The rumors of the artifact's powers were true; the creature could not bear to see the visage and was held in check.

Nick continued reading as the portal began to appear next to the creature. The room filled with cobalt sparks shooting from one object to another and a mystical cyclone began to swirl through the room.

Nick and Sarah held their ground. Once he finished the passage, there was a blinding flash of blue light and an ear shattering boom from the power of the dimensional gateway being ripped open.

Nick closed his eyes in time, but Sarah was caught off guard. She went to shield her eyes from the light, but when she did, the cross got knocked from her hand. It landed on the floor just on the other side of the holy oil barrier... the side that the beast was on.

The moment it hit the floor the creature, no longer a prisoner to the artifact, was able to roam around the room freely. In an instant, he shot from one side to the other. He went to the window and initiated his escape. He looked back over his shoulder with a toothy smirk as he flicked the latch and raised the window up. He began to step out the window when his foot hit the holy oil barrier that Sarah had placed earlier.

The beast winced in pain the moment his foot touched the oil. It caught fire. Enraged, the fiend wheeled around on his assailants, stamping out the flames and letting out a horrifying roar of frustration.

Nick knew that the portal would only stay open for a little while, if they could not get the creature into it before it closed, they would most certainly be his latest, but not his last, victims.

The unholy creature slithered back and forth around the room avoiding the power of the dimensional gateway. It knew that if they crossed over the barrier of the holy oil, he could easily overpower them. He hissed, "I have a proposition for you. Surrender to me now and I will make your deaths quick, perhaps… even painless. How do you feel about my snapping your necks?"

Sarah slowly slipped down behind Nick trying to reach for the cross. She cautiously stretched her hand out toward it while keeping an eye on the beast.

The creature shot up to them and grabbed Sarah by the wrist as her hand crossed the line of holy oil to grab it. He yanked her toward him. "A noble attempt at deception, chippy," he jeered at her as he kicked the crucifix across the floor.

Nick tried to reach for her.

"Nick, no!" Sarah shouted, knowing that it could

easily slaughter them both if he crossed the holy oil.

The creature stood in front Nick, his hand around Sarah's neck. His confidence was growing. "No... perhaps I should allow you to run... I do love the thrill of the chase... it is... delicious," he taunted as his black tongue slowly traced up the side of Sarah's face.

"If you hurt her, I swear, I... swear." Nick could smell the stench of death and rot wafting from the beast's putrid garments. It was as if the hundreds, if not thousands of souls that the creature had taken over the years were festering within him. "You will not *win* this," he continued defiantly, "You will not escape."

The demon pointed at the cross on the other side of the room, his hand tightened around Sarah's neck as her body started to spasm from his stranglehold. He stared directly into Nick's eyes. "I would thoroughly love to observe how you plan to make that protestation come to fruition," he grinned secure of an inevitable victory.

Sarah tried valiantly to fight against the creature's hold, punching and scratching at its arm, but it was futile. Her body flinched again as she gasped for air.

The demon grinned and tightened its grip even more.

Nick's heart raced and he shook with anger, dread, and fear. It was overwhelming. Then suddenly from behind him, he heard a steady beeping.

His focus on the situation waned as the beeping continued.

In fact, everyone's focus was now on the beeping, even the creature, who turned his head to try to find it, and loosened his grip on Sarah's throat.

She dropped to the floor.

They were now all turned toward the door as they could hear it getting louder.

Nick's eyes shot open, and he found himself in his bed. He had awakened from another nightmare, the third one this month, about an old mansion and the creature that resided in it. His heart was still pounding as he flung the covers off and sat at the edge of his bed. He blinked and rubbed the sleep out of his eyes as the sun shone through the window and beads of sweat dripped down his forehead.

The nightmares were so vivid, so *real*. He had so many questions. Where was this old mansion? Who or what was that thing, why were they about to fight to the death? Why on earth was Grandpa Joe there with him? And who the hell was this woman, Sarah?

Nick reached into the top drawer of his nightstand and pulled out a small, well-worn cardboard box. Opening it, he saw multiple odds and ends from his past: an old army man, a few bottle caps, a yo-yo, and the old silver dollar that his Grandpa Joe had given him when he was a child. He held it up and stared at it for a moment, his mind awash in memories. Then he grabbed his wallet and put the old coin into the inside pocket.

CHAPTER ONE

It was a gorgeous morning in Savannah, the sky was a near perfect azure blue. Nick hopped off his bike, took off his helmet, and locked both to the metal pipe that came out of the side of the building. It was going to be another standard day at the office: one early appointment, then working on the statistics sheets for the hospital and another set for the police department, lunch, more statistics, another client, then off to the martini bar on Bull Street to meet Wayne and the guys for a Moon Pie Martini. After that maybe ordering Chinese take-out on the way home, then notes, some housework, emails, and finally catching up on some shows.

He smiled as he walked up the stoop and saw the gold foil lettering on the door. "Dr. Nicholas J. Williams." He had made it, he thought to himself as he opened the door.

"Good morning, Dr. Williams, your 10:00am appointment called and is running behind," his receptionist informed him as he was walking into his practice.

Nick replied while taking off his jacket and heading toward his office, "Really? Ms. Krabbe with her fear of commitment and relationship anxiety is late? Who would have thought it?" he joked. "Thank you, Lisa, I will head upstairs, let me know when she arrives."

Lisa nodded, "Of course, Doctor Williams."

He took a few more steps, stopped and turned. He reached into the pocket of the jacket that he had just thrown over his arm and pulled out a small gift box. "Happy Birthday, Ms. Davidson."

Lisa was delighted that her boss remembered her birthday. But in all honesty, she was not surprised at all, it was who he was. She accepted the gift cheerfully.

"Go ahead, open it!" Nick urged.

Lisa smiled, placed the box on her desk, and carefully pulled off the ribbons that held it together. Her eyes opened wider as the contents of the small box were revealed.

"Oh Goodness, Dr. Williams... wow..." She laughed awkwardly as she reached into the box and pulled out a bumper sticker that said, "I love the ballet and I vote."

"I don't know what to say... but I have one of these... already." She said pointing toward her car in the driveway. Sadly, she was beginning to think that her positive judgement about her boss was a bit misplaced.

"Keep looking, there's more," Nick continued.

"Oh, really" she said reaching into the bottom of the box.

This time her eyes widened with true delight and surprise, "Two box tickets to Swan Lake?" Lisa's excitement couldn't be hidden. "That is so very generous!"

Nick smiled, tapped his knuckle against the wooden desk and said, "I hoped that you would like it. Oh, the bumper sticker is to replace the old one on your car... you can barely see the little ballerina dancing anymore!"

Lisa chuckled softly.

"Now you and Robert have a great time. They are for this coming Saturday. I have a reservation for you set up at The Olde Pink House in the Vault at five, which should give you plenty of time to make the curtain at seven-thirty... dinner is on me, enjoy!"

Lisa held the tickets close to her chest. "We will, Dr. Williams. We will."

"Excellent!" Nick waved as he continued to the elevator. He cranked the large brass lever to the third floor and just before shutting the gate, he stuck his head out and called back to her, "Have a great time! I don't know how I could have gotten this practice off the ground without all your help!"

Her positive judgements about Nick had been reaffirmed. Lisa laughed. She was very lucky to have landed a job that fit her schedule so well so close to where her family lived; and even luckier to have an employer as kind and generous as Dr. Williams.

She and Robert were saving everything they could for the wedding next spring, and this job was a huge help. The fact that she did not have to pay for parking alone was a lifesaver.

If only she had a little sister that was single for Nick, she found herself thinking often... even if he *was* one of those northern *Yankees*. She giggled and instantly started dialing the phone to tell her fiancé the news. She was sure that he would be delighted. They had talked about dining at The Olde Pink House for some time; it would be a night to remember.

The elevator stopped on the third floor and Nick opened the gate, took out his keys, and walked to his Office. He opened the door and clicked on the lights. The old brownstone still had all the antique light fixtures and switches. The ones that you still had to push a button to turn on and off and he thought that was just spectacular... in fact, he occasionally muttered it to himself as he turned the light switches on. He hung his coat on the tall wooden coat rack inside the door.

Nick walked over to the large bay window, opened the curtains, and marveled at the historic beauty of his new hometown. The sun was shining brightly, the locals were walking their dogs, and the tourists were heading toward Forsythe Fountain to take their obligatory pictures with the famous landmark.

He turned and placed his hand on the old telescope to the left of the window. "Dr. Nicholas J. Williams," he thought to himself as a smile came over him. He couldn't help but feel a bit of pride.

"Nick," he said to himself, "Life could not be going better!"

But it was time for work, and Ms. Krabbe was a client that needed his aid. He headed over to his desk and began to go over files and take notes. He took out the old silver dollar that Grandpa Joe gave him and fidgeted with it in his right hand as he wrote. It wasn't long before Lisa would buzz him.

"Dr. Williams, your 10:00am has arrived."

Nick looked at the clock. It was 10:18am. He laughed to himself and hit the reply button, "Yes, Lisa, thank you. Please make sure that Ms. Krabbe has some sweet tea, and I will be right down."

And with that, Nick's workday began. It was a rather plain day, no surprises and before he even knew it, it was five o'clock. Nick typed the rest of his notes in his laptop and locked his office. He closed the elevator gates and cranked the brass lever over to the first-floor notch.

"You have a great birthday, Ms. Davidson," Nick

said opening the gate from the elevator and walking toward the door.

Lisa replied, "Yes, thank you, Doctor Williams, ride safe."

Nick tapped the old wooden door with his knuckle for luck. "Always do," he said as he walked out to unlock his bike, strap on his helmet, and ride off.

It wasn't a long bike ride to the rest of the historic parts of town, but tourists were tourists, so you always had to be careful. He made his way down Drayton Street, heading toward Broughton.

Once he hit Broughton, he would take a left to Bull Street and soon he would meet Wayne, Bryon, and Kevin for a quick one (or two) at happy hour.

Wayne was a relatively new member of the Savannah police force with three years under his belt coming from the big city of Atlanta, but he was by no means a rookie, in fact he was training for the detective's exam coming up in a few months.

Nick was helping him with some of the psychological terms and identifiers to classify patterns in criminal behavior. Bryon and Kevin worked at the hospital. Bryon in billing and coding. Kevin in physical therapy.

It really had been a gorgeous day. Locals were out walking their dogs, the SCAD students were milling around their seemingly endless campus, and of course the tourists were taking full advantage of the Historic

District's open container policy of adult beverages or "taking a traveler" as the locals called it.

Suddenly, at the corner of Broughton and Bull a blue Volkswagen ran the light. It screeched to a halt, but it wasn't in time. It smashed into the front tire of his bike, bending his front wheel to the right, smashing his left knee against the car's fender, and catapulting him through the air over the hood.

Every moment of the incident moved in slow motion. He could hear people screaming. He felt his body hurtling forward. He got a fleeting look into the windshield of the car and saw the horrified look on the driver.

The pain in his left knee was excruciating; he had felt his kneecap crash against the car, he knew that it was broken. He tried to pull himself into a position to prepare for the impact of the pavement that was soon to follow, but it was too late.

The landing was brutal, and his body twisted into a heap. His right shoulder and back took the worst of it. The helmet he was wearing ground against the road making dull, hollow thuds as it skidded across the hot Savannah pavement.

He felt and heard the snapping of bone, more explosions of pain shot through him, and he could taste the blood in his mouth from what had to be cracked or broken ribs hitting his lungs as his body finally came to a stop. There were flashes of light, muffled noises and more screaming, and he was barely able to move.

Hearing the commotion outside the martini bar, Wayne Miller leapt to the door. He ran through the gathering crowds toward the accident which was barely a block away.

Reaching into his pocket, he pulled out his phone. It was then that he saw the mangled bike against the blue car. He recognized it immediately... it was Nick's. His heart sank as he approached the scene and kneeled over his friend. "Nick, it's Wayne, can you hear me? Stay calm. Don't move. Try to stay awake, ok?"

Wayne dialed Nine-One-One, "This is Officer Wayne Miller, Badge Number Three Hundred Forty-Two, reporting a Vehicle versus Bicyclist collision on the corner of Broughton and Bull... you've got the call already... good, they are on the way... More information... Life threatening injuries to the cyclist. Male, Twenty-Eight, looks like multiple broken bones and he is bleeding and losing consciousness fast."

Nick groaned and tried to focus his eyes on his buddy. He went to speak, but the moment he tried, the pain in his chest was too much and he started coughing.

"Tell them to hurry... tell them the injured party is Doctor Nicholas Williams."

He put the phone down next to his barely conscious friend and took off his windbreaker to put over him. "Try to stay awake, man. Help is on the way. They will be here soon," he said draping the coat around

Nick.

Nick couldn't respond; he wanted to but couldn't. His eyes could no longer stay open.

The driver of the Volkswagen had gotten out of her car in a panic and ran over to them. "I looked down for a second! I'm so sorry! It was just a second! Oh, my God!" she sobbed as she stood over them.

The heat of the pavement radiated through Nick's blood-soaked clothes as a light rain began to fall and an irony weighed upon him as everything was becoming a blur; through the fog of his mind, he thought to himself, "Life could not be going better."

Then everything went black.

CHAPTER TWO

Young Nicholas Williams was a kind-hearted boy and a very quick study. So much so that with the help of his Grandpa Joe, he had converted part of his basement into an animal hospital to nurse the injured animals (chipmunks, birds, turtles, and other small creatures) that they would find in the neighborhood back to health. Those that were not able to be nursed back to health, he and Grandpa Joe made sure were given a proper burial in the large field behind the house.

"All creatures, great and small, have a nobility and purpose, Nicholas. Never forget that... *even* those whose purpose is yet to be understood," Grandpa Joe would say.

At school, along with being at the head of his class, Nick was the child that everyone just "got along with." He had an open ear and caring heart for those who needed to talk at the lunch table, and he was the first to come to the aid of a classmate that needed help carrying their books or class project.

His was a happy life with a hardworking, middle class, mother and father. Supper was on the table promptly at 6:00pm... and there was always a spot reserved for his best friend, Grandpa Joe, his dad's father, who lived just a few doors down the hill.

The Williams House was an old Victorian era house on the edge of the small farming community of East Troy, Wisconsin. Of course, there were factories there as well, Nick's father, Rory, worked at one but the population of the town was clear... the cows outnumbered the people forty to one.

Grandpa Joe would say, "It's a damned shame that cows don't have the right to vote in this town! Cows are matter of fact, no nonsense... we sure wouldn't have to put up with so many jackasses in public office."

Grandpa Joe was never shy about his opinion on the ways of the world.

Nick's mother, Fran, kept the house in show room condition. After all, they had a *very* extended family, and anyone could drop in to visit. Especially now with Grandpa Joe getting older and the recent passing of Grandma May, relatives dropped by at least three or four times a month. Sometimes they would stay for a weekend, but mostly, it was just for a quick visit. Either way, Fran made sure that the house always felt like home. It was incredible considering that she had to be to work at 4:00 am, Monday through Friday at Lois's

Bakery, home of "The Best Buns in Town Since 1955."

As gratifying as nursing the little animals back to health with Grandpa Joe was, Nick had the most fun when they would go into Grandpa Joe's attic.

On cloudy or rainy nights, Grandpa Joe would turn on a small reading lamp, sit in an old rocking chair and read from Moby Dick. Nick was enthralled by the story and Grandpa Joe's heavy baritone voice was great for narration. Grandpa Joe always told Nick that he wished he could find his father's copy, Nick's Great Grandfather's, but it was sold a long time ago during the depression. Just like Grandpa Joe had done, his father had written his name on the inside cover, "This book belongs to Tobias Williams of East Troy, Wisconsin." He hoped one day that he would run across it at a yard sale, so he could bring it back to the family.

But when the nights were clear, that's when they had the best time! They would use Grandpa Joe's antique telescope and do some star gazing. Nick loved those nights most of all.

He loved the history that was tucked away in the old dusty suitcases and trunks; Grandpa Joe's attic was a museum unto itself.

The telescope was always at his attic window, and they made sure that it was always cleaned and polished after every use. That also meant making sure that the purple felt cover went over the top of it to make sure it stayed clean for their next adventure into the stars.

One night late in the summer after dinner, Nick and his grandfather walked back to his Grandpa Joe's house to do some star gazing. The sky was unusually clear that evening and Grandpa Joe was a little more talkative than he normally was. Grandpa Joe asked about Nick's schooling, his dreams, and ambitions.

Nick replied, "Grandpa Joe, I told you what my grades were."

Nick's grandfather smiled with pride, "I know Nicholas, I just wanted to hear it again. I don't want you to forget and cast aside the talents you have been given."

"I know. I know," Nick was always uneasy drawing attention to himself; he was far more comfortable talking to others about themselves... he learned more about them that way. Nick continued, "As for the future... I'm not sure, Grandpa, I do like helping people find answers, maybe I'll be a lawyer or a doctor, like a psychiatrist."

Grandpa Joe bristled a little bit. "Well, if you ask me, there are already too many lawyers... but a doctor, even a shrink, that would be something! I can see you as a doctor! Dr. Nicholas J. Williams! I like the sound of that. I like the sound of that indeed! It is always good for a young man to have dreams and ambitions," he continued, "Stay focused and you can do anything you put your mind and heart into!"

Grandpa Joe reached into his wallet and pulled

out a silver dollar. He held it up so that Nick could see the face of the coin, "You see this, Nicholas? This was the first dollar that I ever earned. I still have it."

Nick leaned forward to get a better look. It was from 1934 and had the head of what looked like the Statue of Liberty on it.

"That there is a genuine 1934 Peace dollar. I promised myself that I would never lose it... and I am giving it to you." With that Grandpa Joe reached out and placed the heavy coin in Nick's outstretched hand.

The coin was cold to the touch. Nick had never seen anything like it.

"I was nine years old in 1942 when old Ben Featherstone gave me that for mowing his property, feeding his chickens, and doing chores for a whole week."

"You only got a dollar for a whole week of work?" Nick asked aghast.

"And I was lucky to get that much! Times were different back then. Times were tougher and things were leaner... we had just entered World War Two, but I tell you, Nicholas... that coin was the most beautiful thing I had ever laid my eyes on... until I met your grandmother, of course," he smirked as he ruffled the hair on the top of Nick's head. "Not because I loved the money, Nicholas, but because of what it represented. Hard work. Honest work. My effort and sweat. I knew how tough times were and I had made my mind up to do my part to help the family get through it... and I did. I worked the entire summer at Ben Featherstone's; I earned enough to cover groceries for the whole family."

"But Grandpa, you aren't keeping your promise. You said that use would never lose it," Nick said trying to hand back the coin.

Grandpa Joe stopped him, put up his large, weathered hands and closed Nick's hand around the coin. "I'm not losing it, Nicholas. I'm entrusting it to you. You hold on to that dollar there and I will always be with you."

With that, Nick smiled; put the coin in the shirt pocket over his heart. The idea of always having Grandpa Joe around was comforting.

———————

The next morning was a Saturday; Nick got up and proceeded to go through his normal Saturday routine. He put on his slippers and walked down into the basement hospital to check on the few animals that he was tending.

The robin flittered about in its cage, there was no doubt, the wing was looking much better. Nick carefully opened an old butter container full of dirt and picked out a worm. "Here you go," Nick said as he dropped the worm into the cage. "Let's make sure you have plenty of water too," he said pouring water into the little cup in the cage.

"And don't worry, see... I have been feeding your little ones right here," Nick continued as he opened the cage next to the mother robin and used an eye dropper to feed the three little hatchlings still in their nest, cheeping and begging for food. He adjusted the heat lamp to make sure it wasn't too warm for them as well. "Pretty soon, everything will be back to normal, and you will be one big happy family."

Nick went back up into the kitchen and poured himself a glass of milk and a bowl of cereal – no milk was to go into the cereal itself...it just got in the way of cartoon watching. Dry cereal was easy to grab a few pieces at a time and pop them in his mouth, plus it had the added benefit of never getting soggy. His mom hated it when he did it, but she figured that if that was his worst vice, she could live with it.

With his cereal bowl in one hand and his milk in the other, he sat down in the recliner in front of the television, turned the volume down just low enough so that it didn't wake his mom and dad, and began watching the cartoony goodness that was Saturday Morning television.

Right when the coyote was just about to drop the anvil on the road runner, the phone rang. He heard his mother's muffled voice talking to his father. There was a commotion and his dad burst out of the bedroom door, running down the stairs while throwing on his clothes. He unlocked the door and ran down the street toward Grandpa Joe's house.

Nick sat stunned. What was happening?

He heard his mother coming down the steps. She paused only for a moment as she reached the bottom and gave a concerned look to Nick.

He felt a wave of fear wash over him and his stomach sank. Something was clearly wrong. He sat up in the recliner.

She continued into the kitchen and picked up the phone. She began dialing. Hello, Janet, it's Fran..." she looked over at Nick and turned away, Nick was unable to hear the rest of what she was saying.

Nick got up and slowly walked toward his mother, when he heard the sirens coming down the street. That's when he realized something was wrong with Grandpa Joe!

His world began to spin as a panic came over him, he turned, and started running toward the door. But as he reached it, he felt his mother's firm hand on his shoulder, and she turned him toward her.

"Nick, there is nothing we can do for now. Your father is there. The paramedics are there."

Tears welled up in his eyes, "What happened? What's happened to Grandpa Joe?"

"Grandpa Joe had a heart attack."

The sinking feeling in his stomach now took second behind his heart pounding, "Is he... is he..."

"No, Mr. Welch found him on his front porch and

got help, he is in bad shape, but he is alive, that's what the paramedics are there to help with... your dad is there for him too. We will get dressed and meet them at the hospital. Now go upstairs and make yourself ready. We will leave as soon as possible." She ushered Nick up the stairs and started dialing the phone again to call more relatives that lived in the area.

The rest of the morning was a blur of activity. There were times it seemed like everything was moving in slow motion and at other times it was too busy to keep up. The next thing he knew, he was standing outside a curtained off section of an emergency room, holding his mom's hand and watching his father walking toward them, "Dr. Snelling said we can go back and see him now. He is stable, but still in critical condition."

Nick's heart was in his throat and his mouth got dry. He could smell the antiseptic that just seemed to hang in the air. Together with his parents, Nick walked up next to his grandfather's hospital bed.

The machines and tubes were everywhere. Oddly, it reassured him to see all the technology there to help his grandfather. This was a real hospital... not at all like his basement.

Grandpa Joe slowly opened his eyes and looked and his family around him. He saw the fear in Fran's face, he noticed the concern behind Rory's eyes... and he saw the wonder in Nick as he marveled at the different machines in the room. "They got some pretty fancy equipment here, don't they Nicholas?"

Nick was startled by the weakness behind the words coming from Grandpa Joe. "Yes, sir. Fancy."

"Well, they damned well should be, not only are they keeping me alive, but they are costing me a fortune!" he teased.

Nick's parents laughed softly and shook their heads. Even in his weakened condition, Grandpa Joe couldn't resist making a statement.

"Come here, Nicholas," Grandpa Joe said reaching out with his right hand.

Nick came to him and put his hand in his grandfather's.

Grandpa Joe held Nick's hand with a gentle firmness. "Don't be scared. This is nothing; I'll be home before you know it. In the meantime, I need you to take care of these two," he said motioning to Nick's parents. "Between you and me, they worry far too much."

"Yes, sir," Nick replied obediently.

"Don't lose focus, Nicholas. One day, if you keep your heart in it, you can be a doctor. Doctor Nicholas J. Williams," his grandfather said as his grasp on Nick's hand became slowly weaker. "Yes, sir... I do like the sound of... that... in... deed..."

His grandfather's eyes closed as the machines' alarms started going off in the room. The heart monitor was no longer showing angular rhythmic blips but a flat line.

Almost instantly, nurses and doctors rushed into the room, some yelling, "Code Blue! Code Blue!" One nurse grabbed Nick and his mother and escorted them out of the room. His father was right behind.

The world began to spin again, as it did earlier. Surely, Grandpa Joe would be ok. He had to be.

Nick and his family stood out in the lobby of the emergency room and waited; after what seemed an eternity, the doctor came out and told the family the news. There was nothing left that they could do... Grandpa Joe was gone.

Grandpa Joe's last words kept circling in Nick's mind over the blur of the next week, Doctor Nicholas J. Williams... Yes, sir... I do like the sound of... that... in... deed."

Before he could even catch his breath, it seemed, the funeral service was happening, then over, and the vault holding the casket of his best friend was being lowered into the ground.

Nick looked at the double headstone. "Here lies Mavis Williams, Beloved Wife and Dearest Friend," he then looked over to the right and read "Joseph Williams, Veteran and Loving Husband." The dates weren't yet engraved on Grandpa Joe's side. Nick remembered hearing something about them being done soon when his father was talking to the funeral director.

Nick was jolted out of his reflections by the

sounds of men throwing the dirt onto the vault; filling in the ground that would be Grandpa Joe's final resting place. Soon, the family was back in the car, driving to the house where the rest of the town and relatives were gathering.

It wasn't long after the gathering that the family got together to start getting Grandpa Joe's house ready to sell. The family memories that were kept in the attic went back decades. They decided that the best thing to do was to place it in storage in Fran & Rory's basement until more of the family could help decide on what was going to happen with the items... that meant that the animal hospital had to go. This was hard for Nick, but he understood.

Nick made sure that the robins were in good condition to move outside and took great care in putting the nest back in the high bushes where he and Grandpa Joe found it. As he was walking away from the nest, he could have sworn he heard his grandfather voice his approval, "Well done, Nicholas." He turned but no one was there. He shrugged and chalked it up to wishful thinking.

In the meantime, the table was still set every night at six, and every night there was a setting for Grandpa Joe. Nick insisted on it.

———————

The holidays came about faster than usual that

year and Nick's parents were concerned about him. Sure, his grades were fine, he still did his normal routine, but there were minor things here and there that he seemed to be holding on to a little too long... like insisting on setting a spot at the table for Grandpa Joe. So, after two months, just before Thanksgiving, Nick's mom and dad sat him down and had a long talk with him. It was time for closure. Grandpa Joe's place would no longer be set.

Nick understood that you shouldn't hold on to everything from the past and perhaps it was time to move forward.

But that evening, Nick remembered the silver dollar and took it from his top drawer and placed it in his Velcro wallet. That way, he knew that Grandpa Joe was still with him. This made him smile.

At Christmas, Nick came down the stairs to see something that he thought he ever would again. There, all polished with a large red bow tied around the stand, was the old telescope. It had a handwritten tag that said, "To: Nicholas. From: Grandpa Joe." Nick recognized the handwriting instantly as his grandfather's and there was another smaller present wrapped on the tray of the telescope. Nick opened it carefully and read the card on top of the old book.

"Never let your passions exceed your common sense, Nicholas. Remember Ahab." Nick looked at the worn cover; he held it close. His eyes welled up with tears of fondness as he read to himself, "Moby Dick."

The telescope and book held so many memories for Nick. He loved them because they reminded him of Grandpa Joe. Oh, he kept the silver dollar in the inside pocket of his wallet, and it was something that he would obviously see and look at every day. But the book and telescope represented years of memories, and he cherished them.

He lovingly placed the telescope next to his bedroom window that faced in the same direction as his grandfather's attic window and that's where it stayed throughout his high school and college years. Every chance he got, he would look through it and keep it clean; he remembered fondly all the conversations that they used to have.

The book was always placed on his nightstand. At times, he even thought that he felt Grandpa Joe with him when he would read it. He reluctantly had given up his animal hospital but the telescope and Moby Dick... those were his and he would never lose them.

———————

Years passed and even when he moved out to go to Graduate School, the telescope and book stayed put, he did not want to take the chance of one of his roommates messing with them or worse. When Nicholas became "Clinical Psychologist, Dr. Nicholas J. Williams, PhD," he decided that he finally had a safe place to keep them. They would be reminders of the past and a way to symbolize looking toward the future. He placed them in his Office on the third floor of his practice facing the park.

Nick had opened his practice in historic Savannah, Georgia and found an incredible old brownstone that allowed him to look over Forsythe Park and have an unimpeded view of the night sky.

It was a fixer upper, but it actually had a lift elevator in it that *worked* which allowed him to have his office on the top floor, a file room and a meeting room on the second floor that he used to go over his findings and studies with his corporate clients and a fantastic, quiet little lounge room that he was able to use to meet his individual clients on the first floor without much fuss.

What was even better, was that in a mere fifteen minutes, he could ride his bike to work every day. Not only was it great exercise, but it allowed him to save money on gas.

With his keen eye for the practical, his discerning statistical analysis, gentle nature, open heart, and fantastic listening skills, Nick's practice was an instant success. He had landed contracts with the local hospital, police department, and a couple of manufacturing companies that wanted to improve the morale of their workforce within a few days of his arriving in town *and* it still allowed him to take on a few individual clients during the week as well.

Now, only in his mid-twenties, he was having the time of his life. He was a young single man in a vibrant, historically and culturally rich city. He had a good group of local friends, a fantastic apartment in the heart of town, and pretty much every weekend to do whatever he pleased. He thought to himself, "Life could not be going better."

CHAPTER THREE

The morning air was slightly chilly; there was a sparkling opal-blue hue in the air from the morning fog, giving the world a magical shimmering look to it. Nick hopped off his bike, removed his helmet, and locked both to the metal pipe that came off the side of the building.

It would be another standard day at the office: one early appointment, then working on the statistics sheets for the hospital and another set for the police department, lunch, more statistics, another client, then probably off to the martini bar on Bull Street with Wayne and the guys for an Elvis Martini, then ordering Chinese on the way home, notes, some housework, emails, and finally catching up on some shows.

He smiled as he walked up the stoop and saw the foil lettering on the door. "Dr. Nicholas J. Williams." He had made it, he thought to himself as he reached for the door handle of his office.

"Good Morning, Dr. Williams, your 10:00am

appointment called and is running behind," his receptionist informed him as he was walking into his practice.

Nick replied while taking off his jacket and heading toward his office, "Really? Ms. Krabbe with her fear of commitment and relationship anxiety is late? Who would have thought it?" he joked. "Thank you, Lisa, I will head upstairs, let me know when she arrives."

Lisa nodded, "Of course, Doctor Williams." He took a few more steps, stopped and turned. "By the way… is this normal around here? This fog?" He asked, pointing around to the sparkling opal-blue hue outside.

Lisa nodded. "Oh yes, Dr. Williams. Morning fogs are pretty normal around these parts."

Nick thought about it for a moment and accepted her answer, he smiled, "Well, you must know… you're the local… I'm just a *Yankee*," Nick said as he reached into the pocket of the jacket that he had just thrown over his arm and pulled out a small gift box. "Happy Birthday, Ms. Davidson."

Lisa was delighted that her boss remembered her birthday. But in all honesty, she was not surprised at all, it was who he was. She accepted the gift cheerfully.

"Go ahead, open it!" Nick urged.

Lisa smiled, placed the box on her desk and carefully pulled off the ribbons that held the box together. Her eyes opened wider as the contents of the small box were revealed.

"Oh Goodness, Dr. Williams... wow..." She laughed a little awkwardly as she reached into the box and pulled out a bumper sticker that said, "I love the ballet and I vote."

"I don't know what to say... but I have one of these... already." She said pointing toward her car in the driveway. Plus, she was beginning to think that her judgement was a bit misplaced.

"Keep looking, there's more," Nick continued.

"Oh, really" she said reaching into the bottom of the box.

This time her eyes widened with true delight and surprise, "Two tickets to the ballet?" Her excitement couldn't be hidden. "That is so very generous!"

Nick smiled, tapped his knuckle against the wooden desk and said, "I hoped that you would like it. Oh, and the bumper sticker is to replace the old one on your car... you can barely see the little ballerina dancing anymore!"

Lisa chuckled softly.

"Now you and Robert have a great time. They are for this coming Saturday. Oh, and I have a reservation for you set up at The Olde Pink House in the Vault at 5:00pm... dinner is on me, enjoy!"

Lisa held the tickets close to her chest. "We will, Dr. Williams. We will."

"Excellent!" Nick waved as he continued to the elevator. He cranked the large brass lever to the third floor and just before shutting the gate, he stuck his head out and called back to her, "Have a great time! I don't know how I could have gotten this practice off the ground without all of your help!"

The elevator stopped on the third floor and Nick opened the gate, took out his keys and walked to his Private Study. He opened the door and clicked on the lights. He loved all the history in his building, he swore that he could feel it around him sometimes. He hung his coat on the tall wooden coat rack inside the door.

Nick noticed that the room seemed a little cold, so he figured that he should open the curtains and let the sunlight in.

He walked over to the large bay window, opened the curtains and marveled at the historic beauty of his new hometown. The sun was up there somewhere above the fog, but it couldn't be seen. It seemed odd that it gave everything and everyone below a shimmering opal blue glow and now that he looked around, it was doing the same inside as well. He stared out the window and placed his hand on the old telescope.

"Still take time to star gaze?" a deep familiar voice said behind him.

Nick twisted around quickly. "What's that? Who's there?" But he was speaking to an empty room.

He looked around again. There was definitely no one else in the room. He shook it off, headed over to his desk and began to go over files and take notes.

"You better not just have her here to collect dust," the voice said again.

Nick looked up toward the bay window and the telescope. He blinked in incredulity. He could have sworn that he saw the figure Grandpa Joe standing there in the same opal blue shimmer as everything else.

Nick rubbed his eyes and muttered, "Nick, you have to stop eating leftover Chinese food at 4:00 am."

He opened his eyes and looked again.

There was nothing that wasn't supposed to be there... just the bay window and the old brass telescope, like they should be.

Nick shrugged, turned to get back to work, and began fidgeting with the old silver dollar that Grandpa Joe gave him all those years ago.

"This doesn't seem a little... familiar to you, Nicholas?" the voice returned.

Nick froze. He knew what he had just heard. It hit him like a thunderbolt. There was only one person who ever called him Nicholas. He turned again toward the old telescope and this time could clearly see Grandpa Joe standing there beaming with pride.

Nick's mouth opened to say something, but nothing came out. He was dreaming, he thought. He had to be dreaming.

"You aren't dreaming, Nicholas... it is much more serious than that... you are dying," his grandfather said in his caring, yet matter of fact way.

Nick stood up from his desk defiantly. "What are you talking about? I'm standing right here in my office!"

"Look around, Nicholas. Isn't there something... different?"

"Of course not. I'm in my office. I have a client coming in at any moment."

His grandfather nodded, "And?"

Nick could feel himself getting exasperated, "I rode my bike in this morning, like I always... do." Nick felt that familiar sinking feeling in his stomach as he started to realize what had happened. "I rode my bike in but..."

"... but..." Grandpa Joe interrupted knowingly.

Nick's eyes widened as the events of the crash flashed through his mind. The pain, the sounds, the images were all coming back to him now. "The accident," he stammered.

Grandpa Joe could see how shaken Nick was and started walking toward him. "It's ok. It's not your time. Keep fighting."

Nick stood stunned, "What?"

"Can you hear me, Nicholas?" his grandfather continued, "It's not your time and you need to fight. You have yet to understand your purpose. I am going to help you with that, but you *must* keep fighting."

"What?" Nick asked as the room around him started to lose its shimmering blue hue and fade into darkness.

His grandfather smiled and nodded his head, "Keep fighting. We will chat soon."

"What?" Nick asked again in vain as the blackness enveloped the room.

"Can you hear me, Doctor Williams?" he heard the nurse's voice say softly.

"What?" Nick asked weakly as his eyes slowly blinked. He couldn't see clearly; he could barely keep his eyes open. Through the dull hum, beeps and clicking of medical equipment, he could only momentarily hold on to consciousness.

As he was slipping away, he heard her continue, "Doctor Williams, you've just come out of surgery. You are lucky to be alive. But you kept fighting. The worst is over. Rest for now."

———————

Nick sat in his hospital bed. It had been three weeks since the accident. He had only been completely conscious the last few days after being awakened from the medically induced coma. He was very lucky. The worst was behind him. According to his doctors, he may only come away with a slight limp from his shattered patella. But he was young and in good shape, so that odds were that it was possible for him to fully recover. He would have to walk with a cane for a while, but if he kept up with his therapy, he would more than likely make a full recovery.

The nurse walked in with his breakfast and to check his vitals. "How are we feeling today?"

Nick smiled and gave her a thumbs up, "Good. Ready to go as soon as they let me!"

She laughed and set his tray on his bedside table, "Well, you were in an induced coma for a while to keep your internal organs stabilized after the amount of surgery needed; actually, four surgeries to mend internal lacerations and damage. Your right arm is in a sling from a broken collar bone, and I imagine that the prospect of having to use crutches for a while probably seems a little daunting."

Nick rolled the table with his food in front of him. "You paint such a rosy picture," Nick said to the nurse as he lifted the lid off his tray to see an amazing breakfast of scrambled eggs with cheese, fresh roasted potatoes and two strips of bacon. He smiled gave her a thankful nod, "My compliments to Chef Rich."

"Well, we are all pulling for you," she smiled as she adjusted his pillows behind him.

Nick was, actually, very grateful to the entire hospital staff. He technically worked *for* them, but his colleagues treated him like one of their own. They really had done an amazing job considering the number of injuries that he had sustained.

"Thank God you were wearing a helmet!" she said as she checked his blood pressure. "Really, they lost you for a while during that last surgery. Any more trauma from the initial incident and you might not have pulled through."

Nick paused a moment to reflect on how lucky he was. "That's what they told me, yes." He tried to remember as much as he could of that day, but he really couldn't. He remembered bringing Lisa her birthday present and he remembered the strange bluish fog that morning. "So, how often do you get that blue fog in the mornings?"

She looked at him baffled. "Blue fog?" she replied taking off the blood pressure cuff.

"Yes, the ephemeral blue fog that morning. It made everything seem to... well... sparkle. I mean I know that I am new in town for the most part, so I was just wondering, does that happen often? It was really remarkable to see, actually."

The nurse slowly shook her head, "Well, of course, we get fog... but sparkling, ephemeral, and blue? I can't say as I recall ever having seen a fog like that."

Nick looked at her as if she were joking, "No, seriously. C'mon. My receptionist told me that it happened all the time."

"You must have had a dream about it," his nurse continued, "Remember, you did suffer a terrible amount of trauma."

Nick looked down to think. He couldn't have made it up. He was certain of the conversation... it was the only thing he really remembered from that day. But he didn't want to cause a scene, so he acquiesced, "Yes, I suppose you're right." Even though the memory was so real and vivid to him.

The nurse wrote a new daily protocol on the dry erase board by the dresser. "Well, the doctors will be in around 11:00am to check on you. There will be another round of x-rays. Oh, and another abdominal CT scan..."

"To make sure that the surgeons fixed what they were supposed to fix," Nick finished.

"Exactly," the nurse nodded.

"Aye, aye, Captain," he joked, giving her a salute with his good arm.

"In the meantime, finish your breakfast and rest. You are going to be here for little while longer."

Nick grimaced at the sound of being in the hospital any longer. He had so much work to catch up on and clients that were counting on him. Not to mention, he was so incredibly bored.

His musings were interrupted by a few hearty raps on the door. It was his friends: Wayne, Kevin, and Bryon. Wayne had literally saved his life the day of the accident, if he hadn't been there to stop some of the bleeding and keep him from going into shock, who knows if he would have even made it to the hospital in time.

Bryon worked in the billing and records department of the hospital. He often bragged that he had the best job in the hospital; nine to five, weekends and holidays off, plenty of free time, and all the free coffee he could drink... unless he could snag some espresso from the machine in Chef Rich's office. Bryon's work schedule worked well for Nick on the weekend that he needed his furniture moved into the office.

Kevin was part of the physical therapy unit at the hospital. He was a clown, but he knew his field of study better than anyone else that Nick could think of. Plus, he was Bryon's slob of a roommate, which made for an amusing real life "Odd Couple" situation.

"Any room in here for a couple of hoodlums?" Wayne asked as they barged into the room.

Kevin clapped his hands together as he looked at the remarkable breakfast plate that was prepared for Nick, "Smells good! You aren't gonna eat all of this are you?" He reached for a strip of bacon on the tray.

"You boys *are* hoodlums!" the nurse said slapping Kevin's hand away, "Leave his food alone, you all know where the cafeteria is!"

The rest of the room laughed as Kevin recoiled his hand.

Bryon piped in chuckling, "Sure we do, but the food in there never looks this good!"

Nick warned sarcastically, "Don't let Chef Rich hear you say that!"

Kevin flexed his feeble biceps, "Awe, heck, I ain't afraid of him, look at these guns! I had to call the vet just this morning, 'cuz these pythons are sick!"

The room burst into laughter.

"You should have called a taxidermist," Bryon jibed. Then, switching to his best Hulk Hogan impression, continued, "Besides, I think it's too late for your pythons, brother!"

Again, the room erupted in laughter.

"Okay... okay," Wayne said, trying to calm the comedians down. "Remember, Nick needs to relax too."

Almost simultaneously, Kevin and Bryon responded, "But laughter is the best medicine!"

Nick shook his head and chuckled as Wayne just rolled his eyes.

"No seriously, Nick," Bryon continued, "How are ya feeling today?"

Nick nodded and made a slight grimace. "Better... not going to run any marathons soon, but better."

"That's good to hear, man," Kevin said patting Nick on his good shoulder. "That's good to hear... because the ladies behind the bar at Martini's are feeling neglected. They miss your face."

Nick's nurse stepped in with a word of caution, "Oh goodness no! It will be a while before that is going to happen."

"Thanks for the cheerful outlook there, Nurse Ratchet," Wayne dug. The nurse caught the reference and gave Wayne a playful pinch on his arm.

Nick's cell phone vibrated on the tray table. He

looked at the screen. "Mom," he said to the guys picking up the phone, "I better answer it... otherwise; she will be on a plane and calling out the National Guard."

The nurse smiled, pushed the boys out of the room and started to leave. "Ok you three... leave him alone for a bit, so he can talk to his mother."

"But we just got here!" Bryon objected.

"Yeah, we have not yet begun to cause trouble!" Kevin continued defiantly, raising his fist in the air.

Wayne shook his head and grabbed the other two by their collars, "C'mon, fellas, Nurse Ratchet is right... Besides, you haven't seen his mother worried... I have! We'll swing by later." Wayne tossed the other two out, shooting Nick a quick thumbs up and smile as he left.

"Be sure to finish your breakfast and take your pills, I'll keep these hooligans out of the way," the nurse whispered," as Nick picked up his phone.

"Hi, Mom," he said in his most accommodating voice as he answered the phone. "Yes, I am doing just fine... why did it take so long to answer the phone... well, the nurse was here and the guys, so it took a minute to get them out... of course, I'll say hi to Wayne for you... no, there is no reason for you to come back down... Really, I am doing just fine, they are saying that I will be released in a few days." He tried desperately to change the subject, "How's dad doing with retirement? Has he put on the "New Yankee Workshop" addition to the garage that he always said he would do?"

It didn't work.

"What? No, mom, I will be just fine." He tried to shift his mom's attention again, "Besides, you have your hands full up there with Uncle Bill since his forklift accident... how is he doing?"

His second attempt at distraction didn't work either.

"Seriously, Lisa and her fiancé have been fantastic. Everything is all set for when I leave... yes... yes, I have been following the doctor's orders... I've been getting plenty of rest too..."

There was a knock on the door frame and Nick looked up to see a professionally dressed, stunningly beautiful, auburn-haired woman with the most captivating eyes that he had ever seen standing at the door with a large hospital gift shop Teddy Bear and Mylar "Get Well Soon" balloon.

"What, mom?" Nick said, turning his attention back to the phone. "Oh yes, I will, I promise... I will... look, mom, I gotta run... I have a visitor here... what?" Nick motioned the young woman into the room, "Okay sure, mom," Nick looked at the young woman and mouthed, "What is your name?"

She mouthed back, "Sar-ah."

"Well, mom," Nick continued on the phone, "Sarah is here, I don't want to be rude to her... what? Who's Sarah?" Nick looked back over to the young woman with a 'please help me' look. "Aw, Mom, you know Sarah," he looked back at her and gave her an apologetic look. "Sarah... from the... Savannah Society of Psychologists," he knew this was a lie, he really had no idea who she was, but somehow, she looked incredibly familiar, and he *knew* that he didn't want her leaving the room. "Right... yes, exactly... well, I better get going.... Yes, mom... love you too... and tell dad the same."

Nick stopped the call and put his phone on the stand next to his bed. He raised the back of his bed so that he was sitting more upright and turned to Sarah. "So, now that the Spanish Inquisition is over. Hello... have you got the right room? Do I even know you?"

"First, no one expects the Spanish Inquisition," she said, trying to break the tension.

Nick recalled the old Monty Python sketch and laughed.

There was something about her that captivated him... she was so familiar, he didn't know her, but he knew that he couldn't let her out of the room without getting to know her better.

She looked down at her feet. It was clear that she was uncomfortable.

Nick immediately saw this and changed direction. "I'm sorry... my memory is a little touchy lately... is the Teddy Bear for me?" he asked.

Sarah looked up at Nick and nodded, "Yes, of course, sorry about that." She walked toward him and put the bear and balloon on the stand next to his phone. "We haven't officially met, Doctor Williams. I am not surprised at all that you don't recognize me... I am so sorry about ... all of this," she continued.

Nick tried as hard as he could to recognize her face, her voice was vaguely familiar, yet for some reason, somehow, all he could recall was hearing her crying.

When it was eluded him and he couldn't place it. He could see the pain etched across her face too. Nick tried to break the tension, "Well, you nurses, you have all been doing a phenomenal job, really."

He could see her getting agitated. "Of course, I have only really been fully conscious the last few days. You guys haven't just started to treat me good since I woke up, have you?"

Sarah choked back the tears welling up in her eyes, and shook her head, "No, no... of course they haven't."

"You're not a nurse," Nick kept pressing. "You will have to tell me eventually," he smiled, "after all, complete strangers don't just walk into hospital rooms carrying large teddy bears and balloons. Are you a hospital volunteer?"

Sarah finally responded with an affirmative nod.

"Oh, then you have nothing to feel bad about! Seriously, everyone here has been great."

Sarah took a deep breath, looked like she was

going to say something, but then stopped.

"So, have you volunteered at the hospital long?"

Sarah shook her head. "No, I... am pretty new... kind of... community service."

Nick laughed, "Community Service? You? What did you do, teach a group of visiting Girl Scouts to jaywalk?"

He simply couldn't believe that the woman in front of him, with her countenance and demeanor, could have done anything that would have caused her to have to do Community Service. "Did you try to shoplift from the Art Supply store? I hear that those Bob Ross painting kits are much bigger than they look."

Sarah looked wounded and took a step back, "Actually, I have come to visit you many times, Dr. Williams."

"Please, call me Nick... you did bring me a teddy bear after all," he smiled.

"Very well... Nick," she smiled back apprehensively. "I have read to you almost every day." Sarah paused as she started to open up to him, then continued, "I have always been intrigued by the classics... I figured that you, being a doctor... probably would be too."

Nick couldn't comprehend it. What on earth could she have done to warrant Community Service? As far as he could see... she was pretty much perfect. He was also impressed that she was intuitive enough to know that he enjoyed the classics. "Wow," he replied, "I actually love the classics... my grandfather used to read to me all the time when I was younger."

"I have an entire collection of old classics that I have been collecting for years: from Dickens to Poe, from H.G. Wells to Melville," she said. "It helps when your family has been in the antique business for multiple generations... and well, like I said, it just sort of made sense to me," she smiled hesitantly as she went to reach onto her large purse for a book to read to him.

"So that's why I recognize your voice," Nick concluded. He shook his head, trying to recall a memory, "That's funny, because I somehow thought I remembered you crying..."

In that instant, all the progress that had been made in breaking down the wall between them was lost.

Sarah stiffened with fear and began to tremble. She cleared her throat and mustered up some courage. "Doctor... I mean, Nick... I have to tell you..." Sarah stopped and took a few calming breaths.

"Tell me what?"

"That I was driving the car from your accident," she said breaking down in tears.

Nick was instantly flooded with emotions: anger, shock, disbelief, pain... all of which opened a door in his memories that showed him every exacting detail of the crash.

He saw the front of her blue hatchback. He

remembered briefly seeing her terrified face inside the car as he was tumbling over it. His knees and ribs began to throb with pain.

The monitors in the room began to tick up and accelerate.

He remembered landing and skidding on the hard, hot pavement... and he remembered his grandfather standing in that glowing bluish light, telling him that he still had work to do.

Nick turned to focus his anger on Sarah, preparing to unload on her about her carelessness and how it nearly cost him his life. But when he looked at her, he saw that she wasn't alone.

There with his hand on Sarah's shoulder was Grandpa Joe in shimmering opal blue. He smiled at his grandson, "It's okay, Nicholas. This was meant to be. Now let's talk about your purpose."

CHAPTER FOUR

Nick sat frozen in his hospital bed awash in disbelief. Grandpa Joe *was* standing there. Of that there was no question... but how? Exactly *how* was he seeing his grandfather? And what was his grandfather saying that he was about to know his purpose?

"You have a lot of questions. That's good. I did too. But don't take your frustrations out on this lovely young lady. She made a mistake, and she feels awful about it. You should not live in the shadows of our worst moments, Nicholas, and you should never force others to do so either."

Nick, dumbfounded, stammered out a, "But... but..."

Sarah covered her face and turned away, "I know. This is my fault. It was an accident. I hope you can forgive me... but... I understand if you cannot."

Grandpa Joe looked at Nick, with a "you know what the right thing to do is" look and motioned toward

Sarah.

"No, it's not that... I just... have so many questions," Nick said over her shoulder to his grandfather.

Sarah, thinking he was talking to her, jumped in and rushed through a stream of consciousness, "I really don't know what to tell you... I looked away for a second and the next thing I knew, I was in the middle of the intersection, slamming on my brakes... and well... you know the rest. I've been reliving the nightmare every day since, I can't eat... I can't sleep... not that it even comes close to comparing to the pain and suffering that I've put you through..."

Nick's eyes shot back and forth between his grandfather and Sarah. It was confusing and all so surreal. Until finally, he spoke, "Sarah?"

She humbly nodded.

"Sarah, eh.... I want you to know that... I hold no ill feelings toward you." Nick saw his grandfather smile. "I would very much like to have you read to me..."

Sarah couldn't believe how gracious Nick was. For the first time since the accident, she began to feel a weight being lifted off her shoulders. "Of course," she smiled as she wiped away her tears.

Nick looked at his grandfather and had so many questions, questions that he couldn't begin to ask with Sarah in the room, "But not now... right now, I have to sort through some things and I kind of need you to go away."

The smile left Sarah's face and was replaced with a look of confusion.

Grandpa Joe shook his head in disapproval.

Nick realized how his reaction must have sounded to her and quickly adjusted. "I mean, I have to finish breakfast and take my meds... you know. So maybe come back in say ten or fifteen minutes? Then you can read to me some more and we can talk. After all, there is only so much HGTV one can handle." He looked at his grandfather, who was giving him a "thumbs up" on the recovery, and continued, "Besides... it will be great getting to catch up."

Sarah looked puzzled, "Catch up?"

"I mean... get to know each other."

Sarah felt the pit of her stomach dissolve. She took a deep breath, "Of course, Doctor... I mean... of course, Nick. I'll be back soon." With that, she picked up her oversized purse, walked right by Nick's grandfather and headed toward the door.

"Oh," Nick added, "would you do me a favor and close the door for me?"

Sarah turned back with a shy smile. "Of course, Nick," she said closing the door behind her.

"I'm telling you, Nicholas," Grandpa Joe piped in as Sarah walked out, "that young lady is something special. You would be wise to keep her around."

"Well," Nick supposed, "I suppose if she's with me

and in the passenger seat of my car, she would be less of a menace on the roadways."

Grandpa Joe chuckled, "Just don't let her hear you say that. Your grandmother was a far better driver than I ever was… just ask her someday."

Nick couldn't believe that he was looking at his grandfather.

"Yet, here I am, Nicholas," Grandpa Joe answered.

"You can read my mind?" Nick said with wonder.

"No, son, it's more like I am reading your heart. In fact, I can read everyone's heart. It's one of those abilities that you acquire on this side… that's how I knew that Sarah there was a good soul. Now eat your breakfast, Nicholas, or that nurse will come back and give you what for."

Nick dutifully began eating. "So, Grandpa Joe, were you here the whole time? How come I am just seeing you now?"

Grandpa Joe walked over to the chair on the other side of the bed and sat down. "Well, for a little while, Nicholas, you crossed over. Remember that day that seemed so familiar; the one where you first saw me by our telescope in your office?"

Nick nodded as he continued eating his breakfast.

"That was when you crossed over, boy… you had breached that threshold between the living world and the spirit world."

"But wait, Lisa was there... she's hasn't... crossed over."

"No, not at all, but her consciousness is part of the Universal Consciousness... which is everywhere. What you saw was the part of it that made an impact on what you were doing."

"Going through my day... so I saw the image of her that I would have expected... she wasn't really there."

"Exactly," Grandpa Joe affirmed. "And it is because of *our* connection that I was the first one in this state that you saw, Nicholas."

"First?"

Grandpa Joe nodded. "It won't be long before you will see many, many more of us... *that* is your purpose, Nicholas and it will be happening soon."

Nick put down his fork and looked incredulously at his grandfather with a raised eyebrow, "Seriously? My purpose is to see dead people?"

"No, Nicholas, your purpose is to help lost spirits, the fact that you can see them is a... byproduct."

Nick pushed his rolling table to the side of the bed. "How do you mean, *help*? How am I supposed to help them? They are already dead!"

Grandpa Joe got up and pointed to the curtains on the window. "Open these, Nicholas."

Nick grabbed the remote control for the room on the side of his bed and opened the curtains.

"Tell me what you see."

Nick looked out the window of his ground floor room. It was a typical sunny day in Savannah. "I see tourists," Nick said in an exhausted manner.

"What else?"

Nick looked back at his grandfather and begrudgingly looked again. "Tourists... and girl scouts... locals having lunch on park benches... a few artists sketching...."

"And?"

Nick squinted a moment and leaned forward to look again. "I see a little boy in blue overalls running around that tree there... Holy Crap! He just jumped fifteen feet up that old oak tree!"

Grandpa Joe smiled knowingly.

"Oh God! He just fell out of the tree... and disappeared!" Nick looked with bewilderment at his grandfather. "What did I just see?"

"What you just saw was Adam Kensington. He died in August of 1876. Poor little guy fell out of that tree ... still thinks he is climbing trees in the park... he is 'Pinned' to those moments and as such hasn't moved on."

"Pinned? What does that mean?"

"Well, son, there are a number of different categories of spirits that remain Earthbound... the main two are *Affixed*, those who don't even know they have died and are stuck to a single day or point in time and those that are *Wandering*, those who know that they are dead but have things that are unfinished. Now here is where it can get tricky... an Affixed or *Pinned* Spirit can become a Wandering Spirit once their consciousness is awakened and they are broken from the cycle. Once that happens, the clock starts ticking."

"Right... Affixed or Wandering..." Nick pondered what his grandfather had just told him while he leaned back in his bed and tried to rationalize what he had seen, but he could not. "He wasn't wearing blue overalls, was he? I just thought they were blue... he was all blue... like the fog, right?"

"You always were a quick study," Grandpa Joe continued, "But he's not the only one out there who needs your assistance, Nicholas. There are many, many others. You are someone who has an open heart and can help them find peace."

Nick shook his head, "No. No way. I'm sorry, Grandpa Joe, but I am the furthest thing from Jennifer Love Hewitt. This isn't gonna happen. I am just getting started here in Savannah... I have bills to pay... a car to pay off... a full workload already... of *paying* clients. I don't have time to deal with more."

Grandpa Joe turned to Nick and sternly walked toward him. "Jennifer who now?"

Nick shook his head, "It doesn't matter."

Grandpa Joe shook his finger at his grandson. "Look here, young man. I have two things to say to you and you better listen. One, take your medicine," he said with a grin as he leaned against the wall by the window, "and two... try as you might, you cannot deny what is your true purpose."

Nick looked back out the window to see who he could see. "Tourists... girl scouts... locals... artists..." He recoiled a bit when the visage of little Adam Kensington reappeared and jumped into the old oak tree, "He's back?"

"I told you, Nicholas, to him... he still thinks that he is climbing trees."

Nick looked at his grandfather, "So, what does all this mean for you? Are you my... my spirit guide or something?"

The corner of Grandpa Joe's mouth curled upward as he sat down on the chair by the window, "Indeed, a quick study."

Nick finished his last bite of bacon and reached down to take his paper cup of pills. He tossed them into his mouth, took a swig of water and swallowed. "Well... this should be fun."

"This isn't some kind of joke, Nicholas. These souls will be counting on you. Without someone like you to help them through their individual trials... they may be stuck here instead of crossing over... never seeing their loved ones again because they are holding themselves back... for whatever reason. There worst part of it is, especially if they are a Wanderer, if they don't move on, they eventually become empty shells of themselves."

"The clock is ticking... right." A terrible thought swept over Nick, "Grandpa Joe... is that why you are here? Are you Pinned or Wandering?"

Grandpa Joe sensed Nick's unease, "Oh goodness no, Nicholas. I am here to help you. Call it a Spirit Guide Hall Pass. I am good. I have the rest of eternity to fish, star gaze- by the way you wouldn't believe how close I can get to the stars now.... and, of course, spend all the time I want with your lovely grandmother."

Nick breathed a sigh of relief. "Ok... because if not..."

Grandpa Joe motioned to calm Nick down, "I know, boy... I know."

"So... these wandering and affixed spirits... they are just going to come to me, and I am supposed to talk them through their issues so they can cross over?"

"Not entirely. I am your guide, so I would be leading them to you. Now, don't get me wrong... you are going to start seeing them everywhere... because they *are* everywhere. But that doesn't mean you should always engage them. Sadly, there are plenty of souls out there that are happy to be miserable and even happier to make others miserable. They don't want to be helped, they only want to cause pain... and they don't care if they are causing pain to living people or not; it just doesn't matter to them. They were miserable rotten people in life and death hasn't changed them. Just leave them alone for now."

Nick replied, "Got it. If you were in jerk in life, you're going to be a jerk in the afterlife."

"Pretty much, yes."

Nick found himself looking out the window again as a wave of doubt rushed over him. "I just wish I knew this was all really happening... that this was real."

"Oh, you need evidence?"

"I'm sorry, Grandpa Joe... but you must see how bizarre this all is. This... *paranormal* stuff."

Grandpa Joe rubbed his chin, "No, no... this is good. Healthy skepticism is always better than reckless or blind faith. So how do I prove to you that this is real... without you being able to say that it was in your head the whole time and I am just a manifestation of that knowledge?"

"Well, yes, something like that, I suppose."

Grandpa Joe snapped his fingers and pointed to Nick, "I got it... well, I will soon... should be any second now," then he stood up to stand next to the chair.

Nick looked at his grandfather. What was he waiting for?

There was a quick knock on the door as Sarah slowly opened it. "Am I good to come back in?"

Nick gestured her in, "Of course, please."

Sarah walked over to the chair and sat down. She looked up at Nick and saw him staring out toward the hospital door. "Pardon me for asking this, but... you seem preoccupied. Like you are waiting for someone... should I come back?"

Grandpa Joe put his finger up to his mouth to remind Nick to be quiet about him.

Nick snapped out of his thoughts and apologized. "No, no. I just thought I had saw someone I knew just now and... well, it's... nothing."

Sarah understood and reached into her purse for the book. "Would you like me to start at the beginning? Or pick up where we left off... of course, you probably can't remember where we left off," she babbled nervously.

"Let's start at the beginning."

Sarah reached into the large purse that she was carrying on her arm and pulled out an old copy of Moby Dick and started opening it.

Nick watched as Grandpa Joe pointed, "Look there, Nicholas."

Nick looked down at the inside cover of the book, sat up and exclaimed, "Good God!"

Sarah froze, "I'm sorry, have I done something wrong?"

Nick's eyes grew larger as he anxiously tried to read the words written across the top of the inside cover.

Sarah looked at Nick with unease, "Should I go?"

Grandpa Joe chimed in, "No." But, of course, only

Nick heard him.

"No!" Nick repeated. He couldn't believe it, but he had to confirm it, so he asked, "Where did you find that book?"

"I have been collecting books since I was a teenager. I got this at an estate sale, just north of town.... the day of ..."

"The accident." Nick thought about the words his grandfather told him about hoping to find his great grandfather's book one day at a yard sale and about the timing of finding the book. "The writing on the inside cover of your book... what does it say?"

Sarah was baffled by his question, but started to read, "Oh, it is just an inscription from the first owner probably... This book belongs to Tobias..."

"...Williams of East Troy, Wisconsin," Nick finished.

Sarah's mouth was agape, "How did you... I'm mean, how did you..." Then it all added up in Sarah's mind, "No... no way... Williams... was this book in your family?"

Nick nodded as both of them felt the hair on the back of their necks raise.

"It was my great grandfather's book. He sold it during the Great Depression back in the thirties."

They sat motionless.

Sarah looked up at Nick as if in a confessional. "Actually, this was what took my eyes off the road... it was in such amazing condition after all these years... I was looking down at the book when I ran the light."

Grandpa Joe spoke up.   "This is called synchronicity, Nicholas... it is what we call it when what looks like just a coincidence is *far* beyond a mere coincidence. That book is entangled with our family. It is bound to us just as I am bound to you... and now it is bound to Sarah here. You will learn about this in your studies. How's that for evidence?"

Nick was at a complete loss for words. He sat dumbfounded. He just slowly nodded.

Sarah looked with concern at Nick, "Maybe, I should go. I will leave this with you," she continued as she got up to leave.

Grandpa Joe, knowing that he had to do something to break the tension spoke up, "Perhaps, you should just let her read to you for a bit and relax, Nicholas. The book is hers now."

Nick put his hand up. "No, please... you bought the book, don't be silly. It is yours! Stay and read. I would enjoy that very much... of course, I may fall asleep on you." He chuckled, "the meds make me very sleepy."

Sarah sat back down and smiled, "Are you sure?"

"I am sure," Nick said looking over at his grandfather as he lowered his bed back to a more reclined position. "Please, go ahead."

"Very well," Sarah said, and she began to read.

"Moby Dick by Herman Melville... Call me Ishmael. Some years ago - never mind how long precisely - having little or no money in my purse, and nothing particular to interest me on shore, I thought I would sail about a little and see the watery part of the world. It is a way I have of driving off the spleen and regulating the circulation."

Nick's eyes were growing heavy, he knew that they would be. He blinked a few times and looked toward Grandpa Joe.

His grandfather raised his hand slightly and made a soft patting motion as if to reassure Nick that it was ok to fall asleep.

Sarah kept reading, *"Whenever I find myself growing grim about the mouth; whenever it is a damp, drizzly November in my soul; whenever I find myself involuntarily pausing before coffin warehouses, and bringing up the rear of every funeral I meet; and especially whenever my hypos get such an upper hand of me, that it requires a strong moral principle to prevent me from deliberately stepping into the street, and methodically knocking people's hats off - then, I account it high time to get to sea as soon as I can. This is my substitute for pistol and ball."*

Nick saw his grandfather looking over Sarah's shoulder and heard his comforting voice reading along with her. Nick closed his eyes listening to the story he had heard so many times before. It was good to hear the words again and soon, he was asleep.

"With a philosophical flourish Cato throws himself upon his sword; I quietly take to the ship. There is nothing surprising in this. If they but knew it, almost all men in their degree, sometime or other, cherish very nearly the same feelings towards the ocean with me."

Sarah looked up from the book.

"Poor fella's tuckered out already; looks cold," Grandpa Joe stated.

Sarah got up and put the book on Nick's nightstand. She turned and made sure his blanket was covering him up, "Don't want you to catch cold. They always have hospitals so chilly." She took a deep breath and headed to the door. As she left the room, she whispered, "I'll come back soon... ok?"

Nick heard his grandfather's voice. "Nicholas, say goodbye to Sarah and you will see her soon."

Barely awake, Nick mumbled, "Byesarah... seeyasoon..." and drifted back asleep,

---

Nick opened his eyes and looked up from his desk in his study. He surveyed his office and saw everything in shimmering blue. "I know where I am," he said confidently. "Grandpa Joe?" he asked, looking around the room. "I'm in the Spirit World again, aren't I?"

Grandpa Joe materialized by the telescope. "Indeed. One heck of a quick study. This is a safe haven for you. No harm can come to you here as long as you are alone when you enter here. You are outside the concept of time."

"Will I only be able to get here when I am sleeping?"

"For now, it is the easiest way for me to guide you. But eventually, you won't even need me to get here."

"So, I have my own metaphysical Fortress of Solitude! Sweet." Nick smirked.

Grandpa Joe wasn't terribly amused, "Let's call it a place to study, find answers, and prepare yourself for those souls that may need that little extra work."

"Are we expecting a lot of those?"

"I suppose it all depends, really. Probably not many." Grandpa Joe continued, "There are going to be a lot of different folks coming to you though, Nicholas. Some have led harsh lives, others may have had charmed ones, some may have died of old age or accidentally but just don't want to let go... and others may have had their lives taken from them."

"Murdered."

"Yes, or perhaps in a battle. You have to remember; Savannah is a very old town with a very rich history about it. It is the final resting place of generals and foot soldiers, wealthy plantation owners and slaves, even pirates and a signer of the Declaration of Independence."

Nick knew the city had a history... but this

was quite an amazing list of his potential clients. A thought crossed his mind, "Grandpa Joe, I don't know any foreign languages really... I mean, yes remember a bit of Spanish... but what if the souls who come to me for help don't speak English? How will I know what they are saying?"

"Everyone's heart speaks the same language, Nicholas. You will understand them, and they will understand you. Just remember the first statute. *Do no harm.* If you stick to that guidepost, you will do just fine."

Nick's grandfather walked over to the bookshelf in Nick's study. He picked up the top left volume of many very large tomes and put it on the desk in front of Nick. "Now, it's time for you to study, Nicholas."

Nick looked at the giant book and back to his grandfather. "I'm already a doctor, Grandpa Joe."

"Yes, yes you are... and a damned fine one too... but you haven't studied *anything* that you need to for this new mission in your life."

Nick scoffed and looked back at the book. "The Science behind Metaphysics, Volume I, Application of Quantum Physics and Its Impact on Multiple Universes." He looked back at the bookshelf in astonishment and did a quick count, "...Thirty-Eight, Thirty-Nine, Forty, Forty- One ... Forty-Two? Forty-Two volumes... all this size? I thought you said that this was something that would need to start right away."

"Which is one more reason why you will be doing your studying here; remember, right now in the living world, you are asleep, time is barely moving, if it is moving at all. This world exists outside the boundaries of time... but you will read about that in Volume XI," Grandpa Joe said as he gave Nick a wink, "Now get to your studies."

With that, Nick got down to work studying all the aspects of his newfound calling. He pored over the volumes. He took notes. He cross referenced. He found himself looking out the bay window of this study and noticed that, although people were moving around outside and doing things, the shadows never moved. Time itself was standing still, just like his grandfather had told him.

He learned about Quantum Theory and its multiple universes. He became well-read about the Laws of Thermodynamics and Super Position. He read about the power of belief and influence that the fear of death had on the living as well.

In what seemed to be days to him, so very much. He closed Volume Forty-One, got up and put it back on the shelf.

Nick looked at his grandfather playing with the spirit version of the old telescope and smiled. "I wrack my brain studying and you get to play with the telescope?"

Grandpa Joe snickered, "Well, you don't have a

creek to fish in running through your study. I already played about a hundred games of chess against myself, and I could only play so many hands of solitaire."

Nick rolled his eyes and reached for the last volume. But when he went to grab it, his hand began to fade. Horrified, he turned to his grandfather, "Grandpa Joe?"

Grandpa Joe looked at Nick. "Relax, Nicholas, they are just waking you up for your tests."

Soon, the spirit world dissolved into his hospital room. Nick opened his eyes; the nurse who had brought him breakfast was standing next to him, "Welcome back, Doctor Williams. Are you ready for your all your tests?"

Nick looked at the clock on the wall, he had only been sleeping for seconds, when had had been studying for what had to be a few weeks or more. He took stock of everything that he had just studied in the Spirit World. He was secure in the fact that Grandpa Joe would be with him. "Yes. Yes, I believe I am."

CHAPTER FIVE

Nick took a steady pace as he made his way to the office. He wasn't quite ready for biking, yet he longed for the day that he could.

For now, he measured his steps and used a beautiful silver handled cane with an ebony black stick that he picked up at Sarah's family's antiques shop. He was proud of himself that he only needed it for every other step. After all it had only been four months since the accident and he didn't need the bulky knee brace any longer, just a compression sleeve.

As Nick walked past Monterey Square, the sparkling blue spirit of a tall, slender built man with a mustache leaned against one of the white pillars of the old red brick mansion on the corner. He took a genteel puff on his cigar and watched Nick as he went by. "Looking good there, sport. The cane gives you an air of sophistication. I believe that society in general could use more of it."

Nick acknowledged, "You are too kind, sir."

"Oh, my! Please, sport... the name's Jim. Stop by sometime and I shall regale you with tales of my legendary Christmas parties!"

It was something that Nick was getting used to, the spirits really were everywhere. He had helped a few of them cross over in a short amount of time since leaving the hospital and he was getting remarkably good at it. But when he encountered them outside of those that Grandpa Joe guided to him, he made sure he remained guarded- as his grandfather had cautioned.

Nick smiled politely as he continued on his way, "Why, thank you, Jim. Perhaps someday."

"Well, I have all the time in the world, sport... and then some," and with another puff on his cigar, a slight flourish with his free hand, he turned and faded through the front door.

It wasn't long before Nick arrived at his office. He took a deep breath and made his way up the steps. He opened the front door and saw Lisa sitting dutifully at her post.

"Good morning, Doctor Williams," Lisa smiled. "You're ten o'clock cancelled and you have a video conference call with the hospital board to go over their employee satisfaction surveys at two."

"Slow day?" Nick questioned.

"Just today, besides, it's good that you take the

time to warm back up to things."

Nick walked over to the elevator and went inside. "Well, I suppose that is true." He closed the gate and turned the handle to the third floor. As he did this, he saw the luminescent blue glow reflecting in the polished brass of the elevator. "Hello, Grandpa Joe."

"Good morning, Nicholas, you seem to be healing up well."

Nick looked at his cane. Then up to his grandfather, "Not too bad, I guess."

"I have a client for you today."

Nick exited the elevator and entered his study. He put his jacket on the coat rack and opened his laptop.

"You will have to do a quick refresher on your American History."

"I'm sorry, what?"

"Button Gwinnett, Nicholas. He has been unable to rest for over two hundred and forty years… it's time he gets to. If we don't help him soon, he will lose himself and just be a shell wandering aimlessly for eternity."

Nick nodded in agreement, after all, two hundred and forty years was a very long time to be held back from moving on… and the prospect of wandering aimlessly for eternity did not sit well with him.

"Get your Encyclopedia Britannica and look up Button Gwinnett."

"Umm, Grandpa Joe, we don't really use

encyclopedias like that anymore. We have the internet. I can get multiple sources of information from around the world in an instant," Nick said, pointing to his computer.

Grandpa Joe smiled, "Isn't technology a marvel! You truly live in astonishing times, Nicholas. I will be back in a bit for your session." And with that, Grandpa Joe dematerialized.

Nick turned to his laptop, took out his notebook and began to research. He read along as he took his notes, "Button Gwinnett was born 1735 in the parish of Down Hatherley in Gloucestershire, Great Britain. His father was Welsh, the Reverend Samuel Gwinnett, and his wife, Anne. He was the third of his seven children. There is no confirmation to his exact birthdate, but he was baptized at St. Catherine's Church in Gloucester on April 10, 1735. He began as a merchant in England and moved to Wolverhampton in 1754. In 1757 he married Ann Bourne at St. Peter's Church. In 1762 they left to go to America."

Nick reached into the small refrigerator by his desk, pulled out a can of ginger ale, and opened it. Then he continued, taking a sip now and then, "Gwinnett's business activities took him from New England to Jamaica. But he was never very successful. He moved to Savannah in 1765 and opened a store which failed. He then tried to become a gentleman farmer and that venture failed as well. But it was during this time that he made a name for himself in politics."

Nick rubbed his eyes and kept taking notes.

"Gwinnett did not become a strong advocate of colonial rights until 1775, when St. John's Parish, which encompassed his lands, threatened to secede from Georgia because of the colony's traditionalist response to the events going on around them. During his time in the Assembly, Dr. Lyman Hall became his good friend and closest ally. But he also had a rival in Lachlan McIntosh. This began when McIntosh was appointed as brigadier general of the Georgia Continentals in 1776."

Nick looked up from the screen and muttered, "Now we are getting somewhere."

He went on reading, "Gwinnett voted in favor of the Declaration of Independence, adopted by Congress on July 2, 1776. This was two days before the "fair copy", or scribed version (dated July 4, 1776) was presented to the Congress. He signed the parchment copy on August 2, 1776, and started his journey back home."

"He was accompanied to Virginia by Carter Braxton, another of the signers, carrying a proposed state constitution drawn up by John Adams. During his service in the Continental Congress, Gwinnett was a leading candidate for a brigadier general position to lead the 1st Regiment in the Continental Army. However, he lost the position to Lachlan McIntosh."

Nick thought a moment, "That must have been

like a poison to his soul... no wonder there were such bitter feelings."

He continued, "Gwinnett went on to serve in the Georgia state legislature, and in 1777 he wrote the original draft of Georgia's first State Constitution. He became Speaker of the Georgia Assembly, a position he held until the death of Archibald Bulloch, the Governor of Georgia. Gwinnett was elevated to the vacated position of Governor by the Assembly's Executive Council and while in his new position of authority, he tried to undermine the leadership of McIntosh."

Nick shook his head and mumbled, "So much drama." Then moved forward with his reading, "Tensions between Gwinnett and McIntosh reached a boiling point when the General Assembly voted to approve Gwinnett's attack on British Florida in April 1777 and as commander-in-chief of Georgia's military, he was now the superior of his rival Lachlan McIntosh. Gwinnett had McIntosh's brother, George, arrested and charged with treason. He also ordered McIntosh to lead an invasion of British-controlled East Florida, which failed. They blamed each other for the defeat and McIntosh publicly called Gwinnett a scoundrel and lying rascal."

Nick paused, "And I thought the politics of today were crazy."

"Gwinnett challenged McIntosh to a duel, which was fought on May 16, 1777, at a plantation owned by the ousted Royal Governor James Wright. The two men exchanged pistol shots at twelve paces, and both were wounded, but Gwinnett was hit mortally and died of his wounds three days later on the date of May 19, 1777."

"McIntosh, although wounded, recovered, and went on to live a long but tumultuous life for although he had a successful military career under George Washington, when he returned home after the war, he found that the British had left his plantation in ruins. He was never able to recover financially and although friends of Button Gwinnett tried to, he was never charged in connection with Gwinnett's death."

Nick sat back in his chair and let out a deep sigh. It was no wonder that Gwinnett's spirit was in a state of unrest. Nick took the rest of his time to formulate a diagnosis and how he might be able to help Governor Gwinnett. And it wasn't long before he would have the opportunity to see if his hypotheses were correct.

A glimmering blue radiance grew in the room. He knew that his grandfather had returned with his first supernatural client.

"Good morning, Grandpa Joe... Good morning, Governor," Nick said bowing his head slightly to the statesman.

"Good heavens, lad, I am well past the expiration that title," the statesman chortled, "However, I appreciate that you have made the effort." He tapped his walking stick a few times on the floor, showing his approval. "But, if it pleases you, let us dispense with the formalities, call me Button."

"I do hope that I can help you... Button," Nick said offering the Governor a seat on his couch.

Gwinnett acknowledged the offer with a courteous nod and sat down. "I have been at the crossroads for longer than I care to remember. I have borne witness to the remarkable achievements that our fledgling nation has accomplished... and sadly done the same with its failures. I have longed to be at peace, but the entrance to the realm of Heaven eludes me. However, if you are indeed the man that your grandfather says that you are, doctor, I believe that you can help me."

Nick grinned slightly, "Well, belief is a very powerful force. There are many that would say that belief is the most powerful force in the universe."

Gwinnett thought for a moment about what Nick had just told him. "Yes, I suppose that is true. I have known many men within my life, some that were successful and others that were not... and it almost always came down to the power of commitment or belief that made the difference. Look at Adams, for instance. Not as brilliant as Franklin, not as lauded as Jefferson, but, Sweet Lord, that man was committed to his belief of American Independence! Without him, the dream of becoming a new nation would have never become a reality."

"Fascinating... and a very wise assessment, Button, he must have had an incredible belief in himself as well," Nick observed, trying not to let the enormity of the situation overwhelm him. He was, after all, *speaking* with a founding father!

Grandpa Joe cut in, "Well, gentlemen, this is a personal conversation between the two of you. I will leave you two to your talk." He started toward the telescope and began to fade away. "See you in an hour," he said pointing to the clock on the wall.

"Until then, Good Man," said Button as Grandpa Joe faded away.

Nick turned back to the former governor and began to get to know him. They talked about Button's life, his beautiful wife, Ann, of whom he longed so much to join in the Great Beyond. They talked about his career and meeting George Washington. "He was the noblest and Christian of men that I had ever had the privilege of knowing," to Benjamin Franklin, "a man who was a philanthropist and philanderer. By far the most intelligent man I had ever known... perhaps too intelligent for his own good."

Nick could not help but reel in the moment... he was talking *to* history.

Button continued with his reminiscences on Dr. Lyman Hall, a true friend and confidant, and "his rotundity" the agitator, John Adams of Massachusetts, who was without a doubt, the most infuriating man in congress but as stated earlier, *the* driving force behind American Independence.

Nick listened intently and took notes; he noticed that Button was very keen on his accomplishments and triumphs over adversity but not forthcoming with what it was that he was not at peace with.

"Button, your life was a fascinating series of events," Nick said, "you did so much for your family and your country, but what is it that you feel is keeping you from finding the peace that eludes you?"

Button sat for a moment, when a sudden torrent of antagonisms washed over him. "McIntosh, it has to be... he torments me in death as much as in life."

Nick knew that had been correct on his assessment. Now they were getting to the root of the issue.

"When you say he torments you... do you mean that Lachlan McIntosh is trapped as well?"

"No, *that* bastard crossed over the moment he... how did the bard put it? *The moment he shuffled off this mortal coil.* He held no guilt whatsoever about his actions, nothing held him back. Yet I... I am confronted with guilt constantly and find that stench of discontentment hangs on me like distillates of rum on old Stephen."

"Old Stephen?" Nick asked.

Button laughed sheepishly, "Stephen Hopkins of Rhode Island... the only man to ever have his rum provisions garnished by Hancock. He was a glorious statesman and governor but, heavens, that man could drink... possibly even more than Franklin."

"I see," Nick replied, astonished about the amount of insight he was gaining on the Founding Fathers. But he pressed on with his patient, "So this 'discontentment' you speak of, it stems from your dealings with Lachlan McIntosh?"

"Goodness! No! That was a mutual animosity. In the end, I challenged him to the duel... and I hit my mark too... he simply hit his mark... better than I," Button shrugged, "But his younger brother, George... that... vexes me."

"And why is that?"

Button contemplated, he looked back over his life and his interactions. "In supposition... I did not put my best foot forward... I was rather harsh with the young man. I used him as a pawn in the game between Lachlan and myself."

"Would you say that is where your discontentment stems from? That your treatment of Lachlan's brother was unjust?"

Button looked sternly at Nick as if to snap back at him for the presumption, then paused and lowered his head, "Aye. I suppose so. I was a... I *am* a better man than that... I let my passions override my common sense."

Nick leaned forward with a reassuring smile,

"Button, this is phenomenal. You have identified a source of conflict that is keeping you here! Now we can go forward and get you to a place where you can move on!"

Button looked over at Nick and smiled, "Well then, there it is. All this time, my loathing of his detestable sibling kept me from seeing it." He leaned back in a bit of relative comfort, "For the first time in centuries, I can feel a weight lifting from my shoulders. I am ready, this is wondrous! Your grandfather was astute in his observance you, young man. You have a wonderful gift."

Nick appreciated the compliment but needed to caution his patient, "I am glad that you feel that we have made progress, but I am sure that you still have work to do."

"But whatever for? Clearly, this was the spigot that was preventing me from moving on!"

Nick cocked his head to the side slightly, "Well, we haven't really addressed your animosity toward Lachlan. I am certain that is also a large part of it. And you have been holding on to the animosity for Lachlan for centuries... anger is just as much of a weight as guilt. It prevents you from reaching peace. If you want to cross over, you must find a way to let it go."

Grandpa Joe returned awash in the glimmering blue hue. "Time to get going, Button."

Nick looked at the clock and stood up, "We can go

over this in our next session, if you would like?"

Button, likewise, got up and gave a slight tug to the lapels of his jacket. "If I am ever to see my dear Ann again, I must." he said with conviction as he picked up his cane.

"Thank you, Button. I think we made tremendous progress today. Work on that; we will talk again soon."

"Undeniably! Thank you, doctor. I shall," with that, Button tapped his walking stick on the floor with approval, strode toward Grandpa Joe and they faded away.

Nick stood in the middle of his study, still unable to fully grasp everything that had just happened. He chuckled to himself, "My unreal real world," and went back to his desk to work on the surveys from the hospital.

He didn't get to work very long, when he saw the familiar glimmer of blue over his right shoulder. He looked up. "Grandpa Joe, I know that our work together is important... but I kind of have to do *this* job if I am going to be able to pay my bills."

Grandpa Joe smirked, "Yes, Nicholas, I know, but this is important, there was a murder... and it is unsolved... we need to help her."

Nick turned toward his grandfather, "Unsolved murder?"

"You can read about it on your computer there, it

was mentioned in the news today."

Nick turned back to his laptop and went to the local news station's website. He read over the headlines. "Stock market has record day. Unease in the Middle East. Pedi-Cab Drivers: Earning While Learning. Opioid Epidemic Hits Home."

"That's the one," Grandpa Joe pointed.

Nick clicked on the article and began to read, "Last weekend another death from an apparent opioid overdose was found on Montgomery Street. This marks the fifth such occurrence in the last month and the twelfth this year. The victim of the apparent overdose, Misty Mahler, was a junior attending Savannah's College of the Arts. Her classmates are in shock…" Nick looked up, "Seems like she was a troubled college student… probably had some emotional difficulties and, sadly, couldn't handle the pressures."

"That's not what she says."

"What does she say?"

Grandpa Joe raised his eyebrows, "I better let her tell you that herself." Grandpa Joe walked toward the bay window, "I will bring her by shortly," and faded away.

Nick looked back at the article and looked at her picture. "Poor thing, college can be brutal." He kept reading, "Her classmates are in shock as Ms. Mahler seemed to have everything going for her. She was near the top of her class and had just had an outstanding exhibit that garnered rave reviews on her artwork."

Nick paused a moment to think. He took a deep breath, took out his notebook and began to research. He made a quick call to his contacts at the police station and with his high level of clearance he was able to read what the police had said about the case, which in turn, was backed up by another phone call to the medical examiner.

It wasn't long before he had a basic psychological make-up. Nothing that he came across would have suggested an addictive personality... but the only way to make sure was to speak directly with her. Fortunately, he possessed a unique ability that allowed him to do so.

Nick saw the blue glow fill the room; sure enough, there was Grandpa Joe and standing next to him was the young woman from the article. He stood up with his notebook and pen in hand to welcome them as they coalesced.

Misty stepped slightly behind Grandpa Joe as Nick approached.

"She's still a little... apprehensive, Nicholas," Grandpa Joe explained. "It's alright, Misty," he continued turning to her, "this is the young man I was telling you about. He's my grandson. He can help you."

"Hello, Misty, I'm Dr. Williams," Nick said trying to break the ice.

Misty looked up at him in wonder, "You can see

me? But you are alive! How?"

"That's a long story... but yes, I can. More importantly, I am here to help you. Let's figure out why you can't move on, ok? So why don't you come over here and sit on the couch and we can talk." Nick ushered Misty to the couch and sat down in the chair as Grandpa Joe walked over to the telescope.

Misty sat down, "I know why I can't move on. I was murdered!"

"You mean that you were given tainted pills? They were laced with something?"

"No, I was murdered but everyone thinks that I killed myself. That's why I cannot move on. Do you know how terrible it is to have the world think that you would do something so awful to yourself?"

Nick wrote down a few notes. "The reports said that it was a clear overdose."

"Tell me, Doctor Williams, how does one overdose, when you have a hard time taking aspirin? My doctor always gave me the chewable kind."

"What?"

"The strongest medication that I have ever taken was a prescription antibiotic for a lung infection two years ago... even that I had blend into a strawberry-banana smoothie just to take it."

"But the medical examiner and police reports both agreed that there was a multitude of prescription drugs in your stomach."

"They may have been in my stomach, but I didn't put them there."

Grandpa Joe interjected, "Nicholas. Misty. This is where I should probably go. These are things that are personal. Doctor and patient stuff."

"No, Joseph," Misty entreated, "Please stay. You have been so kind since this all happened... I trust you."

Nick looked over at his grandfather. "Well, I am sure that in normal circumstances, this would be highly irregular... but these are not normal circumstances." Nick raised a finger of caution to his grandfather, "But, make sure that you don't interrupt." He continued with Misty, "You didn't put them there... what do you mean?" Nick continued,

"That night," Misty recalled, "I was to meet a buyer for a series of paintings from my exhibit. He had contacted me by email; he seemed enthralled by my series called 'Shadows' and was going to pay me three thousand dollars cash for them." She continued, "I had just gotten out of the shower, so I dried off quickly and got dressed. I was getting ready to meet him when I heard a knock at my door, he must have been early. I walked up to the door and started getting a *really* bad headache... like out of nowhere...I opened the door and I... I must have passed out. The next thing I knew, I was like this." Misty looked down at herself and shook her head.

Nick leaned back in his chair and thought. He

looked over at Grandpa Joe. "You were right... this is a mystery." He then turned back to Misty. "This headache... have you had something like this happen before?"

"Now that you mention it, yes. I would get them from time to time... especially when I was younger. I remember once, my parents and I walked into an old antique shop, and I was overwhelmed with sadness and a terrible headache, it made me sick to my stomach. Later we found out that there had been a murder committed there back in the 1950's from a robbery gone wrong... the store owner was killed."

"That was the only time?"

Misty thought back through her life and recalled a handful of other times that it seemed as though she could sense tragic events from the past.

Nick tapped his pen and was direct as he could be with her, "Misty, I believe that you have Post Cognitive abilities, perhaps even some Pre-Cognitive abilities as well. You are able to view events from the past with astounding clarity and perhaps sense some impending incidents now and then. Scientifically, this kind of ability is linked to Quantum Entanglement. Metaphysically, it means that you have a stronger connection to the Universal Consciousness... but sadly, especially for those who have not trained themselves for the intensity of these events, they can make you sick... sometimes for days afterward."

Misty nodded. "That makes total sense now. I wish I would have known; I would have totally embraced it... I had a freakin' superpower... I guess it is too late now."

Nick quickly moved back to the case at hand. "Can you remember anything specifically from the night you died?"

Misty tried to recall more details from that moment but could not. "No," she said dejectedly, "I really can't."

Grandpa Joe interjected, "Seems obvious to me that the guy that she was to meet put the whammy on her, Nicholas."

Nick frowned and looked over at his grandfather, "Grandpa, please."

Grandpa Joe, realizing what he had done, grimaced, turned away, and looked out the bay window.

Nick continued with Misty, "But I agree with my grandfather. The simplest answer is usually the correct one. It seems that your buyer was the one who did this to you."

"That son of a bitch!" Misty exclaimed as she came to a realization.

Nick was perplexed. "What?"

"I had my paintings there. Did he take them?"

Nick got up and walked over to his computer. Misty and Grandpa Joe followed. Nick started going over the police report of the itemized list of items in the room. There was no mention of paintings specifically, but of art supplies. "Maybe they lumped them together with your school supplies?"

Misty folded her arms, "No, there is no way. Those paintings were large... like four feet by six feet each. There is no way that they would have missed them." Misty angrily pointed at the screen and yelled, "I was robbed. He fucking killed me for my paintings!"

Nick put down his pen and turned to Misty. "I need you try to remain calm, Misty."

Grandpa Joe rushed up and held Misty by her shoulders to comfort her. "It's ok, kiddo, we will get this figured out... Nick will get to the bottom of it." He turned and looked at Nick, as if to say, "where is your bedside manner, son?"

Nick guiltily nodded. He looked at Misty, "Grandpa Joe is right. We will get this figured out. In the meantime, go with him. He will watch after you. We will get back together soon after I find more answers."

Nick's phone rang on his desk. He could see on the screen that it was Sarah.

Grandpa Joe smiled and walked Misty toward the bay window and in a matter of a few steps they had faded away.

Nick picked up the phone, "Well good afternoon, my little magnolia."

"Hi, Nick," Sarah replied blushing on the other

end of the phone, "Have you thought about our plans for Saturday night? I owe you, remember... and I don't want you to think that I don't pay my debts."

"Of course, not..."

"I was thinking of doing something really exciting, is that ok?" she asked.

"That sounds wonderful. You go ahead and plan the whole night... but let's lay off the limbo competitions for a little longer."

"Certainly," she laughed. "So, the resort has a great spa as well. I was thinking that a nice couple's massage would be nice."

Nick was the one blushing now. "Ehmm," he stammered nervously.

Sarah started to laugh, "Relax, doctor... I'm kidding with you. I will pick you up at six."

"That should work out great," Nick said with a sigh of relief.

"Perfect, we will do dinner down on River Street and then... well... I hope you don't scare easily."

"Scare easily? What makes you say that?"

"Oh... it's a surprise," Sarah replied with a hint of mischief and excitement in her voice. "Ok, I *must* tell you... I'm just too excited! I got us a paranormal tour of a real haunted house! We get to use equipment and night vision cameras and everything! I have a friend who is a docent at one of the old mansions in town... we are getting a private tour!"

Nick slapped his forehead in disbelief. As if he didn't have enough of the spirit world in his life... now there was this- he was very happy that they weren't video chatting or Sarah would have seen the exasperated look on his face. He mustered up as much feigned enthusiasm as he could. "That's so amazing. Sounds a bit expensive, though... are you sure?" he said, trying to get out of it.

"It's not expensive at all! I had a limited-edition copy of <u>The Old Man and the Sea</u>, it's not a first edition... I traded it for us to have three whole hours to investigate with my friend Jenny! Doesn't it sound just *so* creepy?" Sarah said eagerly.

Nick shrugged, "Sure does... can't wait... I will see you tomorrow then?"

"You bet! Wear gym shoes!" she said as she hung up.

He knew that they would have a good time, he was just looking for some time away from his new extracurricular career. He and Sarah had been spending a lot of time together and he enjoyed it tremendously.

They hadn't done anything too physical, due to his recovery still being in process. But he would bring her lunch occasionally at her family's antique shop and just chat. Or they would go to the farmers' market in Forsyth Park on the weekends. Nothing too extravagant and nothing too serious... yet.

And they had so much in common: from classic

literature to scary, or as she liked to call them *creepy*, movies, even that they both loved pizza- loaded with no onions. They were just always in synch with each other. Nick supposed that the paranormal was just one more thing that they had in common. She, of course, had no idea that they had it in common, but in a sense, it didn't surprise him at all.

His grandfather had told him that they were entangled. This was just more evidence of it on some level.

"Evidence," Nick whispered. He needed to see the evidence logs and photos. He also needed to find out if there were any brochures of Misty's exhibit... maybe it had some pictures of her paintings, perhaps there was a clue there as well; with a few more phone calls and emails the information that he was looking for was being gathered.

Nick looked at the clock, it was almost two, time for his video conference with the hospital. He opened the drawer to his desk and pulled out a package of granola bars. "Big lunch today... at least these extracurricular activities are keeping me in shape," he grumbled as gathered his paperwork and began to prepare for the Video Conference.

CHAPTER SIX

Friday was "Office Day," Lisa's favorite day of the work week. It was the day that kept the office organized and documented. Granted, she knew that Nick only had a few clients in house, but the files and paperwork that had to be kept for the Police Department and the Hospital were quite substantial. They needed to be maintained or it would get out of control quickly. This gave her the time to keep everything filed and cross referenced... and Lisa loved keeping everything organized.

Nick arrived at the office and went straight up to his office. Lisa was already happily organizing the file boxes from the clients and studies that Nick had gone over the past week. When he got to his office, he poured a cup of coffee from the press pot- Lisa always had a press pot ready for him for Office Day- and began to go through his mail and emails.

Nick caught a glimmer of blue from the corner of

his eye, "Good Morning, Grandpa Joe."

There was Grandpa Joe, standing next to the old telescope with his right hand resting on top of it. "I really should figure out a way to announce that I'm coming over, shouldn't I?" Grandpa Joe snickered. "I mean you might be busy with company, now that you and Sarah have hit it off so well."

Nick shot his grandfather an astonished look. "Be busy with? Grandpa Joe!"

"I'm sorry, you aren't hitting it off so well?"

"Well, yes... I think we are. We really have only started to see each other."

"And this isn't the only place that I can show up you know. What if you are having a romantic dinner and I just pop in? That would be awkward, wouldn't it?"

"Seriously?" Nick interjected.

"So, we need to work out a signal; like the old 'tie on the door handle' bit. Something that will let me know that you are... busy."

"Grandpa Joe!"

"What? I'm your grandfather for cryin' out loud, I'm not naive about these things, I was in the Army. You think your father just popped up in a cabbage patch?"

"Ok, that's enough," Nick interrupted, a little on the perturbed side. "Really. I am trying to work here, Grandpa Joe!" Nick was a bit louder than he expected. He composed himself, turned back to his computer, took a breath, and stifled a laugh, "Besides, when I was six, you said dad was delivered by the stork."

Grandpa Joe burst into laughter, slapping his hand down on the front end of the telescope… and the telescope moved downward.

They looked at each other in amazement.

The telescope moved… it most definitely moved.

They both saw it move.

Nick spoke first, "Did that just happen?"

His grandfather was just as dumbfounded as Nick was. "Yes, I believe it did," he said slowly moving his hand up and down and watching it pass through the telescope.

"Has that happened before?"

Grandpa Joe replied cautiously. "I think I would have remembered something like that! I will most assuredly look into it." He stopped and stared at his hand, "I *definitely* have to look into it." He smiled and looked at Nick, "If anything, it'll make for a keen party trick!"

"Whatever just happened, it has some wide-reaching implications," Nick pondered.

"Well, let's not get ahead of ourselves, boy, it's not like I was levitating objects around a room or manipulating lottery balls… hey… that's an idea!"

"Stop it, Grandpa Joe!"

"I'm kidding! I would never!"

Nick raised an eyebrow at his grandfather.

Grandpa Joe made the scout salute and smiled, "I

would never!" He quickly changed the subject, "So any updates on Misty's situation?"

"Well, I'm hoping to get some information delivered today that should help. So, we will see." Nick turned back to his laptop, "But in the meantime, I did some research. Come look at this." Nick pointed at a map of the historic district of Savannah. "Look," he said pointing. "I have marked all the locations of an opioid overdose that has happened so far this year."

"That's quite a grouping," Grandpa Joe noted.

"Twelve of them all within thirteen blocks of each other. Heck, it's almost a perfect circle, except for these five locations... these are where they found the victims outside and not in a residence. I have the clerks from the Savannah P.D, sending me the reports, to see if there is anything that connects the victims that might be considered *unusual*."

Grandpa Joe clapped his hands together, "Well, I guess that's where I will go check out things from my end. There's an old orphanage in that area of town that has a lot of otherworldly witnesses."

Nick looked up and nodded. "Could you? That would help tremendously!"

"I'm on it, Nicholas," Grandpa Joe declared and faded away.

With that, Nick got back to work, organizing his notes and making sure that his presentations were sound for the upcoming police conference. It wasn't long before the parcels that he was looking for arrived by bike messenger.

Lisa buzzed him. "Dr. Williams, there are some parcels here for you, would like me to bring them to you or..."

Nick knew what she was going to say, Lisa was constantly riding him to keep his legs moving and getting his steps in for the day, especially since the accident.

"... Would you like to come down and collect them yourself?"

He smiled and shook his head; he *knew* she was going to say that. He took a deep breath, hit the reply button, and said, "I will be right down."

Lisa smiled with accomplishment. So much so that she was still smiling smugly as Nick stepped off the elevator. She held out the large manila envelopes to Nick as he walked with purpose to her to get them. "Here you are, doctor," she declared proudly.

"Thank you, Ms. Davidson," Nick said as he took the packages from her. "And thank you for keeping me moving too."

"Just making sure that you are following the hospital's orders. Got to keep that knee from locking up, you know."

"Oh, I know... I know!" He opened one and examined the contents; it was Misty's Exhibition Booklet. The other had to be copies of the police reports.

He turned and headed back toward the elevator.

"Perhaps, you should take the stairs up to your office, doctor," Lisa said as she walked around her desk and cut him off from the elevator.

Nick shrugged, he knew that she was right, he needed to keep that knee moving or it would lock up and he would be using a cane for the rest of his life. "Okay, okay... you are worse than Kevin!" and he started up the steps.

"The funny therapist from the hospital? He's adorable. I'll take that as a compliment." Lisa watched to make sure that he was doing all right and went back to her organizing, happy in the knowledge that she was helping him whether he liked it or not.

Nick made it to the top of the stairs and felt a sense of accomplishment. Yes, he still needed his cane, but he made it up the steps without too much trouble at all.

He went back into his study and sat down to take a closer look at Misty's Exhibition Booklet. It was clear that she was a very talented young artist. Her sculpture work was fluid and precise, showing a balance and depth well beyond her age, but nothing that would show that she was troubled and "battling with her demons" so to speak. He paged through a little further and came to her paintings.

Her landscapes were light and cheerful, celebrating the wonders of nature without a hint of negativity. Her "Pups are Family" series of dog photos were all very expressive and again showed no sign at all of subjugation.

Nick got to the page of her "Shadows" series of paintings and was struck by the absolute and shocking turn. Gone were the happy pastels, the bright colors, and celebrations of nature. They were now replaced by large, sharp and gutting slashes of paint. There was nothing "forgiving" about them. The angst was palpable. The prevailing sense of fear was omnipresent in every corner of the canvas. They were four paintings that were completely different from all of her other works. It was as though she was expressing an oppression that was profound.

Nick leaned back from the computer and thought, "Oppression." His mind went back to his studies... soon he found himself reaching for book Thirty-Four in his Spirit Library.

He paged through the tome. "Demonic Oppression," Nick muttered as if guided by instinct.

Grandpa Joe appeared in the room. "Demonic Oppression! That's a mighty weighty subject... any particular reason?"

"I thought you were checking things out on your end... what are you doing here?"

"What part of 'outside the concept of time' did you miss, Nicholas? I am never early or late. I am always where I need to be when I need to be there," his grandfather replied sarcastically.

"Ah, yes," Nick replied, realizing his mistake, "Of course."

"Now, what's this about Demonic Oppression?"

"Misty," Nick continued as he traced his way through the volume. "I believe that there *may be* something paranormal when it comes to her murder. I remembered reading about Demonic Oppression in this Volume... I'm sure of it."

"What made you think that?"

Nick stopped his hand on the page and looked up at Grandpa Joe, "All of her other work is light, positive and done with a zest for life... her 'Shadow' paintings are completely different."

"Maybe she was expressing herself differently... everyone carries their own baggage..."

"One shouldn't have to live in the shadows of one's worst moments."

"Oh," Grandpa Joe remarked, "That's a good one."

"I heard it somewhere," Nick answered with a smile, then pivoted back to the subject. "I don't think she was living in the shadows of her worst moments... this was different... there was an outside presence that was affecting her. At least, she could sense its presence."

He flipped through the pages and checked his notes until he found what he was looking for. "There it is!" he continued reading, "Demonic Oppression is believed to be one of the first stages of the process in which individuals are possessed by malevolent beings. These beings are preternatural and often referred to as demons. It is the first stage of a possession. The individual with the oppression will often have erased memories, actions, and can be prone to fainting and outbursts as if they are not in control of themselves."

Nick looked up at his grandfather, "The entity did not want to be found out... Misty's dark paintings were a clue to its identity. She was basically painting an artistic representation of what was trying to attack her."

"You think the girl was possessed?"

Nick thought a moment. "No... I think that she was being *oppressed*... perhaps the entity was using the 'buyer' angle to get closer to her to do here harm. But her latent abilities were trying to warn her. It must have been too late."

He continued reading, "It seems that these malevolent entities need a way *in* before they can do damage," he continued pointing at the section below the one he just read. "But I am beginning to think that her killer did so in order to hide themselves."

"You've lost me here, Nicholas..."

"I would be willing to bet that Misty's killer was someone possessed by a preternatural being. But if that is true, that leads to something more terrifying."

"There is someone walking around possessed by a serial killing demon inside of them."

Nick nodded. "I suspect that Misty's subconscious was able to see the true killer's identity with her abundant but completely untrained gifts. Ultimately, that is why she was killed, she did mention that she had always felt like she could sense things, but she never thought that they were anything of use, so she never developed them... I should talk to my contacts at the police department."

Grandpa Joe shook his head sternly, "And tell them what, Nicholas? That an evil supernatural being is murdering the good people of Savannah? And the person who is possessed by this killer demon doesn't realize that they are even doing it? They'll demand a psychological evaluation of you! And probably lock you away!" Grandpa Joe paused and composed himself, then continued in a more measured tone, "I'm afraid that this is a situation that you and you alone are uniquely qualified to manage."

"Perhaps, you are right... but I'm not alone. I have you... *we* will have to work on this by ourselves for now."

"Indeed," Grandpa Joe affirmed.

"How did things at the orphanage go?"

"I'm glad you asked. There have been several sightings of a shadowy figure of a man wearing a top hat in the area. The local spirits say that it has only been seen recently..."

"... Like since the beginning of the year?"

"Yes... but here's the problem, Nicholas... none of the ones that I had a chance to chat with have caught a clear sighting of him. Just a blur of activity here and a vague vision there. And before long... another victim."

"So... this shadowy hat guy is a spooky version of Sasquatch? A ghost story for ghosts to scare little ghosts?"

"Oh goodness, no. Sasquatch is very much real," Grandpa Joe mumbled.

"Wait... What?" Nick asked, leaning in.

"We can talk about that later, Nicholas... right now we need to focus. Give me time in the physical world, we will get a solid reading on this Hat Man. I have more sources to cultivate. This is a big city after all."

Nick nodded, "Just be careful, Grandpa Joe. If this is a preternatural being, then it will have a lot more muscle than the average spirit... even one that was a *jerk* in life."

Grandpa Joe started to walk toward the bay window, he stopped and turned back to Nick. "Don't let this consume you, Nicholas."

"I won't, Grandpa Joe."

"I mean it now... You have to remember that you can only help these spirits in need if you *remain* on your side. I understand the sense of urgency, but you have to live your life as well. Don't become Ahab."

Nick nodded with the acceptance of the lesson.

"Yes, sir."

Grandpa Joe gave his grandson a wink and faded away.

Nick turned back to his desk and the spirit world dissipated into the real world of his office. He began to look at Misty's works again. There was something about her "Shadow" paintings. There had to be clue in them, he could feel it in his gut... but he just couldn't figure it out.

CHAPTER SEVEN

Sarah and Nick had a wonderful time at dinner. They made small talk throughout the meal. Each of them sharing a little more about themselves and getting closer.

"My family has lived in Savannah nearly since its founding back in 1733," Sarah shared. "My ancestors were fabric and spice merchants. According to Aunt Mary, Oglethorpe would *only* buy his tea from our family... but then again, she always said to burn sage once a month in your house to ward off evil spirits."

Nick giggled nervously, "Oh... she was a..."

"A bit looney," Sarah interrupted, "It's okay, she freely admitted it."

Nick's eyebrows raised a bit, "I was going to say that she was a believer in ghosts... but that takes it a step further."

"Oh, I don't mean it in a negative way. She was just... always more... intrigued about things of the mystical nature. Constantly on the lookout for strange antiques." Sarah looked at Nick and leaned in, "I'll be honest, I have always been fascinated with the supernatural myself and I have been told my whole life that Savannah is just bursting with ghosts, but I have always had a hard time believing that. Probably just the old cemeteries or a few historic mansions. I just don't think that they are all over the place... *I* certainly haven't seen any."

Nick shifted uncomfortably in his chair as the spirit of an attractive and full bosomed prostitute walked behind Sarah's chair and blew him a kiss. "You don't say... I thought it was all a tourist thing."

Sarah took a bite of her key lime pie that was just delivered, "Oh yes, there is that too. There are tons of charlatans out there, you know, just trying to make money. Lord knows they make a fortune in t-shirt sales and ghost tours in this town, but there is such a rich history here and they say that ghost sightings that have gone back centuries." She smiled, "I am rather excited about tonight though... no corny ghost stories, just the history of the building, real ghosts... and us."

Nick sipped his coffee and tried to steer the conversation back to Sarah's family. "So, your family comes from a long line of merchants?"

"Oh yes, and we have had our brushes with history that actually *have* been documented... not just through Aunt Mary," she joked.

Nick smiled and took another sip of coffee.

"We know that we had a relative named Roger Forsyth, who conspired with the Habersham brothers to help spark the American Revolution in the basement of the Olde Pink House."

Nick was fascinated, "Wow, Roger Forsyth!" He leaned in to listen better, when he saw the prostitute stop, turn and rush back to their table. Nick tried desperately to ignore her and started to take a longer sip of coffee.

"You know Roger?" she shouted with excitement. "Ah, good ol' Roger," she reminisced, "aptly named too! He's my best customer! Endowed like a pack mule!"

Nick spit out his coffee. Fortunately, it didn't hit Sarah, but it most definitely made a mess on him and the table. "I am so sorry," Nick tried desperately to recover and clean himself up, "I had this... this tickle in my throat."

"It's okay," Sarah consoled him, "It happens. No big deal."

"You can give me a tickle in my throat for a shilling, your highness," the prostitute teased, licking her lips. "The name's Josette... any friend of Roger's is a friend of mine."

Nick started coughing and got up from the table. "Excuse me, I'm so sorry," he said to Sarah. He picked up his cane, then gave the prostitute an angry "follow me" head nod as he walked briskly toward the men's room.

The prostitute dutifully followed.

Nick checked to make sure the bathroom was clear as soon as he got in and locked the door behind him. A second later, Josette phased through the locked door.

"I knew you were a goer, the second I laid eyes on you, you randy little fiend. So, what'll it be?" she asked as she pulled her hair back.

Nick put his hands up to stop Josette from any further advances. "Look, I brought you in here to try to help you."

"I don't need help... unless it's a proper servicing that you are offering," Josette badgered.

Nick, again, put up his hands to stop her. "I don't think you realize the situation that you are in."

"What? For Christ's sake. Are you a constable? Shit."

"No, I am a psych... a... scientist and I need to ask you a question," Nick looked at his watch, he had seven, maybe eight, minutes to get back to Sarah before she would begin to think something was physically wrong with him. "I have to ask you... do you know what condition you are in?"

"Condition? Oh, you're French," Josette bristled. She took a step back, reached up to her shoulders, unbuttoned her top and let her shirt fall, exposing herself to him. "You like to see before you buy."

Nick turned away and covered his eyes. "That's not what I meant at all! Put your top back on!"

Josette was very confused as she pulled her shirt back up. "Well make up your mind! Roger would have already had me bent over that bench over there. You better not be wasting my time!"

"That's just it," Nick said cautiously making sure that she was fully covered before engaging. "I am not sure how to tell you this but... look, before you walked into the restaurant... I mean the pub here and saw me... what do you remember?"

Josette looked at Nick with mild disgust. "You just want to talk?" she asked rolling her eyes. She let out an exasperated sigh, "This morning, I was down at the docks, finishing my employment with the Captain of a West Indian Tea Company ship, thank you very much... but apparently that isn't happening tonight... then I was crossing the street when the runaway carriage came out of nowhere... I still don't see how those horses didn't trample me."

Nick gave her a look of concern.

Slowly, it dawned on Josette. A look of horror crossed her face, "Wait... they *did* trample me? I didn't make it." Tears welled up in her eyes, "Am I... I cannot be... am I... dead?"

Nick was compassionate as he could be when he replied, "You are."

Josette crumpled to the floor and began to weep, "Oh, God. What is going to happen to Liam?"

"Liam?"

"My baby brother. He was to start working as a cabin boy on Sunday... now, he will end up in the orphanage."

Again, Nick was trying to be as sympathetic as possible, "Josette, you don't have to worry about Liam."

"I don't?"

Nick took a moment to try to form his thoughts carefully, "Josette, Liam is not in an orphanage. You see, the accident happened a long time ago."

"What?"

"What year is it?" he asked.

"Why, 1775... I know that much."

"You think that this is 1775, but it isn't. It is over two hundred and forty years later. You have been Affixed to the day that you died. We are now in the Twenty First Century."

"So... I'm in hell?"

Nick leaned against the sink next to her, as his knee didn't quite bend that much yet. "Josette, I know a lot about these things... it is because you have such bond with your brother and that you passed so unexpectedly, that you weren't able to process the events that happened. So, you stayed *Affixed* in the day... even though that day was over two hundred forty years ago. We need to help you find peace before irreparable damage is done to your spiritual self."

"Oh no! I wasn't there for him at all. He must have felt so alone. What have I done? Don't you know what happens to people like me when they die? It's not all harps and clouds, your highness... not for my lot."

"That's not necessarily true at all. I consider myself a remarkably good judge of character, and you seem like a good person overall; it is just that you were handed a rough go in life. Do you have a religious teaching that you follow?"

"Yes, I was raised..."

Nick stopped her. "It's ok, I don't need to know. But, perhaps, if you make peace with yourself through your beliefs, it will help."

She nodded.

"One should never have to live in the shadow of their worst days, Josette. Let me see what I can find out about Liam, okay? It may take me some time, but we will get through this, and you will move on. We will work on it together."

Josette sniffled and wiped her tears, "You would help me even though you know who I am?"

Nick smiled, "That's just it, Josette, I don't know who you are, I know what you did for a living... that's all... and that is not *you*."

Josette looked up at Nick and started to smile back, "Yeh, you are right... I am so much more than this!"

"Exactly!" Nick encouraged her. He glanced down at his watch, "Oh boy, I have to get going... I'm on a date... I mean, I am courting the young lady who is at my table. How about we get together and chat at the Colonial Park Cemetery next Wednesday?"

"Where is the Colonial Cemetery? There is only one cemetery in town... Christ Church Cemetery just south of Oglethorpe Square."

Nick thought quickly. Of course, Colonial Park Cemetery wouldn't have been called that back in the late 1700's... and it is just south of Oglethorpe Square... that had to be it. "Yes, that's the one," he said standing back up. "I will meet you there at noon on Wednesday and we can try to work through this."

Josette composed herself, "This is so much to grasp. I'm... deceased. I thought I was alive this morning... hell, I felt that I was alive just a few moments ago. It is all becoming so much clearer now." She stood up and looked at Nick, "I suppose that I have a considerable amount of soul searching to do. I thank you, good sir."

"Nick. Call me, Nick."

"You have a very kind heart to take pity on one such as myself, Nick."

Nick bowed his head, as he wasn't abreast of the customs of the period, but it seemed to pass as a proper greeting with Governor Gwinnett. "There is nothing about you that requires pity, Josette. You are a good person, I do not know your life story, and what the circumstances were that put you in this business to survive. We will work together to help you move on."

"Yes, that would be... heartening," Josette obliged, "Christ Church Cemetery at noon on Wednesday," Josette went to hug Nick and passed right through him.

The sensation hit Nick like a frozen wall of static electricity. He saw his breath in the air, he looked at his arms and every hair was standing on end.

Josette turned to face Nick as she started to fade away and smiled, "Well, that wasn't the rise I was expecting to give you... but I suppose it is the proper one after all. See you Wednesday." She blew him a kiss and vanished.

Nick took a deep breath and looked at himself in the mirror. He mumbled to himself, "Got to watch the freelancing, Nick. You can't keep disappearing on Sarah like this."

He washed his hands and looked at his clothes. "Not bad," the coffee spots had evaporated, good thing he was wearing a plaid shirt. Rolling his eyes, he grumbled, "Even though you are going to smell like a coffee cup the rest of the night." He looked at his watch. "Seven minutes... perfect," he said as he unlocked the bathroom and headed back to the table.

"Everything alright?" Sarah asked cautiously.

"Everything is fantastic!" Nick replied cheerfully. He waved down their server and pointed to his cup, "I'm sorry, can I bother you for a fill up? I let this one get cold."

The server nodded and headed to the side station to get more coffee.

"Now," Nick said, as he gazed across the candle lit table, "Where were we... oh yes, Roger Forsyth and the Habersham brothers."

Sarah was impressed that Nick really was listening on their date... not like so many others before. "Yes, and then there was my great, great grandmother Josephine. She actually *married* a Yankee named William!"

"You don't say! That must have been quite the scandal."

"Oh, it was! He was a lieutenant in Sherman's Army during the War of Northern Aggression."

"The what?"

Sarah smiled at Nick's naivete. "The Civil War."

"Oh... right! I knew that," Nick covered sheepishly.

"You see, the story goes... wait, I should preface this by saying that *this* part of the history was from Aunt Mary... although Josephine *did* really marry a Yankee lieutenant from Sherman's Army. Anyway," she continued taking another bite of her pie, "the story goes that when the town fathers of Savannah heard of the path of destruction that Sherman and his troops had waged, they gathered the prettiest single ladies in the city, of which Josephine was one, put out a huge spread of food and drink and met them invaders under a flag of truce as they approached."

The server brought Nick a fresh cup of coffee.

Nick thanked the server and turned to Sarah. "Go on. This is fascinating," he said enthralled.

"Well, as the Sherman and his officers came forward. The mayor handed the key to the city to Sherman saying that the city was theirs. But please don't destroy her, she is far too beautiful."

Nick smiled, "Really?"

"Well, according to Aunt Mary, Lieutenant William Sexton saw great, great grandmother Josephine by the Chatham Artillery Punch Bowl and was instantly smitten. He looked at General Sherman and encouraged him to take the offer. The rest as they say is history."

Nick took a sip of his fresh coffee and couldn't help but smile. "If that is even remotely true... it is genius!"

"I know! Right?" Sarah laughed. "But there is more!"

"Oh, please continue!"

"As you can imagine, Josephine's family wasn't pleased that their Southern Belle of a daughter had fallen for a no-good Yankee Scoundrel!"

"I *can't* imagine."

"They did everything that they could to discourage her. But then one day... remember, this is from Aunt Mary... Josephine's family was walking along the riverfront on a windy day when suddenly a rogue wave swept her little brother and a friend into the river."

"Oh no!"

"Without hesitation, William dove into the water in his full uniform and saved the boys. After that, Josephine had the blessing of the family and as such," Sarah paused to have the last bite of her pie for dramatic effect. "My family tree continued and here I am," she smiled mischievously at Nick.

Nick was fascinated by every word she spoke. They had been seeing each other for a while now and Nick could feel the bond growing stronger between them.

"Now... before you finish your coffee... tell me about you, your work and your family."

Nick laughed, "Well it certainly isn't as colorful as yours. You had brothers in the Revolution. I'm from Wisconsin, our history pretty much goes back to great grandpa's tractor."

Sarah giggled. "Okay, smarty pants... what about work?"

Nick tried desperately to make the field of psychology as exciting as he could.

He talked about statistics and using proper profiling techniques. He talked about how the hospitals use his information to create a more inclusive and welcoming work environment and he talked about how the police department used his methodologies to rate their officers' psychological tendencies… "This is really boring isn't it?" Nick asked already knowing the answer.

Sarah tried to be as kind as she could, but she had to be honest and answered, "Yes… it really is."

They both laughed quite a bit at that.

"Hey," Nick began to wonder and look around, "Where is the check, I need to pay it if we are going to meet your friend on time."

Sarah smugly grinned, "Well… remember when you excused yourself to go to the bathroom?"

Nick knew what was coming.

"That's when I paid the check. This night was on *me*, Doctor Williams. Remember, I owed you for those lunches you brought over to the antique shop. I hope that doesn't offend your manly sensibilities."

"Not at all! As long as I get to pay next time."

Sarah smiled, reached her hand across the table and agreed, "Deal!"

A sharp static spark shocked them as their hands touched… they both jumped when it happened. Nick fought the urge, but made the corny joke anyway, "Looks like there's really a spark between us."

Sarah gazed across the table at him and smiled, "Good Lord, I hope it hasn't taken this long for you to realize that."

Soon, they were on their way to "investigate" the old mansion that Sarah's friend, Jenny, had arranged.

Nick had to admit to himself that the evening was not going as poorly as he had worried, he was certain that there would have been more spirits interrupting their dinner, but aside from the brief interruption from Josette, this night was actually going very, very well.

CHAPTER EIGHT

Sarah and Nick walked up to the old mansion. The whitewashed exterior seemed to glow in the moonlight. Sitting by the gate was Sarah's good friend, Jenny, who got up and opened it for them.

"Welcome, guys! I hope you are ready for some excitement!"

"We are!" Sarah replied eagerly.

"Great!" Jenny continued, "Now the whole house has closed circuit night vision cameras going twenty-four – seven and I will have a copy ready at the end of the session for you to take home."

"You don't have to do that!" Sarah insisted.

"And *you* didn't have to find me a rare edition of The Old Man and the Sea!"

Nick looked around the grounds on the outside of the mansion. He didn't see any spirits hanging around. "Maybe this will just be a fun night of goofy ghost hunting after all," he thought to himself.

"Well, come on in! I will show you the equipment and we will go over the plan for the next three hours," Jenny said, leading the way inside.

Sarah and Nick followed Jenny up the back stairs, Nick was still using his cane to carefully climb. Suddenly, a flash of blue caught Nick's eye from a reflection in the window. His heart sank, he turned his head to get a closer look and it was gone.

He looked around.

He knew that glow all too well. Someone was there and wanting attention... but then why did they disappear so quickly?

He looked up at the window again and saw the cause, it was in the upstairs window of the building behind them across the courtyard. Nick turned and saw the spirit of a young woman in the upstairs window staring at across the courtyard to the house they were entering, her lips were pursed, and her eyebrows were furrowed. Nick quickly asked his host, "Jenny, what is the building behind us?"

"Jenny held the door open for her guests and replied, "That is the old servants' quarters... the original owners of this house never owned slaves, they had servants. Legend has it that one of the last maids died of grief after losing her son to Pleurosis in the 1930's."

Sarah, being so very eager, jumped in, "Are we going to get to investigate there too?"

Jenny laughed, "Sure, that shouldn't be an issue.

But remember, the walls there are not as thick as the main house here. Some of these walls are more than a foot thick of brick, so sound doesn't get in as easily."

Sarah looked puzzled, "What does that have to do with ghosts?"

Jenny explained, "Well, in case you go and get some EVP's from that building, you have to remember that the walls are very thin, so it is probably coming from outside."

Sarah nodded.

Nick nodded along with her in solidarity even though he kept on eye on the young woman in the window. She shook her head with concern and folded her arms as if she was waiting for someone.

"Are you coming inside, Nick?" Sarah asked as she stood next to Jenny in the back-kitchen area of the mansion.

Nick snapped out of his thoughts, "Of course... sorry," and he went up the last few steps to join them.

Once inside, Jenny brought them into a room that used to be the dining room for the residents. In it, there was a table that had multiple video monitors from around the house.

"This is base," Jenny said decisively. "This is where I will be most of the evening, keeping an eye on everything." She pointed at the monitors, "If I see something or hear something in any of these rooms, I can direct you to it, so you have a better chance of interacting with the entities."

"Cool," Sarah whispered impatiently, "so cool."

Nick couldn't help but smile at her excitement.

Jenny continued as she pointed at the electronic devices laid out on the other side of the table, "This is your equipment for the investigation." She picked up one, "Here is a K-II meter, it is used to detect fluctuations in the electromagnetic field... see these lights?"

Sarah leaned in and nodded.

"If you see these flicker... that means there is a ghost present. Well, in theory anyway. These work best when you use *Yes or No* questions."

Sarah was totally immersed in the moment, "Got it. *Yes or No* questions."

Jenny went on to explain the rest of the items on the table; from a laser thermometer to dowsing rods and from REM Pods to laser grids.

"Oh, I can't wait to use them all! But what about audio recorders?"

"Actually, if you have a cell phone, we encourage you to use the Voice Memo App... this way you can review them at your leisure."

"That's so interesting... I would have never thought of that... would you have, Nick?"

"No. That is very clever."

Jenny advised them, "But make sure that your phones are on Airplane Mode so that they don't interfere with the other equipment. We should do that now, so we don't forget."

As they switched their phones over, Nick observed that, although Sarah seemed rather nonplussed about the ghost tourism industry in Savannah... she sure seemed to be enjoying herself as she hit her Voice Memo App, started recording and put her phone in the pocket of her light sweater.

Again, he smiled at her enthusiasm.

Jenny then walked them through the house, talking about getting Baseline Readings, informing them of the history, and telling them stories that were said to have occurred in it.

Sarah listened intently.

Nick kept looking around for anything that had a sparkling blue hue.

But there was nothing. This really struck him as odd, considering that nearly everywhere else he had gone recently, he would see at least one spirit.

They made their way back to base and Jenny encouraged them to take what equipment that they thought they would need for the next hour. "After an hour, I will call you guys back here for a break and to talk about anything interesting or anomalous that might have happened."

"Awesome," Sarah gleefully chirped as she grabbed the equipment she wanted, which was pretty much all of it.

"You are going to leave something for Nick, aren't you?" Jenny laughed.

"You snooze, you lose!" Jenny beamed.

Nick shrugged his shoulders and picked up a flashlight. "Guess this one's mine then," he joked.

"Well, they *do* say that aside from your own senses, a flashlight is one of the most important pieces of equipment that you can have with you... so... good choice Nick!" Jenny smirked.

"Well, Sarah *did* make my choice pretty easy."

"Both of you need to shush!" Sarah objected, "I'm just a little excited, that's all."

Nick and Jenny laughed, "Clearly!"

"Oh, stop it," Sarah teased back, sticking her tongue out at them. "Come on Nick! Let's make our way upstairs after we do those things... what were they called again, Jenny? Base reading?"

"Close... Baseline readings, to get the normal temps and EMF, etc."

"Right! Then upstairs to the loft by the attic!" Sarah called as she was halfway out the door.

Nick followed, bracing himself on his cane.

"Good hunting, kids!" Jenny called as she sat down at the table, put on her headphones and began to look at the monitors. "They are *so* cute together."

Sarah led the way.

Up in the loft, Sarah and Nick set up for their investigation. Sarah turned on all the equipment.

While Nick dutifully held the flashlight as he leaned against the wall.

Sarah turned on the K-II meter and waited.

After a few minutes, she looked at Nick. "Think anything is with us?"

Nick looked around. The loft was completely empty. "Nope, I think we are sitting alone in a dark room on the top floor of an old mansion."

Sarah gave him a look, not realizing that Nick was just relaying what he was- or wasn't- seeing, "Are you being a stick in the mud?"

"No, not at all. I just don't..." Nick had to be careful, being in an old and potentially haunted mansion is not the best time to announce to your *would-be* girlfriend that you can see dead people, "... I just don't feel anything... maybe it's me."

"Okay," Sarah said suspiciously.

"Really, I am having a great time. Believe me, Sarah, if I felt something of the supernatural nature, I would let you know, he smiled, "This is a lot more exciting than I thought it would be."

"Are you really having fun?"

"Let me think a second," Nick quipped, "I'm in a dark spooky building with an amazing, smart, funny and stunning woman who loves getting scared... yes, I'm having a great night."

Sarah blushed slightly, "You flatterer."

Jenny, down at base, heard this entire exchange

over her headset, "Yup, *so* cute."

The K-II meter between Nick and Sarah began to flicker.

Sarah's eyes got big. "Did you see that?"

Nick cocked his head to the side while staring at the flickering lights on the device. "Yeh..." he said quickly glancing around. He saw no one.

"We should ask the Yes/No questions, right?"

Nick agreed, "Yeh, let's try that." He was still confused as to how the K-II was flickering the way that it was, and he wasn't able to see anyone.

"Ok... so, are you looking for something?"

The lights stopped.

Sarah blinked with surprise, "So, I guess that's a no."

"Looks that way..."

"Are you looking for some*one*?"

The K-II's lights began to flicker again, then stopped.

Sarah's mouth dropped, "This. Is. So. Stinkin'. Creepy... but in a cool way. Don't you just love it?"

"This is more thrilling than I expected that's for sure," Nick said as he was still wondering what kind of glitch could be happening with the equipment. He looked around the room one more time.

This time, from under the locked attic door, he saw the familiar sparkling blue glow. "Are you hiding from us?"

The K-II meter lit up again briefly.

Sarah looked over at Nick with a sense of pride that he was taking part.

"Are we scaring you?" she continued questioning.

Nothing.

"Is there someone else out here that you are hiding from?" Sarah asked.

The lights on the meter flickered.

She continued, "Are you playing a game?"

The lights lit up full, then stopped.

"This is so cool," Sarah muttered, "So cool."

"Are you playing hide and seek?" Nick asked.

This time Nick heard the voice of the entity behind the locked attic door. "Have they called 'Olly Olly Oxen Free'? I don't wanna get tagged." The meter flashed briefly as the entity behind the door spoke.

Nick smiled, remembering the same safe words that the neighborhood kids used when he was playing Hide and Seek, "Yes."

Sarah perceived it as him affirming the response of the K-II meter. "The game is over. Why don't you come out and chat with us?"

"Okie dokie!" The K-II lit up like a Christmas tree as the entity stepped out of the attic through the door. "Did I really win?"

Nick looked at the spirit of a young boy, dressed in a checkered shirt, pants and heavy leather shoes as he sparkled in shimmering blue. He looked like he was from the 1920's or 30's. Nick's heart ached. Aside from Adam Kensington, who was so far away across the park, Nick hadn't yet seen the spirit of a child. But here was this adorable little soul, right in front of him.

Nick smiled, "Yes."

Sarah got an idea, "Let's introduce ourselves! My name is Sarah."

She looked over at Nick.

"My name is Nick," he obliged.

The young boy skipped closer to them from the attic, walked right next to Sarah and stopped in between them by the K-II meter which flickered frantically. "My name is Tommy!" he said enthusiastically.

"Did you feel that?" Sarah asked Nick, rubbing her arms.

"Feel what?" he answered.

"That cold… there was a wave of cold air that just rushed by me. I've got chills," she said looking down at her arms and rubbing them.

"That is fascinating," Nick said. He looked at the young boy and gave him a wink while Sarah was looking at her arms; then he looked back to Sarah. "Perhaps you are a bit sensitive like your Aunt Mary?"

"Watch it, buster," Sarah said squinting her eyes at him.

"Or maybe not," Nick said, holding up his hands and recovering as fast as he could.

Sarah went back to questioning, "Are you a child?"

The lights on the meter blipped slightly as Tommy replied, "I'm seven! I'm not a child."

She went on, "Do you like ice cream?"

Tommy replied to Sarah and the meter flickered, "I sure do! The ice cream parlor a few blocks away has the *best* ice cream too!" Then he turned to Nick, "She's nice, I like her! Are we going for ice cream?"

Nick paused to think of a proper response, "I do too. Maybe we can all go for some ice cream together."

Sarah watched as the K-II meter flickered its way all the way to the top red light reading. She turned to Nick, it was adorable how he seemed to be *connecting* with the spirit... well, pretending to anyway.

"That would be so much fun!" Tommy exclaimed.

"Do you know what year it is?" Sarah asked.

Tommy looked at her with a puzzled look on his face. He turned to Nick while pointing back at Sarah, "Is she serious?"

Nick knew that he had to figure out if little Tommy was stuck or had been wondering lost for nearly a hundred years, "Yes, do you know what year it is?"

The meter started lighting up again as Tommy did his calculations. "Let's see, I know I was born in 1918... and it's my seventh birthday... so it is... 1925!" he proclaimed proudly.

Nick breathed a small sigh of relief that little Tommy hadn't been wandering lost but was enjoying his one day over and over again. At least, he wasn't being diminished. He had time... at least more time than he had with Governor Gwinnett.

Sarah saw the lights glimmer, so she took it as a *Yes* answer. "Oh good! So, do you like what you've seen of the future?"

Tommy looked at Nick again with a puzzled gaze, "Huh?"

Nick quickly interrupted the proceedings and looked at Sarah. "Hey, umm, I hate to ask this, do you think we could take a break?" He said as he got up. "I could use some fresh air and stretch my legs."

"Mr. Nick? What is she talking about?"

Sarah stopped her train of thought, looked at her watch and realized that it was a little more than an hour since they had started. "Yes, perhaps you are right. I could use a break too."

Nick helped Sarah pick up the equipment and used his flashlight to light their way downstairs. He subtly motioned little Teddy to follow along.

"Mr. Nick?" Tommy asked as he hopped down the stairs behind them. "What is she talking about?"

Nick and Sarah went down to the first floor and met Jenny.

Nick stood by the door and the ladies chatted. Soon, Tommy came through the doorway and stood next to him. Only Nick noticed the K-II meter's lights blipping on the table.

"What's going on, Mr. Nick?" Teddy asked.

Nick motioned Tommy to stay put, walked over to the K-II meter and turned it off. "Don't want to waste the battery," he said with a nod to Jenny and returned to Tommy by the door.

Jenny glanced at Sarah, "He's so attentive!" Then knowingly, "You got some good interaction up there, didn't you?"

"Oh man, you aren't kidding!" Sarah said piling the equipment back on the table. "But I had no idea that it was this exhausting!"

Jenny laughed, "You are right. People don't realize how taxing it is to sit and wait for things to happen in the dark. Then when they do, the spikes of adrenaline make your heart race like you are running a marathon."

"I know, right," Sarah said reaching into her pocket and taking out her phone.

Nick looked down at the little spirit and whispered, "Can you meet me outside on the back steps in a minute or two?"

"Sure thing, Mr. Nick!" Tommy said, then turned and started skipping down the hall. "See ya later alligator!"

Nick laughed and whispered after him, "After 'while crocodile." He pulled out his phone, turned to Sarah and Jenny. "Hey, I'm gonna step outside for a bit, if that's okay," he held the phone up nonchalantly and rolled his eyes, "Mother texted... such a worrier."

"Oh, that's fine, Jenny and I will talk about the video she has of us! Isn't it so exciting?" Sarah asked.

"Absolutely!" Nick found himself more and more contented seeing her happy. It was thrilling and a bit scary at the same time. He smiled and walked toward the back steps.

Jenny looked at Sarah. "He seems nice."

"He is. I can't believe we that have hit it off so well, especially since... you know... how we met."

"Oh yeh... that's right," Jenny said remembering the incident. "And he doesn't bring that up at all?"

"No and he is so open about his life too. It's like... we don't have a single secret." Sarah took a moment and thought about her budding relationship with Nick. "I know we really just started... but there is such a connection. It's so much more than those other guys that I have dated. He's real. He's honest..."

"And he ain't hard on the eyes either," Jenny teased.

Sarah blushed. "No, no he isn't," she said as the two of them sat down and started going through the video footage of the loft.

Outside on the back steps, Nick made his way down, leaned against the railing, placed his cane against the white brick wall and, carefully, called for Tommy. "Hey, Tommy... you out here bud?"

Nick looked around to see if he could see the telltale glow. Nothing. He gazed up across the courtyard to see if the concerned woman spirit was still there. She wasn't.

Nick was beginning to think that maybe Tommy wasn't going to show. "Tommy? You here?" he inquired again cautiously, he really didn't want the ladies to come out and see him talking to himself.

"Hiya, Mr. Nick! Tommy said as he phased through the door of the house and hopped down on the steps next to Nick.

Tommy had startled him a little. "Hiya, Tommy. Do you mind if we chat about some stuff for a bit?"

"Gosh no, Mr. Nick," the young spirit replied. "Is it about that stuff that the lady was talking about upstairs? Are we going to go get some ice cream?"

Nick shook his head. "No, Tommy, I'm afraid that going for ice cream is going to be out of the question right now."

"Darn," he replied somberly as he shuffled his left foot with disappointment. "That's okay, I had a bunch at the party."

"But," Nick continued, "what if I told you, that you could go to a place that had everything that you would ever need to make you happy?"

"But, I'm happy here, Mr. Nick," Tommy said, "I've got my mom and dad... and my dog, Hercules, and my friends. I just had a great birthday party and we played games too! I am the *best* at Hide and Seek!"

"That's what you were playing when we met, right?"

"Yeh," Tommy thought. "That's kinda funny," he said looking up at the night sky. "Sure, seems pretty late. It's awful dark out here," he continued. "I must have been hiding so long, the fellas just gave up! Ha! Told ya I was the best!" he said proudly.

Nick looked compassionately at him and asked one more question. "Tommy, what's the last thing that you remember before hearing Sarah and I talking to you outside the attic?"

Tommy had a puzzled look come across his face. "What do you mean? I told you... I was playing Hide and Seek and hid in the trunk. I did it good too! I put the extra blankets that were in the trunk over me, so even if they opened the trunk, they wouldn't see me and then I shut it tight... didn't want to get caught, ya know."

Nick now knew exactly what had happened to Tommy. Once the lid was shut tight, he couldn't get any air. Tommy had suffocated. Nick's lips pursed downward slightly at the corners and his eyebrows furrowed; he could not hide his angst.

"What's the matter, Mr. Nick? Why are you getting upset?"

Nick turned to Tommy and looked him in the eyes. He was about to tell him what had happened when a bright blue glow appeared from across the courtyard.

Nick looked up and saw the lady from the servant's house. She was standing at the doorway. Nick instantly realized that she *had* to be Tommy's mother; nothing else would explain why she looked so anxious while staring over at the mansion.

"Thomas!" She called lovingly with outstretched arms.

"Mom!" Tommy yelped as he jumped off the porch and ran into his mother's arms.

"I've been waiting for you! You had me so worried!"

"It's okay, mom. I was just playing Hide and Seek... and I won too!" Tommy pointed across the courtyard. "Mr. Nick told me so!" He cheered with pride.

"Good for you!" Tommy's mother held him tightly as she looked thankfully at Nick and nodded. Then she hugged him again a little tighter.

"C'mon, mom... Mr. Nick is gonna think I'm a sissy," he protested, even though he hugged her back just as tightly.

Nick tipped his head to her and smiled. Knowing that Tommy was in good hands, he picked up his cane and stood on the bottom step.

"Let's go, Thomas... it's time to rest," his mom instructed. "Say goodbye to your friend there."

Tommy looked back toward Nick and waved. "Bye, Mr. Nick! It was sure fun meeting you!" he shouted across the courtyard as he and his mother slowly disappeared into a gold and white sparkling light.

Nick saw a wave of energy wash over the courtyard from where Tommy and his mother once stood. As it crested over him, he felt a deep sense of abiding peace.

He took a deep breath, turned to go back up the stairs and almost ran right into his grandfather.

"Geez, Grandpa Joe!" Nick exclaimed.

"You did good there, Nicholas," Grandpa Joe grinned, "You didn't have to have a single session!"

Nick shook his head. "There wasn't much for me to do, except to *Un*-Affix Tommy. Sarah technically had as much to do with that as I did. It was her idea to go to the loft next to the attic. Plus, it didn't take much to deduce that the lady across the courtyard was his mother by the look of concern and worry that was on her face... the rest was all their doing," he replied with a sense of accomplishment.

"Either way, boy, it was a job well done."

"They definitely aren't *all* that easy are they."

"No... each and every spirit is going to be as different as any other living person would be."

Nick thought of Josette and the shock it had on her, when Nick helped her realize that she was dead; thinking that she was instantly going to hell because of her profession. He thought of Button Gwinnett and how his constant berating of himself over how he treated people, kept him from self-acceptance and moving on... and then there was Misty.

Nick turned to his grandfather, "I haven't forgotten about Misty, Grandpa Joe. I will get to the bottom of this and get her closure."

"Oh, I know, Nicholas. I know. But right now," Grandpa Joe continued, pointing over his shoulder with a smile into the white brick mansion, "you are on a date."

Nick made his way toward the back-kitchen door, "You are absolutely right."

"I usually am more than I am not," Nick's grandfather kidded. "Now, get back in there and finish your date... and if I were you, I'd tell that lovely little lady you love her before she thinks you aren't interested."

Nick's smile grew as he opened the door to the mansion, "Yes, sir." He began walking in when he turned back to his grandfather. "Thank you, Grandpa Joe."

"Goodness, what for?"

Nick paused a moment thinking about all the time that Grandpa Joe had spent with him, making his childhood so amazing. and now helping him with his new calling. He looked fondly at his grandfather and said, "Everything."

CHAPTER NINE

The next morning, Nick was up earlier than usual. It was the weekend, so he didn't have to be up... he didn't even set his alarm, but something about the night before had energized him.

He had already had breakfast, scrolled through his email and caught up on the TV shows that he had recorded the night before... and it was only ten o'clock. Now it was on to the exercises that Kevin had laid out for him.

As he was laying on the floor using the strap to stretch his legs and flex his knees to get their strength back, he came to a stunning realization. There was no real stiffness. His knee felt remarkably better.

He got up, made his way over and turned a chair away from the dining room table and sat. He gripped the strap in his hands and looped the other end down under his right foot. He then slowly moved his foot forward, building tension and extending his leg.

Again, he felt no real stiffness or pain. Could he finally have gotten use of his knee back? He checked again... There was no pain or stiffness. He paused a moment and slowly pulled his leg back. He released the strap and moved his knee forward again.

"This feels great!" he exclaimed... then thought better of it, "Okay... it feels much better." Nick carefully stood up using the back of the chair and table as a brace and gingerly took a few steps. His knee felt loose. He slowly walked into the kitchen and got a glass of water. Still no pain and no tension. "You better keep the compression sleeve on it for a while," he mumbled, "and you need to call Kevin to make sure this is really a good thing or a bad thing that you *think* is a good thing." After all, it was better to be prudent than careless.

Nick finished getting ready for the day. Then made sure to put on his compression sleeve, the extra support felt good. Clearly, he wasn't one hundred percent yet, but he walked outside and down the steps without his cane at all. *That* felt incredible.

Nick placed a quick call to Kevin. "Hey buddy! Got a question for you."

"Sure, Nick, what's up?"

"It's about my knee."

"You in more pain? Is there residual swelling?"

"No," Nick answered with a bit of astonishment, "It feels great!"

"Well, you have been doing your therapy and that

always helps. No pain?"

"No, none and I have been walking on it, carefully, with no pain either! Isn't that great?"

"No pain is always good, pal. But do me a favor and keep an eye on it and if there is any and I mean any pain or swelling, you get back here for x-rays and an MRI... in the meantime, take it easy... no triathlon competitions or competitive cycling, okay?"

That was all Nick needed to hear. "Thanks, Kevin, I will!" he said with excitement as he went out of his house and locked the door. "Take care!"

"You too, Nick... just be careful. But as long as there is no pain or swelling, it sounds like you are going to be fine."

Nick ended the call and went down the steps to the street. He stood outside his house and checked his phone for the weather, it was eleven o'clock and the weather looked to be pleasant and partly cloudy in the upper seventies. A perfect day to hit the farmers' market. Maybe meet up with Sarah for lunch at her family's shop, then come back for some binge watching. He flagged down a nearby pedicab, when his phone rang. It was Sarah.

"Good morning, my little magnolia!" he said gleefully.

Sarah didn't answer right away.

Nick continued apprehensively, "Uh... Sarah, everything okay? Are you still there?"

"Yes, Nick, of course, I'm here," she answered, then went on, "I have something pretty incredible to talk to you about."

Relieved, Nick replied, "That's funny, something incredible has happened on my end too and I have news for you! Are you free for lunch? Want to meet at the Deli on Broughton? I really think you are going to love this news!"

"I'm sure I will…"

"Well, then, what do you say about that lunch date?"

The pedicab driver waved at Nick and silently pointed at his watch, as if to ask, "Are you getting on here or what?"

Nick pantomimed back, begging for another minute.

"How about, you pick up lunch, I will close the shop early. I think we need to spend more time… alone," Sarah said with conviction.

Nick's heart started pounding in his chest and his mind raced. This day looked to be getting more amazing by the second… binge watching could wait; it could definitely wait. "Absolutely! See you in a few!" he said as he quickly put away his phone. He turned to the pedicab driver, "The corner of Julian and Price, my good man!" he commanded to the pedicab driver as he sat down.

"You got it, brother," the college aged driver said

jumping up on the pedals to get a good start.

Nick was finding himself with butterflies. His nerves were starting to get the better of him. Then realized he needed to pick up lunch, "Wait... the deli first! The one on Broughton by the ice cream parlor. Then to Julian and Price!"

The driver shook his head and chuckled. "This lady has you all wrapped up, eh?"

Nick looked at the driver. "How did you know there was a girl on the other side of the call?"

"Brother, there are only two reasons a guy begs for more time while on the phone and keeping a cab waiting. One is business... it's the weekend so that's out... and two, you called her My Little Magnolia... and Sarah. Both are kind of clues," the cabbie laughed.

Nick laughed a bit too, rubbed his newly unhindered knee and leaned back to enjoy the ride.

It really was another gorgeous day in the old city. The ride to the deli seemed almost magical as they passed the old squares with the occasional buskers playing their instruments for donations. The Spanish moss softly waving in the breeze as it hung down from the branches of the ancient oak trees.

Before he knew it; he had already picked up lunch and was at the antique shop. Sarah's family had owned the shop for well over a century. It was much bigger than Nick had imagined as well, taking up both main floors of the building for retail space and having a restoration workshop downstairs.

Nick paid the pedicab driver and stood in front of the store.   He looked at the Mercedes parked out front.   Nick found himself having a moment of disappointment. "Looks like lunch is going to be delayed a bit," he said walking into the building.

The little brass bell hanging above the door jingled brightly as he went inside. Nick shut the door and looked around, figuring that Sarah was with the person whose car was outside.

The shop was, as always, meticulous and organized. It wasn't overcrowded with odds and ends either. This was an antique shop that knew what it was doing. Of course, it still had that antique and unique smell to it. Nick supposed that was just part of the package when dealing with antiques... like a server at an Italian restaurant coming home, smelling of wood oven, garlic and marinara sauce.

Nick no sooner finished his thoughts than Sarah came from around the corner. "Good morning, Nick," she said giving him a quick hug and kiss on the cheek. Then she walked by him toward the front door.

Nick stood there confused momentarily until he saw her pull a set of keys from her pocket and click a button on the key fob. The lights on the Mercedes parked out front flashed briefly, and the horn made a short beep. Then Sarah turned the lock on the front door, flipped the "Open" sign to "Closed," and turned to him.

"So... you had fun last night, didn't you?" she asked.

Nick stood in the aisle of the shop with their lunch. "Yes, it was fun... umm, the Mercedes is yours? I thought you had a Volkswagen?"

"Yes," Sarah said grabbing his free hand and pulling him toward the office area, "I have both... and a Land Rover for when I go camping or estate sale trips. Not to mention the two fleet trucks."

Nick knew that the antiques business had done her family well over the generations; Sarah came from a very long line of the well-to-do, that much was clear, but three personal vehicles? Sarah was doing *very* well for herself.

He followed her back to the office where they usually ate lunch. It was a large oak paneled room with high backed leather chairs and a large wooden writing desk. Sarah's laptop was open on it.

Nick always felt like they were dining in an exclusive upscale niche restaurant when they ate there with the Tiffany lamps and ornate wooden framed family photos of the last five generations of the Beaumont Family on the wall that ran the antique store, including Sarah's photo right next to her Aunt Mary's.

Sarah sat down on the edge of the desk as Nick stood next to his usual chair.

"Did you notice anything?" he prodded.

"I did," Sarah said smiling, "I did indeed."

Nick pointed at his free hand, "Isn't it great! No cane!"

Sarah, in all honesty, hadn't noticed the cane at all; she had something else on her mind but still she was happy for him, "Woah! That is great news! How did this happen?"

Nick shrugged, "I don't know really, just loosened up completely during my morning stretches that Kevin had me doing... and here I am!" He held up the bag from the deli, "You ready for lunch?"

Sarah smiled, looked at Nick and shook her head, "No, not yet... I think we need to talk."

Nick slumped down in his chair. An empty pit grew in his stomach. No good had ever come from a woman telling a man that *they needed to talk.* He felt the blood rushing from his face, and it must have shown.

Sarah went over to Nick and kissed him. "Relax, silly, I'm not breaking up with you... but we need to talk." She took the deli bag and put it on the desk as she sat back down on the edge of the desk facing Nick.

Nick took a deep breath and relaxed, "Okay... what's up?"

"I'm glad you had fun last night. I did too. I have something for you to listen to," she said as she turned her laptop toward Nick.

He stared at the screen of the laptop and saw what looked to be a sound editing program.

"I didn't realize it until I got home from our date last night, but I had my Voice Memo App on my phone going during our whole time in the mansion. Some of it was a little muffled, as the phone was in the pocket of my sweater, but I found a program online, downloaded the recording and cleaned it up."

The pit in Nick's stomach had returned as fast as Sarah had kissed it away. "Really?" he asked, feigning ignorance.

Sarah hit the play button and Nick could clearly hear Sarah and himself in the loft of the old mansion.

First, he heard his voice, "Are you hiding from us?"

Then Sarah's, "Are we scaring you?" ... Is there someone else out here that you are hiding from? ... Are you playing a game? ... This is so cool ... So cool."

"Are you playing hide and seek?" he heard himself ask.

Sarah paused the recording and said excitedly, "Listen to this!"

She hit the play button again and they could clearly hear the voice of a child respond in an almost ethereal whisper, "Have they called Olly Olly Oxen Free? I don't wanna get tagged."

Sarah paused the recording again. "Did you hear that?"

Nick's eyes got big. "Wow... that's amazing!" he replied, "It sounds like a little boy."

Sarah looked at Nick and asked again, "No, Nick, I am asking did you *hear* that?"

Nick paused, "Yeh, I just told you... fascinating stuff!"

She looked at him with a questioning stare, "Because it sounds like, you are answering the child."

Nick could feel the butterflies in the pit of his stomach growing. "I was just relaying what the meter was saying, that's all."

Sarah complied, "Yeh... okay, that could be too." Then she played more of the recording.

Soon they heard the little voice, "Okie dokie!" and Nick replying, "Yes."

It continued, "Let's introduce ourselves! My name is Sarah."

"My name is Nick."

"My name is Tommy!" the ghostly voice responded.

Sarah stopped the recording again. "I want to play you another section."

Nick shifted uneasily in his chair, "Okay, sure... this is amazing stuff, isn't it? I mean, who would have thought you could record stuff like this?"

Nick felt nauseous.

Sarah nodded, pointed at the laptop, and hit play on a new recording, "Are you a child?"

The child's voice could clearly be heard saying, "I'm seven! I'm not a child."

"Do you like ice cream?"

The spirit replied, "I sure do! The ice cream parlor a few blocks away has the best ice cream too! ... She's nice, I like her!"

"I do too. Maybe we can all go for some ice cream together," Nick heard himself saying.

Sarah stopped the recording again. "Are you sure you didn't hear that? It really does sound like you are responding to the voice."

Nick shook his head, "Really, I was just responding to the meter. "How could I have heard that?" he denied. Nick felt like a heel lying to her, but what choice did he have? How could he tell Sarah that he can not only communicate with the dead, but they communicate with him, and that they can see each other just as he looks at her? She would think he was insane.

Sarah played another segment. "Do you know what year it is?"

The spirit's voice said, "Is she serious?"

"Yes, do you know what year it is?" Nick asked.

"Let's see, I know I was born in 1918... and it's my seventh birthday... so it is... 1925!" the child's voice proclaimed proudly.

The segment stopped and Sarah folded her arms in front of her. "Are you *sure* that there is nothing that you want to tell me?"

Nick steadfastly denied any knowledge of the

"extra" voice recorded the night before. "Really, this is amazing evidence. I mean, this is the kind of stuff they make movies about."

"Nick, I want you to know that I want no secrets between us. I want us to be open with each other. I think that we have something here. I don't want to cloud it with obfuscation."

Nick was torn. Every fiber of his being wanted to tell Sarah the truth, but how would she take it? How would *anyone* take it if they were told that their boyfriend talked to dead people... not just in a television physic medium sort of way... but legitimately talked and interacted with the dead?

Sarah stood up and walked over to the wall of her family's portraits. "I told you about my family history, Nick, because I wanted to be open with you. I believe that we have something very special here..."

"So, do I..."

"And, as such, I have to show you something." Sarah grabbed the corner of Aunt Mary's photo and tipped the frame to the right.

The wall behind the desk recessed back and slid open. From his chair, Nick could see inside the hidden room. Nick muttered, "Holy Shit. You're Batgirl."

It was filled with artifacts: crossbows, crucifixes, knives, sabers, goblets, books, and containers of all sorts. He stood up and walked behind the desk. He looked at Sarah and then back inside. It was massive and just as meticulous as the front of the store.

"This was my Aunt Mary's collection. Three decades of rare and mystical objects that she collected during the time that she ran the shop before she passed away twenty years ago. The shop was then run by my father.

But before she died, she brought me into this office, I was maybe eight at the time, to show me this room. It was our secret. She told me that all these items were used for some sort of mystical and metaphysical purpose of warding off, defending, vanquishing and/or protecting someone from evil entities... but I never put much stock in the mystical and paranormal. Plus, I was eight! So, it was all so... creepy. Creepy scary... not creepy fun."

"I can see where you could think that," Nick said glancing over at what looked to be a large, spiked mallet hanging on the wall.

"When my father retired five years ago, I took over the family business. Imagine how surprised I was that it was all still here, my father never knew it even existed. Of course, I have never tested or investigated any of it, except to try to find out when it was made, what it was made from and where. Like I said... I have never seen a ghost."

He turned and looked at Sarah. "Why are you showing me this?"

Sarah came around the desk and took his hands,

"I told you, dummy, I don't want us to have any secrets... there had to be a reason that Aunt Mary collected all of this and a reason that I just never could make myself sell it. There are collectors that would pay millions to get their hands on half of these items, some of them are from the fourteenth and fifteenth centuries and older. Almost all of them are one of a kind and some of them, I can't even find a date for... but something told me to hang on to them."

In that moment, Nick knew that she knew what he was hiding, she just needed him to admit it.

Nick led Sarah back to the chairs in front of the desk and sat her down. He took a deep breath. Then with his voice trembling, he began, "Okay...here it is... in the hours after the accident. I died."

Sarah's eyes widened. He had never said this before. Nick never talked about the accident and hearing this hit her like a punch in the gut. "I had no idea..."

"But only for a little bit... apparently, during that time, I crossed over into the spirit realm." He smiled, "There I met my Grandpa Joe."

A tear slowly began to fall down Sarah's cheek.

Nick leaned over and softly wiped it away. "It's okay, because that was when my grandfather told me of my purpose in life. I was to help those souls that were stuck here in the physical world to move on."

"... like Jennifer Love Hewitt?"

Nick closed his eyes and sighed, "I suppose so, yes. But, because of my psychology training, I am also able to help them work through their issues and help them find peace... then they can move on." He held her hand, "And when you visited me in the hospital, Grandpa Joe told me that you were special... that you and I were entangled... connected... and that I shouldn't let you get away. Then when you pulled out my great grandfather's copy of <u>Moby Dick</u>..."

"It proved it." Sarah sat motionless. She knew that there was something special about Nick, she had felt it from the beginning. Now there was this remarkable aspect of him that she would have never guessed if she hadn't heard the recordings. Yes, she had known for a few hours now, but it still came as a shock to have it confirmed. After a moment, she stood up and hugged Nick. "I am so happy that you told me."

Nick melted into her arms, "I am too. It makes things so much easier... but how did you know? I mean, I made every effort last night to just respond to the meter flickering."

Sarah walked over to the laptop and played the last of her recordings.

He heard is voice repeating, "Can you meet me outside on the back steps in a minute or two?"

The voice of little Tommy saying, "Sure thing, Mr. Nick! See ya later alligator!"

"After 'while crocodile."

She looked up at Nick and smiled. "*That's* when I knew that you could do what you do. Well, for the most part. You mean to say that you see them, like *see* them, and they see you? As if they are real people?"

Nick nodded. "Well, they are..."

"How many are there?"

He shrugged, "Too many."

Sarah looked around, "Are there any in... here?"

Nick laughed, "No... but last night at dinner, when I spit out my coffee..."

"Not a very suave moment for you."

"Thanks," he replied, sticking his tongue out at her, "Anyway, there was a young prostitute there that knew your relative, Roger Forsyth... rather well."

"Shut up!" Sarah said, giving Nick a little shove. "You're joking, right?"

"No... I have another appointment to help her on Wednesday at noon in the Colonial Cemetery."

"At noon? I thought ghosts only came out at night. Like on those TV shows."

"No, if they are stuck here on the physical world, they are here all the time."

Sarah nodded, "I suppose that makes sense."

"So..." Nick asked apprehensively, "are we good?"

Sarah pulled him toward her and gave him a passionate kiss. "Doctor Williams, we are fantastic!"

Nick's heart raced. "You know, when I was eight, I shot the teacher with a rubber band and blamed it on

Billy Shultz, the kid who was sitting next to me... and when I was sixteen, I got a parking ticket but didn't tell my parents."

Sarah looked at him strangely, "What on Earth made you say that?"

Nick smiled devilishly, "I figured if I was getting kisses for secrets, perhaps I should tell you some more."

CHAPTER TEN

The church bells tolled twelve that next Wednesday, and true to her word, Josette, sat patiently on a bench in the old cemetery looking for Nick. She looked around and saw the dozens of others that were stuck in this plain of existence and pondered her position.

It had only been a few days since she had been shown her true state. What had her life become? What could she possibly do to get out of the state that she was in? Could she, even if she tried?

Soon, she spied Nick approaching. She waved, "Good day, doctor," she called.

Nick walked up to the young lady and sat on the bench next to her. "Good day, Josette. How have you been doing?"

Josette shrugged, "As well as I could be, I imagine. Have you received any news on Liam?"

Nick had tried to do as many searches as he could,

but he hadn't gotten a single hit on his searches for Liam, Savannah and orphan. "Sadly, no... not yet, I need more information... but I will keep looking, I promise. Have you given yourself time to reflect?"

"Oh, yes, every moment since our first meeting."

"And what do you want to talk about?"

Josette shook her head, "I must know what happened to little Liam. I am certain that he was lost without me. How could a mere child get through all of that loss without his family? That worries me to my core. Plus, I know where people that aren't up to snuff go when we die... I have known it since I was a little girl."

"But we agreed that your job wasn't who *you* were, correct? Why would you feel that because one part of your life wasn't up to snuff, that it would dominate the rest of your life?"

Josette sat and thought.

Nick took out his leather notepad, began to jot down notes and continued, "Where did you grow up?"

"Right here, in Savannah," she replied.

"Okay then. Tell me about your family while you were growing up."

A little glimmer of a smile began to appear on Josette's face as she recalled her childhood. "My father, Marcus Loughton, was a tradesman, a very accomplished jeweler right down there on Price Street," she pointed.

"He must have been very talented to have his own shop."

"Yes, he was very sought after by the high society families. His goldsmithing was the best in the city, better than most of those in New York as well! He could take an average gemstone and make it sparkle like one twice its price... it was all in the cut, he used to say."

"And your mother?"

"My mother's name was Elizabeth. She was a god-fearing woman. Always kept the house right and proper too. She had the gentlest voice you would ever want to hear. Especially, when she was tucking us in at night."

"Ah, and Liam?"

"Yes, my little brother Liam and myself. It was just the two of us. He was eight years younger than I."

"Eight years? That's quite a gap between children."

"There were three others between us, but they all died in infancy."

"That must have been terribly difficult."

"It was a very difficult period in time, doctor. If you wanted fresh water, you had to go and get it from the well. If you were cold, you added an extra blanket or huddled by the fireplace. If you were hot in the summer, you prayed for an ocean breeze to come across the river. But Liam and I never wanted for anything. We played, learned our lessons and studied our bible teachings."

"What was your favorite bible story?"

"Oh, my, doctor," she laughed, "I haven't thought of those in ages! I don't think that I could remember one if I tried."

"Well try," Nick urged.

Josette thought through her young past. She remembered the family going to church together and her mother making sure that she sat up properly during the sermon. That's when she said, "The story of Jonah."

"Jonah and the Whale?"

"Actually, doctor, the good book says that it was a 'great fish' not a whale."

Nick looked at her incredulously. "Really?"

"Yes, I am quite certain," she recalled.

"Why that story?"

Josette thought and thought, "Perhaps, because it was my father's favorite. A triumph over adversity and learning to walk on a righteous path. They said it at his funeral ceremony."

"He died when you were young?"

"Father died of consumption when I was just fifteen... mother passed the next spring. They said it was apoplexy... I say it was from a broken heart."

"So, you were in charge of the house at only fifteen?"

"I was sixteen when mother passed. I was the only thing standing between Liam and the orphanage. I had several suiters... but they were either young and stupid or very old and fat with horrific teeth! I was sixteen! I could not imagine having to be married to any of them."

Nick started adding things up. "How long did it take for things to turn for the worse?"

Josette lowered her head, almost in shame, "The debt collectors came almost as soon as we had lowered my mother into her grave. They took the jewelry shop straight away. That barely left Liam and I with anything to get by on. I tried desperately to keep the household together. I worked as a seamstress, fixing the hems on ladies' dresses. Ladies who just two years prior, were trying to coerce my father and mother into marrying their halfwit sons. Now, they looked upon me with distain. We needed money, but we did not have a large family and little Liam was only eight... we finally found him work down at the docks, fixing the nets of the fishing boats as they came in. His little hands were able to mend them much easier than any adult could. It wasn't enough."

"That's when you changed... professions."

Josette's eyes welled up with sadness and anger. "I should have just married one of those repulsive suitors when I had the chance... but it was too late for that, so I reasoned that if I was going to have to be with those old, fat men with their terrible teeth... that they would have to pay me for it. At least, it would be on *my* terms... and it paid far better than being a seamstress. Like I said, I was the only thing standing between Liam and the orphanage. Not to mention keeping a roof over our heads."

"You didn't have a problem with people recognizing you?"

"Heavens no, the upper crust wouldn't be caught down by the docks after sundown! No, the two circles of society that I had begun travelling in, rarely intermingled. Except for Captain Roger, I guess... he was very tight with the Habersham brothers... but they only talked politics. Plus, I was never with any local men. I guess it paid to be young and relatively attractive, there were very few officers that came to port that didn't want to share their time with me."

"And how long were you working your new profession?"

"Three years almost to the day. It is funny, because I was just about to quit and move to Charleston."

"Why?"

"I had saved as much as I could by the spring of 1775, and I had parlayed a cabin boy position for Liam on a merchant ship for the East India Company. I was going to sell the house and make a fresh start in a city that didn't look down at me... but then..."

"But then?"

"Well, then the accident happened."

Nick could see how upset she was, but there was a truth that Josette would have to hear. "Josette, everything that you had done was from a good place. They weren't exactly the decisions that you probably should have made in retrospect, but you did your best. Now, we must figure out a way to get you to a place of completeness. One where you can be with Liam and your family again."

Josette wiped the tears from her eyes. "Yes, I cannot stay here... I cannot stand the emptiness and isolation that I feel growing inside of me." She pointed at one of the older lady spirits that passed by, "They all act like I don't exist, even now, they still pay me no attention."

Nick clarified, "Josette, don't take that personally at all. They don't pay attention to you, because they are Affixed in their last days as you were in yours... or worse, they have been wandering so long, that their consciousness has weakened to a point of barely existing."

Josette acquiescent to what Nick was saying to her and with heartfelt pity she replied, "Oh, those poor lost souls."

"Yes... unless they are helped along. Kind of like what we are working on for you."

"Yes," Josette turned back to look at Nick. "Let us work on that with haste, I dare not wish to be in that state."

"Well, we will get you there, but it may take some time," Nick said reassuringly. "First, we have to make sure that you are able to reconcile your decisions with your beliefs," he continued as he got to his feet, "Let's take a walk."

He took out his Bluetooth earpiece and put it in his ear, so if someone *was* watching him having a conversation, they would assume that it was on his phone.

Josette and Nick quietly strolled the paths in the old cemetery. Now and then they would see another entity making their way through the hallowed grounds, but they all kept to themselves.

Occasionally, Josette would stop and look at a headstone and reminisce. The immense history of the city was not lost on Nick. He listened intently, both as an avid history buff and to see if he could glean some information that would be helpful to Josette and her case.

They strode along the long brick wall that was built on the Southeastern side of the cemetery. Along the wall were placed several headstones that had fallen over or were broken to the point that they could not be returned to their initial locations.

Soon, they were up to the southernmost edge of the cemetery, the side closest to the former orphanage. Josette looked over at the building. "At least I kept him from languishing in there... I just wish I knew what happened to him. My poor little brother, all alone in the world."

Nick's phone rang. It was Lisa.

Nick excused himself and stepped away to answer the call. "Hi Lisa... yes, I know that I have a two o'clock session with Mrs. Krabbe... my outside session took a little while longer than expected...no, you wouldn't have it in the itinerary... it just sort of popped up... it's okay, I'm not that far away, I will be just a few minutes late... I promise... yes... of course... remember to have the sweet tea... you're the best, Lisa... okay, see you in a bit."

Nick turned back to Josette. "I know it seems like we just got started, but I have to get going."

"I understand completely, doctor."

"I am glad we had this talk, Josette, and you have made some progress."

"But yet, I am still here."

"It will take some time. And look at what you have accomplished so far. Not the least of which is that you have determined that you were doing what you did, to save the family home and take care of your baby brother... those actions are *not* the actions of a vile person. Are they?

Josette looked down, "No, I guess not."

"There is much more that we still need to work through. I tell you what, next time, let's meet in the park outside my office. My grandfather will show you the way."

"Your grandfather?"

"Yes, he is my guide between your world and mine. I usually take appointments through him, but you were very..."

"...persuasive?" she smiled.

Nick smiled, "Yes, persuasive. Now, I need you to keep working on *you*. You have given me much more to work on in regard to finding out what happened with Liam, so let me do that. Remember that you are *not* an evil person. You are a dutiful daughter and loving sister. You must make peace with that and reconcile it with your beliefs. That is the only way that you will move on."

"I understand," Josette agreed.

Nick looked at his watch. "I really have to go," he said making his way out of the cemetery. He turned to wave goodbye, "Remember, my Grandpa Joe will come get you for our next session." This garnered some odd looks from the two ladies who were walking their dogs.

Josette laughed and faded away.

Nick walked up the stairs to his office after his session with Mrs. Krabbe. He opened the door and saw a very familiar blue glow.

"Hey there, Grandpa Joe."

"Good afternoon, Nicholas. I understand that you have taken on a new client?"

"Ah, you have already met with Josette."

"Indeed, I have, Nicholas. She is quite…"

"Persuasive?"

"Yes, persuasive," Grandpa Joe laughed.

Nick walked over to his laptop and pulled up his calendar. "Let's try to work her in for a session next week."

"Do you think she would be willing to wait that long?" Grandpa Joe pulled out an old notepad from his back pocket and jotted down the appointment.

Nick laughed, "I think that she has plenty of homework, it should keep her busy until then… and what's that? You have to keep notes?"

"What? I'm no different now than I was when I was alive, Nicholas! If I don't write it down, I'll surely forget it. Especially birthdays, anniversaries, and appointments."

Nick looked at his grandfather and shook his head. "Josette gave me a lot to find out about her family situation. The names of her father and mother, even information about her little brother Liam."

"Well, then pop his name into your gizmo there and see what it gives you," Grandpa Joe said pointing to Nick's laptop.

Nick laughed, "I already have… her little brother was eight when he became a cabin boy on a merchant vessel, I tried searching every combination that I could think of for: *Liam Loughton, 1775, & East India Company*… none of them brought up any pertinent results."

"Well, he was only eight then. Did you try later?"

Nick paused a moment. Grandpa Joe was right. Perhaps, he needed to start his search when Liam would have been an adult. A time well after the American Revolution. He turned back to his laptop and typed in *Liam Loughton & War of 1812*.

This time, he had a hit. Nick opened the tab and read, "On 5 September 1813, USS Enterprise sighted HMS Boxer off **Pemaquid Point**. After nearly six hours of maneuvering, they engaged. Blyth, the captain of the Boxer prepared for a fight to the finish. Captain Burrows moved one of his two long 9-pounders from the bow to a stern port, and it is reported that he declared: *"We are going to fight both ends and both sides of this ship as long as the ends and the sides hold together."* Blythe was killed during the first volleys. Shortly after, while assisting his crew run out a carronade, a musket ball ripped open Burrow's thigh. He was mortally wounded. The battle lasted only thirty minutes."

"This is all very interesting, Nicholas, but I haven't heard you mention one thing about Josette's little brother."

"Let me keep reading," Nick said turning back to the screen. "Lieutenant Edward McCall took command of the Enterprise and appointed Corporal Liam Loughton as second in command."

"That's it?"

Nick looked through the other hits, "Looks that way... wait. There is one more." Nick clicked on the link and continued reading. "Retired United States Admiral Liam Marcus Loughton died peacefully in his home in 1855, surrounded by his wife, two eldest sons and nine grandchildren. A decorated war hero and skilled naval officer, Admiral Loughton was instrumental on growing and maintaining the US Naval Fleet under the command of six different presidents. He accomplished this even though he only obtained the office of Admiral from President Andrew Jackson in January of 1837 and retired under President Zachary Taylor in 1849. During the retirement ceremony, he acknowledged that the importance of hard work and dedication were impressed on him at a very young age by his beloved sister, Josette, who passed away tragically when he was merely eight years old. But not before she had secured him a position as the cabin boy on a fine ship, giving him a lifelong love of the sea."

"Well, would you look at that," Grandpa Joe declared.

"Josette will have to be happy with this information. This is going to help her tremendously to find peace and move on," Nick said, saving the information.

"Good work, boy," Grandpa Joe said. "I knew that you would be perfect for this calling... I just knew it."

CHAPTER ELEVEN

Days later, Nick sat at the desk of his office going over the items he gathered to try to help Misty. He went through the artwork and tried to figure out what had changed. In the meantime, he had cut out all of the photos of her work from the brochure that she had for the Exhibit and laid them out in a row across his desk to try to get an idea of the progression. When was it that she began painting her "Shadow" series of paintings? It was something that he wouldn't be able to answer without talking to her again.

The intercom on his desk buzzed. "Yes, Lisa?"

"Dr. Williams, Sarah is here with lunch," Lisa replied. "Should I send her up? … Or would you like to walk down here to meet her?" she continued, still making sure that he kept up his exercises.

Nick sighed, "I will be right down… by way of the stairs."

"Thank you, Dr. Williams. I will let her know. See you soon."

Nick got up from his desk and checked himself in the mirror before heading downstairs.

Sarah stood in the receptionist area next to the large staircase. "So, Nick says that you like the ballet?" she asked Lisa.

"Oh yes," Lisa looked up from her work and smiled at Sarah. "I have always marveled at the sheer talent and strength it all must take."

"You never danced yourself?"

Lisa laughed, "Oh heavens, no. I was never a very coordinated young girl, let alone a prima ballerina."

"Don't sell yourself short. Nick says to me all the time that belief is the strongest force in the universe. The difference between those that are successful and those who are not, is not a question of talent, or strength, but a lack of will..."

"Or belief," Nick interrupted as he finished coming down the stairs, completing the quote. "And actually, I'm paraphrasing Lombardi."

Sarah and Lisa looked at Nick confused, "Who?"

"Vince Lombardi."

Sarah and Lisa stared at Nick blankly.

"The Lombardi Trophy... the greatest coach ever to coach football..."

Lisa looked at Sarah, "I don't recall any coach of the Georgia Bulldogs named... Lombardi, do you?"

Sarah shook her head, "No, can't say as I have. Nor any other coach in the SEC named... what was that... Lombardo?"

"Lombardi! He won the first two Super Bowls for Pete's sake!" Nick entreated.

Sarah couldn't hide her laughter any longer. "Of course, we know who Lombardi is, you dope!"

"No kidding," Lisa chuckled along with her, "You quote him at least twice a week."

Nick knew that he had been had. "I hate you both."

Sarah put her arms around him and gave him a big hug, "Well, I am proud of you for coming down the stairs to see me... reminded me of Scarlet coming down to see Rhett in Gone with the Wind." She started giggling again.

Nick gave her a quick kiss. "I think I hate you more," he jabbed at her with a smile as he led Sarah upstairs.

Lisa, chuckling at what they had just pulled on Nick, got back to work, "Remember, Dr. Williams, you have a call with the police chief at one-thirty."

"I remember, I remember," he called back down the stairs. Nick continued talking to Sarah, "We are going over the detective psychological exam questions."

"The ones that you are helping Wayne with?"

"I'm not helping him with the questions... we are going over example questions from other exams. So, he knows what to expect... it's like tutoring," he said as they got to the top floor.

"You sure do give a lot of your time to others," Sarah observed as Nick opened the office door for her.

"Don't you fret, my little magnolia, I will always have time for you."

Sarah went inside and started unpacking lunch. "You better!" she smiled.

Nick walked over to his desk and started to pick up the pictures of Misty's artwork.

"What's all that?" Sarah asked.

"Oh, nothing... just some stuff for a client," he found himself saying but then he stopped. "You know what? Come over here and look at these. I want to get your opinion."

Sarah grabbed a paper napkin, wiped her hands and stood over Nick's should as he sat down.

"These are from a recent art exhibit of a local college student who passed away. What do you think?" Nick asked as he panned his hand from left to right. "I think that I have them in order of their production... I am trying to find a connection to something, but I just can't put my finger on it."

"Did you say passed away?"

"Yes, she is a... client."

"Then, should I be seeing these? Isn't that against doctor-patient confidentiality or something?"

Nick nodded, "Perhaps... but I think we are in a

grey area considering her state of mortality."

"Oh," she replied acknowledging the implications. Sarah looked at Misty's work. She picked up a few of the pictures and studied them. "Aw, puppies," she sighed, "Adorable!" She flipped through them until she got to the first of the "Shadows" series. She looked at Nick, "Are these from the same artist?"

Nick nodded.

"But they are so... dark and jagged." Sarah put the pictures down on the desk and spread them out, leaving the "Shadows" series by themselves. She leaned in to get a closer look. "No, these can't be made by the same person. I don't have an art degree, but I have seen enough paintings from well-known artists... they don't just change their painting style instantly... if they do at all... it is a gradual implementation."

"That's what I thought as well."

"Unless they are done this way on purpose to obfuscate the real story," Sarah finished.

"Like a puzzle?"

"Sometimes the artist will hide messages in their paintings. Something profound but hidden in plain sight... so to speak." Sarah moved the dark pictures around. "Wait a minute... look... there is something here." She adjusted the pictures again to form a diamond pattern.

The moment she put the last picture in place, she could clearly read something painted through the brush strokes, "Dear Boss..." She looked at the paintings again, pointed at them and looked at Nick, "They say 'Dear Boss'... what is that supposed to mean?"

Nick leaned forward in his chair and sure enough, he could make out the words that Sarah was pointing out. He hadn't noticed them before because he had never looked at them in a shape, just in a row. "Dear Boss?" Nick mumbled. "Maybe it was a suicide note to her employer? Or professor?" He thought a moment, "No, I know that I have heard that somewhere before." He turned to his laptop and opened a search engine. He typed in the words and got a terrifying answer.

Up on the screen, were the words, "Jack the Ripper," in large bold letters. He read on, "The "Dear Boss" letter was allegedly written by serial killer, Jack the Ripper, as (according to the letter) penned on September 25th, 1888. But it was postmarked and received on the same day of September 27th, 1888, at the Central News Agency of London. It was then, sent to Scotland Yard two days later."

"Shut the front door..." Sarah said under her breath. "Jack the Freakin' Ripper?"

A chill went down Nick's spine. Perhaps, this was Misty's subconscious trying to leave information about her would be attacker. Maybe she had sensed that she was about to become a victim and wanted to make sure that somehow, someone would be able to track the killer down after her death? So, it wasn't a demonic oppression of her... it was her innate insight about her killer.

Again, Nick could only get these answers by talking with Misty again... he would have to call upon Grandpa Joe soon... very soon.

"What did the 'Dear Boss' letter say?" Sarah asked, pointing to the small photo of the handwritten letter on the screen.

Nick clicked on the image and a larger, more legible, copy appeared on aging yellowed paper, written in red.

"God! It looks like it was written in blood!" She exclaimed, taking a step back.

Nick took a moment to adjust his eyes to read the Victorian handwritten script, then began to read aloud, "25 September, 1888. Dear Boss... I keep on hearing the police have caught me, but they won't fix me just yet. I have laughed when they look so clever and talk about being on the <u>right</u> track. That joke about Leather Apron gave me real fits. I am down on whores and I shan't quit ripping them till I do get buckled. Grand work the last job was. I gave the lady no time to squeal. How can they catch me now? I love my work and want to start again. You will soon hear of me with my funny little games. I saved some of the proper <u>red</u> stuff in a ginger beer bottle over the last job to write with, but it went thick like glue and I can't use it. Red ink is fit enough I hope <u>ha.</u> <u>ha.</u> The next job I do I shall clip the lady's ears off and send to the police officers just for jolly wouldn't you. Keep this letter back till I do a bit more work, then give it out straight. My knife's so nice and sharp I want to get to work right away if I get a chance. Good Luck. Yours truly Jack the Ripper... Don't mind me giving the trade name... PS Wasn't good enough to post this before I got all the red ink off my hands curse it. No luck yet. They say I'm a doctor now. ha ha."

"God, that is some dark stuff," Sarah muttered. "And they never caught the guy who did it? That's just *so* creepy... in a bad way."

"I'll say." Nick noticed a few more links on the page and was about to click on one. "Look there's more!"

"Nope. Nope. Nope," Sarah insisted, "I don't want to ruin my appetite for lunch." She walked over to the table and started opening the bag. "Besides, I got you a cup of some of your heart attack soup that you love so much, and I know that you don't want it to get cold."

"Wisconsin Beer Cheese Soup?" Nick said as his eyes lit up. "With a crusty roll?"

Sarah held up the small baguette from the bag, "But, of course!"

Nick shut his laptop, "Catch you later, Jack, the flavors of the homeland call!" He spun the seat of his office chair toward lunch and hopped up to his feet. "You really are something amazing, you know that?"

"Yes, I know," Sarah said jokingly as he gave her a kiss on the cheek. "But I also got you a large garden salad with balsamic dressing and a bottle of water to *try* to even out your cholesterol intake. Seriously, I don't know how you are in such great shape when you grew up eating this sh…stuff."

Nick sat down at the table and got ready to have lunch with the love of his life. "I love you."

Sarah froze. She slowly turned her head and stared at Nick. Her eyes filled with joy. She put down her pita wrap sandwich and leaned over the table to get closer to him. "You've never said that before."

"Nick's brow furrowed with thought, "Sure I have…"

"No, Sweetheart. A woman remembers the first time a man says those words to her."

Nick smiled uneasily.

"I love you too, Doctor Williams."

Nick let out a sigh of relief, "Oh good. I was a little nervous there."

"But I need you to know and remember something very important."

Nick prepared himself for some pearl of Southern Charm that Sarah was surely going to bestow upon him. Perhaps about the care and keeping of a Southern Belle. Or a nugget of veracity passed down from generation to generation in her family.

She leaned in and kissed him, then pulled back just far enough for him to see the twinkle in her eyes, "I want you to remember… that you said it first."

Nick finished his video call with the police chief on his laptop. He filed his notes and looked down at his phone. There was a text message from Sarah.

"OMG. UR not going to believe what is in Aunt M's collection," she wrote. Attached was a photo of an ornate iron mirror with a long and pointed handle. "You need to see this in person... have provenance!"

Nick replied, "Sounds intriguing! I will meet you in a bit. At the shop?"

Nick set his phone down and started looking that the diamond pattern of the 'Shadows' paintings... then his eye noticed something odd. He rotated one of the pictures a quarter turn to the right and he could make out something different... different but unfinished. He did the same to the other three pictures and couldn't believe what he was looking at.

The pattern, now seemed to show the pattern of a name, "*H. W. Mudgett.*"

Nick rotated the pictures again, now they spelled out, "*Gien.*"

"What the hell?" Nick questioned as he rotated them one more time. Now it showed the words, "two, three and four," written in a circle.

Nick's eyes squinted as he thought, "Perhaps it's an address? Or maybe a time of day?"

Quickly, he typed in, "H. W. Mudgett."

A twinge of nervousness came over him, when he read the results of his search, "Herman Webster Mudgett, better known as Dr. Henry Howard Holmes or H. H. Holmes, (May 16, 1861 – May 7, 1896) was an American serial killer who confessed to twenty-seven murders. The actual number of his victims could have been up to two hundred."

He typed in "Gien" in the search bar and the results were just as intimidating. He read, "Edward Theodore Gien aka The Butcher of Plainfield or The Plainfield Ghoul. Born August 27, 1906, and died July 26, 1984. He had confessed to killing two women, Mary Hogan and Bernice Worden. Although, when his home was searched the police found multiple items made from human skin, far too many to have come from two bodies. It was assumed that Gien had dug up freshly buried corpses to make his creations. Initially, found unfit to stand trial due to mental illness, he was convicted of the murder of Bernice Worden and remanded to a psychiatric hospital. He was the basis for the movies <u>Pyscho</u> and <u>The Texas Chainsaw Massacre</u>."

Nick sat for a moment lost in thought. He and Grandpa Joe were right. This was a dangerous entity, one that had been around for over a century... and who knows how long before that?

His phone pinged. It was Sarah, "No, come to my place tonight for pizza and a creepy movie," she finished the text with a heart eyed emoji.

"As you wish, MLM," he replied.

Nick leaned back in his chair. He had to let Sarah know what was going on. She knew his secret and he had promised her that he wouldn't keep anything more from her. Plus, he had already told her that his client, Misty, was a *special* client. And she already knew about 'Dear Boss' hidden in the paintings. But this... a serial killing preternatural being of some kind... perhaps this was just too dangerous to involve her any more than she already was.

Nick sat back up and grabbed the photos. He put them in the outside pocket of his laptop case, stowed his laptop, and headed out. He took off his tie, rolled it up and put it in his coat pocket.

He walked into the elevator and turned the crank to the first floor. His thoughts bounced back and forth between the pros and cons of telling Sarah all the way down.

The elevator stopped and he opened the metal gate.

"Heading out early, Dr. Williams?" Lisa asked as he exited the elevator.

But Nick was deep in thought and didn't hear her.

"Dr. Williams?" she said a little louder.

Nick snapped out of his stupor. "Oh, Lisa... I'm sorry. I've got... quite a bit on my mind tonight."

"I can tell," she said with a reassuring smile. "Just be careful and have a good weekend."

"I will. I will," he nodded back and left for Sarah's condo.

CHAPTER TWELVE

Nick stopped off at the liquor store and grabbed a bottle of cabernet. Sarah used to get upset when he would bring things to her house, as she had plenty of nearly everything. But Nick was raised to always bring a gift or something when you were invited over to someone's home. Once he explained that to her, she understood, and it became an endearment.

He entered the foyer of the grand building that Sarah lived in. It had clearly been remodeled and upgraded significantly since its days as an old trade building that sat high above River Street.

"Good evening, Dr. Williams," the doorman at the welcome desk called to Nick. "Ms. Beaumont said that you would be by."

"Yes, Anthony," Nick said holding up the bottle of wine, "Pizza, popcorn, and scary movie night."

"Ms. Beaumont does love those nights, doesn't

she, Dr. Williams?"

"I've been here several times before, Anthony. You *can* call me Nick, and her name is Sarah, you know," he said getting into the elevator that the doorman was holding open for him.

Anthony smiled, "Oh, I know, I know... and it is very kind of you. But I have to maintain a level of professionalism. Something that I take great pride in while on the job," he continued with a wink, "Now, if someday, the missus and I run into you and Ms. Beaumont out and about, I will be sure to call you, Nick and Sarah." With that, Anthony smiled, inserted his pass card, and hit the button for the top floor. "You have a wonderful evening, Dr. Williams."

"And you as well, Anthony," Nick said as the doors were closing.

The elevator doors opened on the top floor. Nick stepped out and walked over to the window that faced the river. He could see all the people crowding River Street as they entered the various shops, restaurants, pubs and bars. He could also see the many other souls that were down there as well. Glimmering in opal blue, they went about their days. Over on the corner, by the alleyway, he saw a gang of ruffians working over a mark from long, long ago. There were sailors and military men, going through their routines, merchants selling their items and even the occasional woman of the evening, making their way up to a living man that was passing by, only to be completely ignored.

Sarah opened her door and leaned out. "You know, there is a better view in here."

Nick turned and walked to her, "It pales next to the view I am looking at right now." He leaned in and gave her a quick peck. "I brought some wine."

Sarah smiled and took the bottle graciously, "Of course, you did!" Then she noticed his laptop. "And... work?"

"Oh, this... well... sort of. We can chat about it later. Okay?" Nick said setting it on the dining room table.

"Sure. I will just open our wine and bring it to the living room. Pizza is keeping warm in the oven; they delivered it about five minutes ago. Can you bring it over to the coffee table?"

Nick and Sarah settled in on the couch and started their dinner and a movie date. The pizza was an easy choice, they both loved loaded pizzas, no onions. But they alternated on who got to pick the movie and tonight was Sarah's turn.

"Are you ready?" she asked proudly, pressing the play button on her remote. "Just when you thought it was safe to enter the water! Jaws!"

Nick smiled and handed her a glass of wine. Then they sat back and enjoyed their dinner and a movie. As Sheriff Brody and Hooper were swimming back to shore, Sarah got up and started cleaning. Nick joined her and brought the wine glasses into the kitchen and rinsed out the empty bottle.

"Such a great movie!" Sarah said excitedly.

"It really is a classic," Nick agreed. "And I couldn't help but look at Quint as a modern-day adaptation of..."

"Ahab! I know, right?"

"Exactly, really well done. Suspenseful and rather tame regarding gore... especially comparing it to the movies of today."

"Definitely," Sarah agreed as she finished putting the dishes into the machine. Sarah dried her hands and walked toward the dining room table. "So, what's this work, that you brought along?"

Nick opened the case and took out the pictures that Sarah had laid out earlier. He arranged them as she had originally done with the words 'Dear Boss' being visible.

Sarah looked at him with a bit of trepidation. "Oh, *that* work! Wait! I have to show you this!" she said as she ran down the hallway and picked up a rectangular shaped, wooden box, about the size of a shoe box,

She brought it to the table and opened it. There inside was the mirror that she had sent pictures of earlier. "Guess what this is called?"

Nick looked puzzled for a moment, "You mean aside from... a mirror?"

"This is a specific mirror. Its provenance dates

back to the late 1800's! 1888 to be specific."

"That is very specific."

"It's called the Whitechapel Mirror; it was found in the room of Jack the Ripper's last known victim."

Nick couldn't believe what he was looking at. An actual piece of history. A gruesome history, but history none-the-less and one that had a direct connection to what was going on now with Misty. "Synchronicity," he muttered.

"Go ahead pick it up and really look at it. I will read you the notes that Aunt Mary had assigned to the box.

Nick picked up the mirror and held it. It was remarkably solid. It was definitely made of iron. The mirror itself was starting to degrade from time, but still held a very good reflection. He turned it over and realized that this was a modified cross. With wonder, he looked over at Sarah.

Sarah smiled at Nick. She opened a large catalogue binder of hand written notes, and began to read, "The Whitechapel Mirror, found in the room of Mary Kelly, who is believed to be the last victim of Jack the Ripper. Taken from the scene by Constable Hugh Foster, who then gave it to the Abbey of the Sisters of Light outside of London. From there it was sent to the Vatican and on to America in 1904 by Pope Leo XIII for use in the ongoing battle against demons and other evil entities. The iron cross was originally forged in the 1400's possibly as part of the crusades, the points of the cross are rather sharp, even though they have dulled over time. Due to the techniques of application, the mirror and bezel were probably added in the early 1800's. This mirror is believed to cause any evil entity to become a prisoner of its own reflection, immobilizing the demon until it can be banished. It was used by Father Francis Dorman and his apprentice, Deacon Joseph Rivers in 1917 for the successful exorcism of Delores Mellwood of Jacksonville, Florida."

Nick looked back down at the mirror, "This could come in very handy."

"I know!" she reacted. "I have to go through more of the items in her collection. Not all of them have notes to help me out. But when I read this, I figured, you *had* to know about it!"

Nick started staring at the mirror again.

"It's crazy, right? You have a client that seems to a connection with Jack the Ripper and me having this artifact?"

"Synchronicity."

"Entanglement."

"Exactly!" Nick placed the mirror back into the old wooden box, pulled out a chair, and invited her to sit. "Now, it's my turn... I noticed something odd about the pictures that Misty painted after you left today."

"More than Jack the Ripper?"

"Well... you tell me," Nick started rotating the

pictures in front of Sarah. He turned them all a quarter turn to the right.

"H.W. Mudgett?" she said looking up at Nick. "She hid *multiple* messages in the paintings!"

Nick turned them again.

"Gein?" she questioned shaking her head.

"And one more," Nick said as he turned the pictures on last time.

"Two. Three. Four?"

Nick opened his laptop, looking for the searches that he had looked at earlier. "Check this out," he said as pulled up the information about H.W. Mudgett and Ed Gein.

Sarah sat in rapt attention. She could not believe what Nick was showing her. A chill went down her spine. "This is... bad, isn't it?" she asked knowingly.

Nick looked at her and nodded, "I looks as though it is much worse than I had thought, yes."

"What does this all mean? And what do the numbers two, three and four have to do with it all?"

Nick shook his head, "I'm not certain, perhaps a time or the start of an address, perhaps... I searched online and came up with nothing... nothing that related to the serial killers mentioned or to Savannah in general really."

"That's disappointing," Sarah replied. "Why would she have felt it necessary to hide all of this information in the paintings? Why not just *tell* people?"

"And who would believe her? Heck, I can barely believe it myself and I am in the thick of the paranormal racket now."

Sarah could see that it was bothering Nick tremendously. She reached out her hand and grasped Nick's. "I know. I know," she smiled, "We will figure this out."

"We?"

"Like you said... or your grandfather said... we are entangled, my dear, Dr. Williams. It seems obvious to me that you need my help, and it was abundantly clear to Aunt Mary that I was to have these items for a purpose, that's for certain," she laughed lightly.

The nerves in Nick's stomach grew. He looked at Sarah steadfastly, "I cannot ask you to help me with this... it is... far too dangerous."

Sarah leaned in and smiled, "You didn't ask. I've just told you, silly goose." She got up from her chair and headed into the kitchen. "I'll put on some coffee... looks like we have some studying to do... good thing tomorrow is Sunday, and the shop is going to be closed. I've got all night! Let's get crackin'!"

Nick was amazed at the enthusiasm of his new partner, even though he still had many trepidations about the path that they were embarking on.

While the coffee was brewing, Sarah brought out two cups. "I will go through Aunt Mary's catalogue and see if there is anything else that may be helpful."

"Look, Sarah," Nick interrupted, trying to keep a position of reason. "This is great and all, but this could be really dangerous… I mean… it may even be deadly."

"Stop being so dramatic," Sarah scoffed. "Besides," she continued, leaning in to give him a quick kiss, "if it is dangerous someone's got to be there to pull your ass out of harm's way."

CHAPTER THIRTEEN

The sun was up and glistening across the ripples of water outside of Sarah's condo. She lifted her head and rubbed her eyes; the river was already busy with freighter ships passing through, and there were conventioneers milling around outside the hotel on Hutchinson Island. The artifact catalogue was lying on top of her, open to the last items that she remembered looking at.

She looked over from her spot on the couch and saw Nick sleeping at the dining room table in front of his laptop. Sarah carefully got up, put the catalogue on the coffee table, and stretched. It had been a long night going through the binder looking for anything that would help them gain a leg up on their, yet to be identified, adversary.

She went to the kitchen and started making some breakfast, nothing fancy, just some coffee and cinnamon rolls. She and the doughboy with the chef's hat had a love/hate relationship, but to her, there was something magical waking up to the scent of fresh baked cinnamon rolls. As they baked, she got herself ready for the day.

Once the pastries were ready, she brought a tray with coffee and the freshly baked goodies to the dining room table. Carefully setting them down, she gently woke Nick. "Good morning, Sunshine."

Nick woke up a bit startled. It had nothing to do with Sarah's approach, it was just that the last thing that he read was about the lamp shades that Ed Gein had made from his victims. Quickly, he realized where he was and apologized, "Sorry."

The heavenly aroma of Sarah's efforts in the kitchen brightened his mood. Nick felt his stomach grumble a little bit in anticipation. "Wow, fresh baked cinnamon rolls? I haven't had those in years. Ms. Beaumont, I do believe that you are taking a shine to me."

Sarah smiled, "And again, Dr. Williams, I certainly hope that it hasn't taken you this long to figure that out." She handed Nick a plate, "It's a bit of a switch from our usual bagels, I admit. But I figured we needed the sugar to get us going after all the studying last night." She dished up a cinnamon roll and placed it in front of Nick. "Did you find anything?"

Nick tried not to devour the sweet treat in front of him, but his inner child had gotten the best of him. "There seems to be something different about this set of killings," he said taking a huge bite out of his breakfast.

Sarah poured herself a cup of coffee. "What do you mean?"

Nick continued, "Well, in the other three events: The Whitechapel Murders of Jack the Ripper, The Murder Hotel of H.H. Holmes, and even Ed Gein's horrific acts... the murders were gruesome and made headlines... but now... it is as though the killer was trying not to get caught. Having everyone think that they were accidental overdoses." Nick poured himself a cup of coffee.

"So, maybe it isn't the same creature that is doing it?"

Nick took a sip of his coffee. "I have to trust my gut on this... or at least Misty's. I don't think that she would have left those names as clues if it weren't the same entity that had caused all the other events."

"So then why?" Sarah asked, as she cut into her pastry.

Nick took another bite out of his cinnamon roll. "These are *so* good," he said, letting his taste buds take over his train of thought momentarily.

"Buy *why*, Nick?"

Nick composed himself and continued, "I think it

has something to do with those numbers."

"Two. Three. Four."

"Yes, every other clue that Misty left was a name, or something directly attributed to the killer. The numbers *have* to be as well."

"You said that you checked the addresses with those numbers involved, correct?"

"Yes."

Sarah thought a moment and looked at the circle of numbers. "Two. Three. Four," she thought out loud. "Two. Three. Four... or maybe..." Sarah reached down and spun all four of the pictures as one unit to the right. "Maybe it's four – two – three?"

"Or three- four- two," Nick finished. "That opens up a whole lot more addresses! And look," he continued, "I noticed this the other day." Nick pulled out the map of all the documented deaths due to opioid overdoses. "They all seem to be in an almost perfect circle here around the old orphanage. Perhaps there is an address that corresponds to the area inside the circle."

Sarah leaned over the map. "Wait a minute..." Sarah got a piece of wax paper from the kitchen and placed it over the map. She took out a pen and drew over the dots. First, she made a circle, then she drew straight lines between the five deaths that weren't found in buildings Her eyes widened as she finished.

Nick's mouth dropped open.

Sarah stammered, "Nick...isn't   that   a...

pentagram?"

Nick took a deep breath, "Actually, it's an inverted pentagram... the Sigil of Baphomet... Volume Thirty-Six."

"Volume what?"

"Sorry... just books that I had to study when this new career of mine was thrust upon me."

"Oh."

"Anyway, a pentagram with the star pointing upward, isn't necessarily considered bad at all, it was used by the Masons even... but this kind..."

"Bad juju?"

"Bad juju," Nick nodded.

Sarah sat down, "So... what's the next step?"

Nick thought a moment, "I suppose, somehow, we have to identify what it is that we are dealing with."

Sarah enthusiastically jumped up, "I think I can help with that!" She ran over to the coffee table, brought over the old register and started paging through it.

"What are you looking for?"

"Aunt Mary knew of a book... a *catalogue* of demons, I guess. I know that I saw it in here..."

"A catalogue of demons? *All* of them? How old is this book?"

"Old," Sarah said, briefly looking up from the index. "It was written in the fifth century by... here it is! Daemones Sicut Scripsit Aurelius Augustinus Hippo Regius."

"You can read Latin?"

"It kind of goes with the territory, you know... antiques."

"Ah," Nick concurred. "What does all that mean?"

"Roughly, The Demons as written by Aurelius Augustinus of Hippo Regius."

Nick thought, "Hippo Regius... I know that from somewhere..."

"The northern part of Africa... it would be... Algeria now, I think."

"That's it... I know who that was!" Nick proclaimed proudly. "That's Saint Augustine! He was from that region. He was like... like... one of the first great teachers of the Catholic Church back then. Patron Saint of... of... theologians."

Sarah looked up from her aunt's old registry book, "And brewers as well... sounds like a fun guy."

"I cannot imagine that a book that old could be in good shape at all. It's over sixteen hundred years old."

Sarah looked back down at the registry, "Aunt Mary said that she came to know of it from a bookbinder that specialized in the restoration of ancient and historic works. It was held in a private collection until the seventeen hundreds. Get this! It was owned a Founding Father, a former Governor of Georgia..."

"Button Gwinnett?" Nick determined.

Sarah looked up from the registry, "Yes." She looked at him with a raised eyebrow. "You know, for a

Yankee, you sure seem to know a lot about our fair city of Savannah."

"Just a lucky guess."

Sarah's feminine instincts told her that Nick was trying to cover something up. She nonchalantly looked back at the registry. "Sure would be nice to know where he might have gotten it from... perhaps, you could ask him, the next time that you see him."

"I should..." Nick stopped and looked away.

Sarah laughed, "I knew it! He's one of your *clients*... isn't he?"

Nick grimaced with frustration, "Now, Ms. Beaumont, you know that would fall under doctor-patient confidentiality."

"I'm sure it also falls in that *grey* area" Sarah continued to chuckle.

"So, you think that will help us to identify who we are up against?" Nick asked, trying to move on.

"Well, it would be great a starting point, that's for sure... if we had it."

"Wait, it's not in her collection?" Nick probed.

"She said that it is be watched over by Father Nicolai Phillipe in the Basilica of... St. Augustine... in Florida."

"Well, that seems appropriate. But how do we get a look at it?"

"*We* probably wouldn't. But I would be willing to bet that *I* could," she said with a cavalier wink.

"Sarah, somehow, I don't think that your Southern Charms will work on an old priest."

"Ha, ha, smart ass... it just so happens that my family gifted the Basilica two sterling silver communion chalices just a couple of years ago. They were brought over by Pedro Menéndez de Avilés, the founder of St. Augustine and were thought to have been lost after the British attacked the town and the entire city had to hideout in the Castillo de San Marcos back in 1702. So, *Monsignor* Phillipe knows me rather well. I'm sure that if I paid a visit, I could get my hands on that book and look over it for an hour or two."

"Then I defer to your realm of expertise, Ms. Beaumont, whilst I partake in another fine pastry," Nick said with a playful flourish, raising a cinnamon roll to her.

Sarah curtsied and laughed, "And I accept your deferment, good doctor."

"But are you going to have time to read that entire text in an hour or two?"

"Goodness, no... I'm going to take photos of each page with my phone!" Sarah smiled as she sipped her coffee. "Then it's just a matter of downloading the pictures into my computer, changing their format and applying translation software... piece of cake."

Nick was momentarily speechless. "Ok, you speak multiple languages, know a ridiculous amount about computer software, come from a long line of antiques experts, are the curator of a mystical weapons cache and," Nick said cutting into his cinnamon roll, "clearly know how to get to a man's heart... anything else I should know about you?"

Sarah thought a moment, "Nah, not much... oh, I did knock out my karate instructor."

Nick dropped his fork.

Sarah burst into laughter. "Nick, relax! It was an accident! I missed the board completely when I was testing for a new belt... clocked him right on the jaw... poor Mr. Tehada didn't have a chance."

Nick laughed along with her, "Geez, you had me going."

"But I was very fortunate that, after he came to, he let me try again. Gosh, that was years ago."

"So, did you break the board?"

Sarah set down her cup, "Oh yes, like I said, that was years ago. I got my black belt when I graduated high school."

Nick shook his head, "Shit. You *are* Batgirl."

Sarah giggled, "Anyway, it's only about three hours to St. Augustine. I could get there and back by dinner tonight if everything goes well."

Still a little stunned, Nick agreed, "Umm, yeah... that's a great idea. Plus, it will give me time to get with Grandpa Joe and try to talk with Misty. See if we can obtain any more insight on her hidden messages."

Sarah smiled, "Sounds like we have a busy day

scheduled. Let's meet back here tomorrow to go over what we've found."

Nick got up from the table, walked over to Sarah and hugged her. "I'm really glad that you are on *my* side."

Nick sat in his study, trying to figure out what the elusive numbers meant in Misty's painting. He stood looking out the bay window on the top floor of his office and contemplated his next steps. The artifact that Sarah had found was impressive, but could they really use it to destroy this creature? How dangerous was this thing that killed Misty and so many others? Could they even stop it if they tried?

Nick walked back over to his desk and sat.

Soon he felt the presence of his grandfather. Nick looked over and saw that he was with Misty as well.

"Hey, Grandpa Joe. Hello, Misty."

"Good afternoon, Nicholas."

Misty still stood a slightly behind Grandpa Joe and peeked around him, "Hello, doctor."

Grandpa Joe looked down at Nick's desk and saw some of Misty's artwork sticking out of Nick's satchel. "Anything new here?"

Nick motioned them both to the desk. "It's funny that you said that... I really need to chat with Misty about some things, if that's okay."

Misty nodded.

"We found some amazing information hidden in your 'Shadows' paintings." Nick pulled out the pictures and laid them out in the diamond pattern, then went through the paces of rotating them.

Misty and Nick's grandfather watched in amazement.

"Remarkable," Grandpa Joe thought, stroking his chin, "I recognize that name 'Gein'... that must be crazy Ed Gein from Plainfield. He was one scary bastard. Had your grandmother checking behind every curtain and closet door for years after they caught him."

Nick rotated the pictures again and again, showing them all the different clues that were hidden in the paintings. He explained that H. W. Mudgett was the name of a man called H. H. Holmes, who murdered people during the Chicago World's Fair in the late 1800's. Then, he showed them the 'Dear Boss' letter and the numbers: Two, Three, and Four.

"I need to sit down," Misty said, "I feel a little dizzy."

Grandpa Joe guided her to the couch, and they sat down.

Nick came over with his notepad and sat in the session chair.

"I painted those paintings," Misty said confidently. "But I don't ever recall putting those messages in them," she continued less confidently.

"How can that be?"

"I believe it was your innate abilities trying to come through. Somehow, they knew that you were in danger from this preternatural creature, but your conscious self couldn't see it. So, your subconscious manifested the information the best that it could... leaving breadcrumbs along the trail so to speak."

"In the painting..." Misty added.

"Yes. But now the question becomes, what does it all mean? Obviously, if we apply Occam's Razor..."

"Occa' what now?" she asked.

"Occam's Razor. You see, Misty, back in the fourteenth century, a Franciscan Friar named William of Ockham basically gave precedence to simplicity and said that given two possible explanations, the simplest explanation is usually the correct one."

Misty interrupted, "But that's not always true..."

"She's got a point there, Nicholas. Heck, right now, we are looking at an explanation that involves an eons old murderous demonic entity... I wouldn't call that simple."

Nick smiled, "Yes, but considering that we already know that it *involves* an eons old murderous demonic entity... it remains the simplest and probable outcome."

"So, to the outside observer," Misty concluded, "because they don't know about the entity... it looks like a bunch of random opioid overdoses."

"Exactly, Misty!" Nick exclaimed, "That is a form of the Observer Effect: which states that the mere act of observation changes the outcome of the phenomenon. We know about a shadowy figure that has been seen in the area since the beginning of this epidemic. But now, we need to see if we can get you to remember more details."

"Like the numbers," Misty supposed.

"Yes, Misty. I have a hunch that those numbers are the key to us finding this menace and putting a stop to his carnage."

Misty slouched back into the sofa and thought. "I really don't remember anything," she said with a look of frustration.

Nick got up, went to his desk and pulled out a crystal on the end of a gold chain. He walked back over to Misty and his grandfather. "Misty, I am going to try something. I'm going to hypnotize you. Hopefully, we will get you to a point where you can see what is going on."

Misty started to fidget.

"Now, Grandpa Joe and I will be here the whole time. You will just be watching what happened. You will not be in any harm at all."

Misty looked up at Grandpa Joe, the only being that she felt safe with during this entire ordeal, "Are you sure?"

Grandpa Joe glanced over at Nick, then back to

Misty, "Absolutely, sweetie. I will be here the whole time. And if anything starts to go sideways, Nicholas will pull you right out. Safe and sound. Okay?"

Misty took a deep breath, "Okay."

Nick told Misty to lean back on the couch and relax. Take some deep cleansing breaths and focus on the crystal swinging back and forth in front of her. He calmly told her to focus on something that made her happy and would connect her to her apartment. It wasn't long before Misty's eyes were shut.

Nick leaned in, "Misty, do you hear me?"

"Yes, doctor."

"Where are you?"

"I'm in my apartment, I'm organizing my work for the Art Exhibit."

"Good. Is all your work complete?"

"All but my last four paintings… it will be a series of paintings on the homeless."

"The homeless?" Nick asked.

"Yes, I want to show the less fortunate in a better light. They all have stories to tell. Did you know that many of them served our country and now we have left them in the streets?"

Nick was expecting her to mention the 'Shadow' Series. He looked over at Grandpa Joe a little confused but answered Misty, "No, I didn't know that."

"It's true, that's why my first painting was to be of Corporal McHugh. He lost his right leg below the knee from an I.E.D. and now can't get work... so he weaves palm leaves into roses to give to tourists. He never asks for money, he has a donation jar, but it isn't enough to live on, he usually has just enough to eat."

"You said that you were going to do a series of four paintings?"

"Yes, one of Bernie "Jazz Man" Smith, down on Abercorn Street. He plays the trumpet and has a glorious voice. He sings for tips. He's the one who introduced me to Corporal McHugh and Ruby over in Colonial Cemetery with sells palm crosses to those who want to leave mementos or honor those interred there, was another one. The last one was going to be Ms. Margarete, who sold trinkets over on Warren Square. She was very sweet but must have had some demons that she was wrestling with."

Grandpa Joe and Nick shared a look with each other, then Nick asked, "Why do you say that, Misty?"

"It's sad, they found her in the park one morning, she had overdosed."

Nick's eyes widened and he got up from his chair to get his map of Savannah on his desk. "That is very sad. How does that make you feel?"

"I am troubled by it. She was a very sweet lady. Very kind. She let me make multiple sketches of her. They all did really, they were looking forward to my Exhibit."

Nick brought the map back to his session chair

and looked where Warren Square was located. A shiver went through him as he realized that the location of Ms. Margarete's death was the bottom point of the inverted pentagram.

"You have many sketches of your subjects?"

"Yes, they were all very excited. But now, I may have to change it. I have to have four more paintings, it's an academic requirement. I have almost a month's work of sketches that I'm not going to be able to use. I suppose that I can ask the others if they are okay with me including Ms. Margarete in the series, even though she has passed."

"Isn't this your work?"

"Yes, but they are a part of it. My subjects are just as much a part of it as I am."

"Ok, so when are you going to ask them?"

"I was going to go now; it is only seven-thirty. Corporal McHugh is still over by the pizza place on Liberty."

"Misty," Nick instructed, I want you to head over to Corporal McHugh. You are perfectly safe. I want you to tell me everything about your visit. Are you ready to visit the Corporal?"

"Yes."

"Ok, you are walking down the street toward your meeting with Corporal McHugh. What do you see?"

"There are customers outside the pizza parlor, so he is around the corner now, kind of on Whitaker."

"On Whitaker?"

"Yes."

"Ok, what do you see?"

"It's odd, he is in a dark shadow, but the sun isn't shining in the right direction."

"What do you mean?"

"I've studied light sources for years. This shadow is wrong."

"Ok, what are you doing now?"

"I've stopped walking. Something is wrong. I can still see the customers at the pizza place, there are a lot of people around, but no one even notices him." Misty paused and a look confusion crossed her face, "The shadow is moving."

"Moving?"

"Yes, I can see it moving around him so quickly. It's like it is everywhere and nowhere at the same time."

Nick thought of the other parts of the Observation Effect and how it related to Quantum Theory. "But you see it?"

"Yes... and now it has stopped moving around him. My God, it is standing up!" She said as the confused look on her face changed to one of horror. "It sees me!" she screamed.

"Misty, you are in no danger, I promise. I need you to tell me exactly what is happening."

Misty sat frozen for a moment, "It sees me. But it isn't coming toward me. It is just standing over him."

"Can you see Corporal McHugh?"

"Yes, he looks... dead," she said as tears welled up in her eyes.

"It's okay, Misty. This is all in the past. You are just seeing what happened that night. You are in no danger at all."

Misty took a deep breath. "Okay, okay."

"What is happening now?"

"It is looking at me."

"The shadow?"

"Yes."

"What does the shadow look like?"

"It is tall, and is... wearing a top hat? Yes, it is wearing a hat!"

Nick looked at Grandpa Joe and nodded.

"And what is happening now?"

"It is standing over Corporal McHugh and it is looking right through me. I can see it smiling...now, it is tipping its hat and shooting down the road from Liberty Street going south. I scream and run toward Corporal McHugh. There are people starting to notice from the pizza parlor and they are gathering around."

"And what happens next?"

"While I am on the phone with the police, just giving them our location, a man in hospital scrubs and a light jacket shows up. He is very nice and consoling. He gets on his phone and calls the hospital that there is an incident."

"Do you remember his name?"

"He is wearing a name badge...it says 'Wells, Kevin.'"

Nick felt the wind being knocked out of him. What was Kevin doing in that area? The hospital isn't anywhere near the pizza parlor... and his apartment is just south of Forsyth Park. Nick had to ask a very important question, one that he didn't want to ask because he did not want to confirm his fears. If Kevin came to the scene from the south, the same direction the creature fled, that would be a terrible coincidence. "Do you remember which direction Kevin came from?"

Misty paused, going through everything that she was experiencing. "He approached from the south."

Nick's heart sank. "Are you sure?"

"Yes, there's a crowd of people gathering behind me on Liberty, and he is definitely coming toward me. He approached from the south."

Nick tried to shake the thought out of his head. He continued his questioning, "What happens next?"

"A squad car pulls up with its lights on and an officer comes over to us. He calls for an EMT and more police to secure the area."

"Do you tell the officer what you saw?"

"About the Shadow? No! He never would believe me!"

He looked up at Misty, "Okay, Misty, I want you to close your eyes and relax, we are going to bring you back now. Back to my office and Grandpa Joe. I'm going to count to three and you will open your eyes. When you open your eyes, you will be back with us in the present, am I clear?"

"Yes."

"One. Two. Three."

Misty opened her eyes and looked at Nick and Grandpa Joe, "Were you able to get anything?"

Nick relayed all of the information that Misty had told them in her hypnotic state.

She sat motionless for a second, "How could I have forgotten all of that?"

"There are a lot of theories in regard to that, but the important thing is that you remembered it… and it is very helpful."

"That must have been the moment I changed my series of paintings," she surmised.

"It sure seems that way to me," Grandpa Joe said.

"Yes, it does… and we have a lot more to go on here… I think we have gone through enough for today. We are making progress, Misty, I promise."

Misty got up from the couch, "I know, doctor. I know. I appreciate everything that you both are doing. You don't know me at all… and this is a lot."

Grandpa Joe stood up next to Misty and put his arm around her shoulder in reassurance. "Don't fret about that, Misty! In our short time together, I regard you as the granddaughter that I never had," he smiled.

"I need to speak with Nicholas here for a little bit now, would you mind heading out and I'll catch up with you?"

Misty nodded, made her way over to the bay window and faded away.

Grandpa Joe looked back at Nick. "So, we *are* looking at a serial killing entity... this would pretty much confirm it to me."

Nick nodded his head.

"So, did you figure out what the numbers mean? Two, three and four?"

Nick slapped his forehead, "The one question I needed to ask. Damn it." Nick gritted his teeth in frustration, "Umm, we think that it could be an address or a date perhaps, but nothing really matches up. I will have to ask Misty the next time we have a session."

"I could just ask her."

"Sadly, Grandpa Joe, these are repressed memories... I had to put her under hypnosis to get this much."

"I suppose that's true. Well, keep looking into it, Nicholas, these things have a way of presenting themselves in the most unlikely of ways."

"Speaking of which, look at this," Nick said pulling up a few pictures of the Whitechapel Mirror.

"Goodness me, what is that?"

"An example of something presenting itself in the most unlikely of ways. It's called 'The Whitechapel

Mirror.' According to Sarah's late aunt, the mirror was taken from the last known crime scene of Jack the Ripper... and can be used to "entrap" any evil entity that looks into it. It is part of a vast collection of mystical items that she had collected over thirty years. Now Sarah has the collection in her family's antique shop."

"What now?" Grandpa Joe looked quizzically.

"That's what her research said."

"So... just so I am clear. Your girlfriend, the woman who hit you with her car and owns your great grandfather's copy of Moby Dick... is also the keeper of a treasure trove of mystical relics..." Grandpa Joe paused. "Well, I believe it."

Nick laughed. "It was a bit of a shock to me as well, but here it is. And perhaps just in time, if we can figure out how to use it properly."

"I better catch up with Misty. You take care, we will get this thing and make things right. You are doing good work here, Nicholas."

"Thanks, Grandpa Joe," Nick said as his grandfather walked toward the bay window and faded away.

Nick took the map and headed back to his desk. Nick looked again at his map and noticed that another point of the pentagram was the location of Corporal McHugh's death. He went through the reports that he had sent over from the police department about the opioid deaths. Specifically, he was looking for the report on Corporal McHugh.

Nick's phone pinged. It was Sarah. "Have the whole book photographed. Heading back now. It's going to take me all night to get these uploaded and translated. Go over them tomorrow," she finished with a heart emoji.

He typed back, "Drive safe, see you soon." He too finished with a heart emoji.

Nick went back to the report. There was no mention of Misty as a witness to anything. There was no mention of anyone finding the Corporal at all, just that when the EMT's arrived, and there was nothing that they could do.

Nick thought long and hard. Could he really be looking at Kevin as a host to this... this beast? Yes, he was a slob and it drove Bryon crazy at times, but to be so broken that he could be possessed? It didn't seem possible.

But Misty's memories from the hypnosis session put him there within seconds of her seeing the Hat Man... and there really was no reason for him to be in that neighborhood.

Nick got up from his desk, laced his fingers behind his neck and tried to stretch out the tension. "Well," he muttered under his breath, "this sucks."

CHAPTER
FOURTEEN

Nick opened the door to Martini's on Bull Street; he saw Sarah at their usual table in the far back corner.

Sarah excitedly waved him over.

"You're not going to believe how many freakin' demons are noted in this book," she said as he sat down across from her.

Nick did a quick reference through spiritual studies, "Considering that there are about two hundred and twenty-five named demons that start just with the letter 'A'... I imagine, quite a lot."

Sarah looked at him in disbelief. "Well... shows what you know... there are two hundred and twenty-eight," she said sarcastically.

Nick smiled, "I suppose I better order.".

"Oh, don't bother, I already ordered."

Nick looked at her slightly offended.

"Stop it. You always take five minutes to look over the menu and when the bartender, Jennifer, comes over, you always end up getting the same thing..."

"One Moon Pie Martini for the gentleman," the bartender, Jennifer, interrupted Sarah's lecture as she placed the drinks on the table. "And a Bourbon Pecan Pie Martini for the lady."

Nick laughed, "Thank you... that's just what I was going to order."

"My pleasure, Doc. If you need anything else, you know where I'll be," she said as she walked away.

"Okay, okay... clearly, I'm getting too predictable," Nick said taking a sip of his drink.

"It's an endearment," Sarah replied. "Anyway," she continued as she opened her laptop and turned it so they both could look at it, "I have narrowed our suspects down to about a hundred and forty."

Nick choked a little. "Just a hundred and forty?"

"I know that it seems like a lot, but as I was going through them, most of these entities try to lead people astray, make the people have a conscious decision to do wrong or sin. Very few of them make it their business to do the work themselves. But even those had to find a host that was flawed to begin with."

"Yes, I know," Nick shuddered to think that Kevin was that flawed of a human. He seemed so normal. "That's not good."

"Not good?"

Nick leaned in, "I have a working theory that is... disturbing."

"What do you mean?"

"I have a witness to one of the victims... Misty."

"What? The dead girl? How could she be a witness?"

"Before she was killed. She was the first person to find the body of a victim. Corporal McHugh... she was going to paint him for her art exhibit. She saw the Hat Man attacking him... the monster looked right at her. Hell, it smiled at her, then tipped it's freakin' hat and fled down the street. Then within seconds... Kevin came running to the scene from the same direction that the Hat Man fled."

Sarah's eyebrows raised, "Your Kevin? Kevin Wells, your physical therapist?"

Nick sighed in resignation, "Yeh. Seems that way."

"That's not good. You don't think that..."

"I don't want to, but... that's quite a coincidence."

Sarah clenched her lips and bowed her head in agreement. "It doesn't look good."

"Exactly," Nick determined.

They sat quietly, pondering the ramifications of what Nick had just said.

After a moment, Nick decided to break the silence. "So, here's a question you don't get every day...

how does one find out if the guy who literally got you back on your feet is under the influence of a preternatural being of incalculable evil?"

Sarah took a moment to reflect, then looked up at him, "Very carefully."

"Gosh, thanks," Nick winced.

"No, seriously. There has to be a way to get a definitive answer."

"Aside from asking, 'Hey, pal? I was just wondering if you might happen to be possessed by an ancient evil that is using you to kill unsuspecting people for its own primal urges?'"

"Yes, aside from that." She thought about the situation, "This is something that has to happen spontaneously. Something that Kevin wouldn't think twice about answering or doing, so *if* he is possessed, the demon inside of him wouldn't try to stop it from happening."

"That is good point."

"So, the question would be, *how* do we make that happen?" She reached down, picked up her drink and took a sip. "We could tell him that I have a girlfriend that I want him to meet, we get him there, and while we are waiting for my quote-unquote friend, we use the Whitechapel Mirror to hold him."

Nick shook his head, "We are a step ahead of ourselves. If we pull the Whitechapel Mirror out in the middle of the hors d'oeuvres and the Hat Man *is* using

Kevin as a host, we are going to find ourselves trapped in a room with a demon."

"But... the Mirror?"

"Even with the Whitechapel Mirror, what would we be able to do then? We can't just hold the mirror in front of us forever."

"Right.... We need more mystical assistance."

"Without a doubt." Nick took a long sip of his martini. "This isn't something that we are going to be able to pull off tomorrow. I will do some research on my end. So far, we have a possible way to hold him with the Whitechapel Mirror... but no way to reveal himself or vanquish this damned thing."

Sarah took a long sip of her drink, "Yeh... definitely not going to happen tomorrow."

A few days later, Nick sat at his desk and combed over his notes. He looked over each and every section of his hypnosis session with Misty. There had to be something that he was missing.

Finally, he took a moment and concentrated. His spirit office appeared before him. He looked up and gazed at the vast amount of knowledge that he had at his fingertips. He had spent so long studying them, he felt that he knew every single one of the forty-one books by heart. He recited the Science behind Metaphysics from Volume One. He recalled the volumes in the middle about the advent of Psychology and Human Nature... then he noticed something.

There were forty-two books. Nick carefully walked up to the shelf and pulled out Volume Forty-Two. He opened it. Nothing looked familiar at all. Then he remembered, "I only had gone through forty-one of the books when they woke me at the hospital." Nick's eyes skimmed over the pages. "The Bible, Necronomicon, The Ancient Egyptian Book of Emerging Forth into the Light, Book of the Damned, and other Religious Texts."

Nick took the book over to his desk and began studying.

"You forget something, Nicholas?" his Grandpa Joe said, appearing next to him.

Sheepishly, Nick replied, "Actually, yes. Things have been so hectic that I completely forgot that I had only gone through forty-one of the forty-two volumes. You remember, back in the hospital."

"Oh, yes" Grandpa Joe commented, "That was a while ago... that would have been bad... but you are here now."

"Yes! Good thing we are outside of time here, this is going to take a while."

"Well, take your time, just remember that I am bringing Button over at two o'clock today for his session."

Nick looked up. "Wait, no, I can't."

"You can't what?"

"I have a video conference call today at two with the Hospital Board of Directors... it's a standing meeting... happens every week."

"Well, you are going to have to move it."

"Grandpa Joe, I can't just move it. It is a standing meeting... in the *real* world... remember, in this world I need to pay bills. No, you and the governor will have to swing by later. I should be done by three."

"You seem out of sorts, Nicholas."

Nick realized that he was a little harsh. He hadn't meant to be, but he was. "I'm sorry, Grandpa Joe, the whole 'Kevin' thing has me on edge."

"I'm sure that you will figure it out. You always were a..."

"...quick study."

"Well, it's true. And don't sass me, boy."

"You're right. I'm sorry," Nick shook his head. "It really is starting to get to me."

"What do you mean? I thought you said that Sarah had that mirror thing?"

"Yes, the Whitechapel Mirror should hold the Hat Man *in theory,* but we don't know for certain. I mean what if it doesn't?"

"It's always good to have a back-up plan, sure, but you can't go through life always second guessing yourself, son."

"Then there is Sarah... she just jumped right

in, like it is some sort of lark... like a vacation or adventure. We are talking about a being that has killed for centuries... this is not a game."

"And I'm sure that Sarah doesn't think that it is either. But I know that you are stronger together, certainly, you can feel that. She gives you balance... support... and you love each other... love is a very powerful force."

Nick agreed. "You're right, Grandpa Joe. It ranks right up there with belief. I would say that love is a very potent form of belief, so yes."

"Good, then what's this problem that you're working on?"

"I have been racking my brain trying to find a way to vanquish the Hat Man, not just keep him at bay, but I'm stuck."

"You will find it," Nick's grandfather continued, "Look, Nicholas, you are a kind and dedicated soul... you always have been... unfortunately, that can lead to letting your passions control you. You know what you need to avoid."

"Yes. Yes."

"Do you? There is a fine line between dedication and obsession. Now that your friend, Kevin, is in real danger, can you steady yourself properly? It is vital that you remind yourself of the difference. Dedication drives you to move forward and do the right thing... obsession consumes you and can compel you to make foolish choices, sometimes even dangerous ones."

Nick looked down at the spirit book, "Right, I know, Grandpa Joe, you read me the story of Moby Dick countless times. It is more than a story about a white whale and a mad captain... don't be Ahab."

"Exactly."

The crowds had dwindled quite a bit from earlier in the day on Reynolds Square. The sun was almost down, and a cool breeze meandered its way through the park.

Standing on the south side by a park bench, stood a slender musician holding his trumpet. His threadbare jacket instantly betrayed better times that he used to have performing. Now, age and bad choices had caught up to him. It was etched all over his face, the pain and soulfulness that only comes with wisdom. But one only acquires wisdom by getting through bad choices.

There was a time that every jazz club from Atlanta to New Orleans wanted Bernie "Jazz Man" Smith to perform at their club... but that was long ago. He wasn't as sharp as he used to be, he knew it. The years of abusing himself with alcohol and drugs had taken its toll and the stints in the county lock up for disorderly conduct didn't help his professional reputation either.

A few tourists passed by and tossed some money his way. The coins made a dull thud as they landed on the felt inside the old trumpet case. Bernie smiled as always and tipped his hat, "Thank you, folks. Would you like to hear a tune?" The couple declined with a wave and continued walking on.

It had been a long, hot day of busking. He had just finished a rendition of Moon River, when he felt the all too familiar patter of raindrops hitting his faded grey fedora. The rain began to fall lightly onto the bricks next to him as well.

He looked up and saw the storm clouds building. "I guess that's the last set for you, Jazz Man," he said to himself as he sat down on the bench and put his trumpet in the case. "Time to get to get out of the rain."

Bernie lifted his jacket over his head trying to cover himself as much as he could in the ever-growing storm. He made his way out of the park and headed toward the Second African Baptist Church.

They had a hall that was for the less fortunate on weekday evenings and it was the closest shelter by far. He could really use a warm meal and a nice cozy spot on the floor after this soaking.

The rain was really coming down now and he did his best to try to keep his trumpet case, which contained his livelihood, from getting too wet.

He looked at the old Timex on his wrist and wiped away the water droplets off the crystal to see the time. "There's still time before the shelter closes for the night," he said, deciding to try to wait out the passing storm in an alcove behind one of the apartment buildings on the way.

Standing in the relative shelter of the alcove, Bernie set his case down and reached into his jacket pocket for his cigarettes. He looked up at the sky. "Looks like it will pass soon enough," he said as he put the cigarette up to his lips, lit it and squatted down against the wall to count his money.

Bernie had made good money on this outing. The tourists were generous, and his voice and trumpet were in fine form.

The alcove began to feel heavy, filling with smoke. He waved his arm around to clear the air, but it didn't help. "Well, ain't this stran…" he said as he began to cough.

"You've been a bad boy, Bernie…"

Bernie looked around frantically, trying to see where the voice had come from. His coughing was becoming more and more difficult. Soon, he could barely breathe at all. "Wait… please…"

"You talk too much, Bernie…"

The air in the alcove was now so thick with smoke that he could barely see at all. His eyes burned from it. He coughed. "I gave you the people that you asked for. We had a deal. I didn't say nothing," he denied, "I mean it… I promised you."

"I didn't say nothing… I mean it… I promised you," the voice mocked. "You are *lying*, Bernie. You talked to your little artist bitch. She saw me with your cripple... so, the little pinch prick had to be eliminated."

"I... I'm sor... ry," Bernie choked out.

The Hat Man growled as he became a solid form and shoved the busker against the wall, "No one even blinked when a few reeking vagrants bit it. They didn't give two shits about the habitual drug addicts offing themselves... but your little artist bitch... suddenly the damned town grew a damned conscience! Articles in newsprint. Headlines splashed everywhere. I told you that I didn't want attention drawn to myself! I've played that tune before Bernie... I've had to stay in the shadows for decades and now because of you and your big... fat... mouth..."

"I... I didn't... think..." Bernie gasped.

"No, you didn't! We both agree on that. But, although I adore your singing voice, I truly do, we just cannot let you continue to share our little secret, now can we?"

Bernie's feet slowly raised off the ground as the Hat Man lifted him by his neck. He flailed against the darkness that had him pinned to the wall. The cigarette dropped from his hand, hit the ground and went out with a sharp sizzle on the rain-soaked cement below.

"Please," he gasped as his eyes bulged; and as he was about to lose consciousness, the Hat Man mocked the aging trumpet player one last time.

"Poor, pathetic, Jazz Man," the demon taunted,

"You really should have taken better care of yourself... don't you know that cigarettes are killers?"

CHAPTER FIFTEEN

Nick made his way into the lobby of Sarah's building where they had invited Wayne and his current girlfriend, Heather, to join them for dinner. He walked toward the elevator. "Evenin' Anthony," he said with a wave.

"Ah, Doctor Williams," the doorman said walking to meet him. I was wondering when you were going to arrive. Ms. Beaumont told me that you were on the way. She's been entertaining tonight."

"Yes, my friend Wayne and his girlfriend."

"No... it was that nice young man from the hospital." Anthony snapped his fingers a few times trying to remember the name, "Ken... Kenny,"

Nick froze for a moment. "What? Kevin?" Nick resolved for him. "Are you sure?"

Anthony stuck his card into the reader of the elevator, "Yup... That's it! She said for you to join them right away."

Nick slowly nodded. "Yes... that is a very good

idea... how long would you say that they were up there now?"

Anthony looked at his watch as the doors started to close. "Oh, probably twenty or twenty-five minutes now."

The doors closed and Nick felt the elevator rise upward as his heart sank. "What the hell is she thinking? This is crazy!" Nick paced side to side impatiently waiting for the doors to open. "C'mon. C'mon."

The doors finally opened outside Sarah's condo. Nick bolted across the hall and knocked on the door. His mind filled with terrible and horrific visions of what might have befallen her. He knocked again. "Open the door, Sarah," he sang tensely under his breath.

Suddenly, the door flew open, and Sarah stood in front of him. "Oh good! Nick's here!" she smiled, jumping into his arms and giving him a big hug. "I don't understand it, he hasn't tried anything," she whispered in his ear. She pulled Nick into the room, "Look, Kevin and I were just finishing up the cheese plate in the kitchen and he brought a nice bottle of Rosa Regale for later."

Nick was very confused. "So, it's going to be a big party tonight? Wayne and Heather are coming too."

"That's not a big party at all, Nick." Sarah called over to Kevin. "Go ahead and head out to the patio, Kevin, Nick and I will be right out with the chicken wings." She pulled Nick next to her, "Watch…"

Kevin slid open the glass door and stepped out onto the patio. Instantly, his head shot from side to side in a frenetic blur.

Sarah's grip on Nick's arm grew tighter. "Oh my God, could this actually be working?"

Nick's level of confusion jumped up three more levels. "What are you talking about?" he asked out of the corner of his mouth.

"I have cloves spread out all over the balcony, they are in the cracks between every board. I even had Chef Pythoud use them as the stems in the marzipan fruit bites on the table there." She pointed to the high-top patio table that sat near the edge of the balcony. "I have it on good authority that cloves help rid you of evil entities."

"Cloves?" Nick questioned, keeping his eyes glued to Kevin's every move.

"Yup."

"Like, the little spice things that my mom would stick into the Christmas ham every year?"

"Yup… now shut up and watch."

They looked on as Kevin shot frantically from one side of the balcony to the other. "Holy Crap! Look at the size of that grill! Six burners? You have an outdoor wet bar and wine cooler? Your TV behind the bar is like three times bigger than mine! Is that a bumper pool table? A freakin' bumper pool table! You've got a firepit?

Geez, this view is amazing!" Kevin surveyed the river from the large patio terrace outside Sarah's condo and ran back up to the doorway. "Hey, Sarah?"

Sarah and Nick took a small step back. They both looked surprised, as nothing was happening to him at all, he was just excited. "Yes, Kevin?" she replied.

"If you ever feel like dumping this doofus, will you give me a serious shot... not for any that stupid boyfriend-girlfriend stuff... just, you know, for the wet bar and the view? I could just live out here on the porch... you wouldn't even know I'm here. This place is awesome! Hey, I'm just gonna grab a beer from the cooler out here. Is that okay? I don't want to dull my senses with the hard stuff... have to keep my dominance as Master of all That is Trivia, once my patsy, Wayne, arrives!"

Sarah laughed nervously, "You got it!" She looked up at Nick, now she was just as confused as he was. "Help me in the kitchen."

Nick followed Sarah as he made his way to the kitchen and kept looking over his shoulder toward Kevin on the porch. He turned to her, "What the hell is going on? We are supposed to be getting together with Wayne and Heather tonight. Now, *Kevin* is here? We said that we needed a plan before we were going to confront him?"

"I know, but Wayne called... he dumped Heather. He has his eyes on a secretary at the precinct now..."

"What? They just met at Martini's last Wednesday?"

"What can I say, your friend is a hoe."

Nick chuckled quietly. She wasn't wrong. Wayne was a great guy. A hell of an officer too… but he would try to bed anything that looked good in a skirt.

"Besides, he said that he would still come over later." Sarah's words drifted off as she looked over her counter to the patio. She watched Kevin hop up on a chair at the high-top table and take a swig of his beer. He reached over to the glass bowl in the center and lifted the lid. "Is this marzipan?" he called back into the condo looking at Sarah. "This is incredible!"

Sarah watched as Kevin grabbed a piece shaped like an orange with a clove sticking into it. He pulled out the clove and held it up to his nose. He turned and looked back at Nick and Sarah in the kitchen, held up the candy and shouted, "Reminds me of my grandma's!" Then he gleefully took a bite.

"I don't get it," Sarah said disappointedly, "that should have made *any* demonic entity reveal itself."

Nick walked into the kitchen and stood next to her as they both stared out at their guest. "Where did you hear about cloves being able to rid you of evil?"

Sarah opened the drawer in front of her and pulled out a ring bound book. It looked to be from the 1950's. The cover was yellowing with age. It had a photo of a kitchen that looked to be heaping with herbs and vegetables. Standing behind the cornucopia was a cherubic, older nun wearing wire rimmed glasses with her arms outstretched. Sarah read, "Schwester Helgas Rezepte für ein dämonenfreies Leben."

"A German Nun's copy of a Betty Crocker Cookbook? That had to have sold at least what... ten... maybe fifteen copies? Is it cursed or something? Found in Hitler's Bunker, perhaps?"

"Stop it. It is rare, there weren't many copies printed at all. But no, it is not cursed. This is Sister Helga's Recipes for a Demon Free Life. Sister Helga Baumgartner worked with the Vatican in the 1950's under Pope Pius XII. Don't let her grandmotherly appearance deceive you. She was part of *La Gilda degli Esorcisti*... one of the only females."

Nick pointed to the cover, "That little old nun performed exorcisms?"

"That little old nun not only performed them but helped to develop new techniques and natural potions in the eradication of malevolent entities."

"That's bad ass... I must admit. But it looks like she was wrong about the whole *clove* thing."

"I know, right. But she was part of La Gilda degli Esorcisti, Nick. Guilda degli Esorcisti... That *has* to count for something!"

"So, maybe there wasn't enough cloves?"

"I have like seven containers of cloves out there! And he touched one of them... he *sniffed* it!"

Kevin held up his beer and called in from the patio, "You guys need help with the chicken wings? I can come in and help!"

"No!" they both shouted.

Sarah smiled anxiously and called back to Kevin, "It's all good. We've got it! Have another beer if you like!"

Kevin looked longingly at the beer fridge, "Oh, you and I are going to be good friends!" Then he raised his bottle to show his appreciation for the ice cold nectar.

She turned to Nick and dipped her head toward the oven, "Grab the chicken wings out of the oven, Sweetie!"

Nick played along, "Sure thing, my little magnolia." He grabbed the oven mitt that was hanging next to the oven and started to open the oven door.

Sarah nodded to Kevin that everything was well in hand and Kevin turned back to face the river as a giant freighter ship went by. She turned to Nick, quietly she informed him, "Look, I have to believe that Aunt Mary kept that book for a reason. Those recipes and notations about the different herbs and exotic spices have to be legit."

"Guilda degli Esorcisti."

"Right!"

Nick pulled the sheet pan of chicken wings out of the oven and set them on the stove top. "Well, something has to be messed up. The clove thing was definitely a bust."

Sarah acknowledged. "That's why, you have a much more powerful recipe in your hands there, Dr. Williams."

Nick raised an eyebrow, "You made mystical chicken wings?"

"No, smart ass. I made them using Templar Oil." She said pointing to a small bottle of oil sitting on the counter.

"Templar Oil?"

Sarah grabbed Sister Helga's Recipe Book and flipped through the pages. "Look," she pointed at the book, "It's a process that she modified from the Knights Templar back in the Crusades. It is supposed to be very powerful... can burn the evil out of a possessed individual *and* anyone anointed with it cannot be possessed again!"

Nick raised his eyebrow again. "The Knights Templar... you better not start babbling about an invisible treasure map hidden on the back of the Declaration of Independence," Nick laughed as he was dishing up the wings onto a platter.

"Nicholas Williams! Seriously? *You* were the one who said that we needed a way to get the Hat Man to reveal himself. Well, this is it. According to Sister Helga, Templar Oil has the same impact as holy water does... except that it is more powerful as it doesn't just evaporate or wiped away easily."

"Wait," Nick realized, "we have to make sure that this Templar Oil doesn't hurt Kevin."

"It doesn't say anything about it hurting the human host."

"I've read enough articles and have seen enough exorcism movies to know that these things don't always end well."

Sarah sighed. "Is it a chance that you are willing to take if it meant the end of the Hat Man?"

Nick bit his bottom lip and took a deep breath. "I guess it is something that we have to do. We cannot let him continue to kill." He reached into the refrigerator and pulled out the ceramic dish of blue cheese dressing and set it in the middle of the wings. "Guess it's now or never."

"Remember to act like everything is normal." Sarah picked up the cheese platter and led the way. "Once more unto the breach, dear friend..."

"Henry V, Act Three, Scene One."

Sarah rolled her eyes as they made their way to the patio. "I thought that Kevin said he was the Master of All that is Trivia."

"It's Shakespeare! Everyone knows Shakespeare!"

"No, Nick... not many people at all know Shakespeare *that* well," she laughed as they made their way onto to porch.

Kevin turned and hopped off his chair as they came to the table. He made his way over to the wet bar. "Can I grab you guys a cold one while I'm over here?"

Sarah put the cheese plate down and turned with her front facing Kevin to grab the wings from Nick. "You know what, yeh, I'll have a beer too."

Nick looked slightly surprised at his girlfriend, "Make it two."

Kevin shot them a double finger point, "You got it!"

"Did you just Isaac Washington us from the Love Boat?" Nick quizzed.

Kevin held up his hands and laughed, "Guilty as charged!" He brought the beers over to the table, "Remember, when I said the marzipan reminded me of my grandma's? Well, she always used to watch that show. So, I couldn't help myself... like I said, Master of All that is Trivia!"

"No question about that!" Nick laughed.

Kevin sat in his chair and reached across the table while Sarah and Nick watched and waited. He grabbed a few pieces of cheese.

"Nick, try the wings, I put some of my family's secret herbs and spices on them."

"Oh really? That sounds phenomenal!" Nick said as convincingly as he could as he grabbed a wing and took a bite. "Mmm, is that a hint of tarragon?"

"Yes, yes, it is," she said, laying on the Southern

Charm.

"Kevin, you really should try one of these," Nick coaxed.

Kevin smiled and shrugged, "Yeh, sure! I'm starving." He reached across the table. "When is Wayne getting here with his Femme du Jour?" he asked as he picked up a wing and started eating.

Sarah's eyes widened. Again , nothing was happening... *nothing.*

Nick shook his head and grimaced, "Well, he's coming stag, I guess. He called Sarah earlier and informed her that he broke up with Heather."

"Already, he just met last week at the bar for Pete's sake. That guy goes through women faster than I go through a taco combo!" Kevin laughed licking his fingers. "Sarah, these wings are dynamite."

Sarah excused herself from the table and slowly backed away toward the patio door. "Nick, look! We forgot the..."

"Napkins!" he said following her inside. "Let me help you with that."

"And plates too, silly us," Sarah added.

Kevin wiped his hands on his pants. "It's okay... I'm good."

"No, no," Nick replied, "We will be right back."

Kevin grabbed another wing. "Seriously though, Sarah, your family recipe is incredible. You should probably get a patent on it," he said taking another bite.

Nick followed Sarah into the kitchen, "Look, I know that you put a lot of faith into Sister Helga... but it's either not working or Kevin isn't possessed by anything other than maybe his ego about how good he is at trivia and veracious appetite."

"He's not our guy.... I'm sorry, Nick, my aunt just wouldn't have collected this item if she didn't have substantial evidence to back it up. Kevin is clean." She looked out to the patio and saw Kevin wiping more chicken grease on his pants. "At least from a demon possession standpoint."

Nick concurred, "Looks like we are back to square one again."

"Hey Sarah!" Kevin called from the patio, "do you have the NFL package set up on your TV out here? Cuz if you do... I might not wait for you to break up with Nick and just move in here tomorrow."

Sarah let out a small sigh of exasperation, "Square one." She picked up a stack of small plates and napkins. "I'm sorry Nick, I really thought we would have exposed the Hat Man. These recipes work, they have to."

Together they walked back out to the patio deck and joined Kevin.

A foul smell hit Nick's nose, "Ugh, the wind must be blowing over from the paper mills."

Kevin chimed in, "Yeh, I promise, I had *nothing* to do with that stench. Speaking of stench... I thought you said that Wayne was coming by?"

"Mighty big talk about Wayne, when he isn't here, little man," Nick jibed back.

"What?" Kevin laughed, "I could take him in a fair fight! And by fair, I mean with both his arms and legs tied together and if he was blindfolded."

They all busted out in hearty laughter. Nick looked at Sarah with a bit of relief in his eyes that his good friend wasn't a part of this nightmare of the Hat Man.

Kevin jumped off his stool and headed to the bar, "I'm grabbing another one... you guys good?"

"I haven't had a chance to have a sip of mine," Sarah informed her de facto bartender for the evening.

"Suit yourself... it's your house!" Kevin smiled as he walked behind the bar.

Sarah's doorbell cut through the pause in the conversation.

"Must be Wayne, I'll get him." Nick got up from the table and walked back into the building. Nick walked up to the door and took a quick look through the peep hole. There was Wayne, standing outside, holding a bottle of dessert wine.

"Welcome to Chateau Beaumont, Officer," Nick said as he opened the door.

Wayne walked in and looked around. "Shit, man... you told me that Sarah's family came from money... you didn't say she had *money*." He gave Nick a spirited elbow to the ribs and handed him the bottle of wine. "So, where's the action at? I know that Kevin and Bryon have to be here already, they are never late when food is involved."

Nick pointed to the patio and walked toward the kitchen. Kevin is out on the patio, I'll just put this in the kitchen for when we bring out dessert after Trivia… oh and Bryon isn't here, it's just the four of us tonight."

Wayne grinned, rubbed his hands together, and headed out to the porch, "Good, makes my challenge easier if I only have to deal with *one* Master of All that is Trivia… not the both of them."

Nick laughed and brought the bottle into the kitchen.

Wayne stepped out on the penthouse patio, "Dang… what's that smell?"

Kevin walked over to the table with a beer in his hand and waving the other behind his backside, already chuckling at the joke he was about to spring, "I already told them; it wasn't me!"

Wayne made it to the high-top and shook his head, "Really, it smells terrible out here."

Sarah apologized, "Sorry, Wayne, sometimes when the wind blows from the direction of the papermills…"

"No… it's…" Wayne's face started to contort from the stench that was bombarding him, "not that… I've lived here long enough to know that smell… this is different... like really strong cheap perfume or bad incense."

Sarah turned and looked over at Wayne. He was searching out the scent. She could see that it was irritating him. Here eyes widened as she came to a frightening realization. "Kevin, can you go give Nick hand in the kitchen?"

"Oh, sure thing! Does he need help making more wings?" Kevin dutifully hopped off his chair and headed inside.

"No, no, but tell him that I need that bottle that I left on the counter... right away."

"You got it!" Kevin said as he quickly went into the building.

Sarah casually placed some wings on her small plate, all the while keeping a watchful eye on Wayne, who was now very visibly agitated, she got up from the table and inched her way toward the patio doors.

Wayne, facing the river, grabbed the edge of the table and gritted his teeth in frustration, "What is that damned stench! It's fucking nauseating" He began to shake the table violently.

Sarah backed her way into the doorway and called to the kitchen, "Nick... I think you better come over here... now!"

Nick looked up from the box of desserts that he was transferring to a serving plate. He saw Sarah at the doorway to the patio and Wayne acting irrationally outside.

Kevin, who was leaning over the counter facing the kitchen was oblivious to what was going on behind him, "Oh yeh, I forgot... Sarah said that she needed the bottle she left on the counter."

Nick realized what was happening, turned, and grabbed the small bottle of Templar Oil. "Stay here!" he commanded to Kevin.

Kevin, who was entranced by the assorted pastries laid out in front of him, continued to lean over the counter and paid little attention to what was going on behind him. "Sure, okay... you don't mind if a have a couple of these now, do you Nick?" He looked around and saw Nick running out of the kitchen. He shrugged. "Guess it's cool then," he said reaching over the counter and picking up a confectionary marvel.

Nick ran to Sarah at the doorway. "It's Wayne?" he stammered in shock.

"Well, there is one way to find out for certain, I guess." Sarah grabbed a wing and called to Wayne over at the table, "Wayne, catch!" she yelled as she threw the wing at him.

"What do you want!" Wayne yelled, instinctively catching the wing. Instantly, he let out a blood curdling scream and dropped to his knees. His hands were smoking and sizzling as the Templar Oil coated them. "You bitch! I will rip your fucking head off!" he said throwing the chicken wing to the patio floor. That is when he saw all the cloves hidden in the cracks of the wood. He looked up at the two of them standing in the doorway. "You think you can stop me from having what I want?"

Kevin, still not turning around as he grabbed another pastry, took a bite, and laughed from kitchen counter, "Geez man! Stop being such a jerk! There's plenty here... besides I'm doing you a favor keeping these empty calories from you!"

Nick glanced over his shoulder and saw that Kevin was not paying any attention to what was going on outside. Then he turned back and watched as the smears of oil on Wayne's clothing smoldered.

Sarah threw another wing at Wayne, hitting him square in the chest. Wayne yelled, pushing it away as another section of his clothing burst into a blue flame. His eyes turned red and sharp, jagged teeth began to appear in his mouth. "It's mine!" it shouted. "You can't have it!"

Kevin called back, thinking that Wayne was talking about the desserts, "Not this one!" He replied picking up another pint-sized dessert, "This one's *all* mine."

"Clearly, we aren't talking to Wayne anymore," Nick said to Sarah as he opened the cruet of Templar Oil. "Let him go now!" Nick demanded.

Kevin dropped the pastry back into the box, "Okay, okay... I'll wait." He got up from the counter

"I hope you guys aren't this way when we're playing trivia." He made his way down the hallway toward the guest bathroom that Sarah had shown him earlier. "I'm gonna take a whiz."

The demonic entity had complete possession of Wayne and it snarled a toothy grin. "Do you think I care what happens to this meat sack? It means nothing to me; I will have another by the end of the night!"

Nick couldn't take any more and threw a stream of Templar Oil from the cruet onto Wayne's torso.

Twisting in agony, as his chest erupted in smoke and flame, he fell forward onto its stomach in a desperate attempt to put the flames out, but it was no use. As he writhed in pain, Nick ran out onto the porch and threw more oil on his back.

A pillar of smoke, cinder and shadows shot up out of Wayne's body and flew over to the far corner of the balcony.

Nick stood his ground, between the entity and his friend laying behind him. As he saw the creature take form, his arm drew back ready to throw the rest of the oil at the creature if it dared come toward them.

The figure of a tall, slender man wearing a top hat began to take shape. "You have stopped nothing, you festering pile of shit," it hissed. "Do you think your little parlor tricks will help you when we next meet?"

Nick looked that the smoke and small blue flames still burning on the creature from the Templar

Oil. "I think we have a good shot. Yes."

The demon cackled, "Good... keep thinking that. Stay overconfident, little feculence, it will make my killing you that much more enjoyable."

"We will stop you," Sarah held firmly as she stepped forward onto the porch.

"Stop me?" the Hat Man taunted, "The entire of your pathetic Scotland Yard could not stop me. Even without my wings and powerful fangs, I kept my genius and the inept constables in Chicago only caught up to my vessel after your so-called World's Fair because he became too grand for his abilities... and as for that rube in Wisconsin, I had long since moved on by the time the sheriff found my handiwork. You seem to think that I am concerned with this infantile dimension. I use it as my plaything, feeding off the fear and misery that it provides me. You pathetic creatures have such deliciously deep wells of fear inside of you. So, no, I will not be going anywhere soon... I've just begun my fun. I have existed long before your civilization even came to fruition. You think that a few trinkets will defeat me? I am the author of bloodlust incarnate. I am the heart of darkness. I..."

"Talk too much," Nick yelled as he flung more oil at the creature, coating its entire front, which burst into flame. The demon shrieked in pain and fell backwards over the railing, plummeting toward River Street below.

Sarah ran up to Wayne, who lay unconscious

on her deck as Nick ran up to the railing to see the creature fall, dissipating into a cloud of cinder, smoke and shadow, then rocket off into the shadows of the night. There was no doubt that they had weakened the Hat Man with the Templar Oil, he couldn't maintain a physical form. But there was also no doubt that he would return, when he was stronger, and they would be facing the menace again.

Carefully, she turned Wayne over, bracing herself for the damage that had been done to him. But there was none. He was groggy, covered with oil, but unharmed.

Nick turned from the railing and went to help Sarah with his friend. "Wayne, can you hear me?"

Wayne's eyes slowly open. "Umm... what the hell am I doing on the floor?" He said lifting himself into a seated position.

Nick put his hand on Wayne's shoulder. "Are you okay?"

Wayne looked at Nick as if he had three heads, "Did I black out or something? Seriously, what happened?"

Nick looked at Wayne, "You don't remember anything that happened?"

"No, man, I hadn't even pre-gamed at the martini bar. Last thing that I remember was marveling at your palace here, Sarah."

Sarah's southern charm accepted the compliment

with a polite, "Aw shucks, that is so very sweet of you to say."

"Lost time," Nick whispered to Sarah, "it's common with possession cases."

Wayne looked even more confused as he got to his feet. He went to dust himself off. Nick and Sarah watched as his hands touched the splotches of oil that were on his chest, and nothing happened. The entity had completely lost its hold over Wayne. "Will somebody tell me what is going on?"

Nick led his friend to the cushioned patio set. "Have a seat, pal."

"I'll go get some towels, to help clean up," Sarah said getting to her feet and going inside.

"Bring some sweet tea as well, Sarah. He's going to need the sugar and tannins." Nick turned to Wayne, "What do you remember?"

Wayne thought through the events of the evening and shook his head, "Nothing, man. I mean it. But I'll tell ya, between you and me... I'm a little worried. I've had some of these black outs before."

"Like, say in the last year?"

Wayne looked at Nick with wonder, "Yeh... just since the beginning of this year. How did you know that? Do you think it is serious, like it would keep me from making detective?"

Nick knew that Wayne was now technically anointed with the Templar Oil, the Hat Man would no longer be able to take possession of him. He comforted his friend, "No, I think you will be just fine," he said patting Wayne on his back.

"You sure? I mean, something like this wouldn't hurt my chances of making detective, right?"

Nick chuckled, knowing that the question of demonic possession would *never* be a part of the detective's exam. "What? Nah, brother... I think you might just be a little tired and maybe had a bout of low blood sugar. Did you eat lunch today?"

Wayne thought, "No and I had a light breakfast too. Yeh, that must be it. Strange though, huh? I mean it came out of nowhere."

"If you are really concerned about it, go to the doctor and get some bloodwork done, just to be sure... but I think you will be just fine."

Sarah walked over with an armful of towels and a big glass of sweet tea. She handed it to Wayne. "And there is plenty more food inside to eat."

"Thanks Sarah," he said taking a huge gulp. "I'm sorry about all the fuss. Your place is really amazing."

Kevin overheard the conversation as he walked out onto the porch, "No way, man! I already called dibs." He looked around at the mess on the porch. "What the heck happened out here?"

"Seagulls," Sarah said as quickly as she thought it. "After you went to the bathroom, Kevin, a whole flock of them swooped in and made a mess of things. I was just going to clean up and move us inside."

Kevin looked at the carnage, "Must have been some pissed off seagulls."

Nick laughed as he helped Wayne to his feet.

Wayne raised the near empty glass of sweet tea to Sarah, "This hit the spot... I'm feeling better already. I can't explain it, but I feel like I just finished the Ruck Course at the Academy. The one that I told you about where you have to carry a guy on your back the entire time."

Nick and Sarah shared a knowing glance.

"Kevin, why don't you and Wayne go inside while Sarah and I clean up out here? You can start setting up the game," Nick said guiding Wayne toward the patio door.

Once the two were inside, Sarah looked at Nick and whispered. "How is he?"

"His is blissfully ignorant of everything that happened."

"He remembers nothing at all? Not any of it?"

"Apparently not, he must have blacked out during all of the times that the Hat Man took over... like I said, it is a common occurrence in possession cases."

Sarah looked inside at the two friends laughing with each other as they set up the trivia game. "Remarkable," she said lifting the table back up into place. "What do you suppose is his flaw that the demon exploited to get to him?"

"I don't know... until he feels that he can open up to me about it, I can only watch and guide."

Kevin placed the last few pieces on the board and sat back onto the couch. "All set to get your butt kicked, Officer Miller?"

Wayne set his glass of sweet tea down on a coaster and stood up, "After I hit the head. Where is the shitter in this castle anyway?"

Kevin pointed. "Down that hall, second door on the right... if it smells bad in there... it was you," he smiled.

Wayne rolled his eyes and took a deep breath, "Thanks for the warning."

CHAPTER SIXTEEN

Nick sat quietly on the park bench next to the fountain in Forsyth Park. The park was full of girl scout troops playing out on the expansive lawn area. He noticed a couple of the troop leaders ducking into the coffee shop next to the fountain, as well, to grab some much-needed liquid energy.

There were a dozen students, who were either taking summer classes at the Art College or trying to get ahead of next semester's curriculum, sketching and drawing various portions of the iconic fountain. And, of course, there were the tourists looking at the monuments and marveling at the natural beauty around them.

They all succumbed to the historic charm of the city eventually.

He was early for his appointment with Josette, but he had to get out of his office and get some fresh air after the events of the past weekend. Plus, he was excited to give Josette the good news about Liam.

A couple walked by holding hands. He was a short, stocky older man, wearing a blue camp shirt, straw fedora and glasses. He looked close to fifty. The woman that he was walking with a was much younger, slender, wearing a light sundress, sunglasses and a large, brimmed hat.

Nick normally wouldn't have paid too much attention to them, but there were two things that struck him about the couple. One, was that the woman was way out of the man's league and, two, he kept yammering on and on about the history of the fountain as if he was a city tour guide himself. He walked a few steps, stopped and turning to the lady, "The fountain was built in 1858."

"Really," the woman dutifully listened as she sipped her drink, thankful for the city's open liquor policy in the historic district.

Then he walked a few more steps, took out his phone to take a picture of the lady with him by the fountain, "It's beautiful, isn't it? Did you know that it isn't even a one of a kind fountain? It was ordered from a catalogue!"

"Amazing," she smiled and nodded along while taking another large sip of her drink.

"The last time the fountain was refurbished was in 1988," the stocky man said with pride.

"Okay, sweetie," The younger woman playfully took his arm in hers. "Let's just walk and enjoy each other's company for a while," she smiled as they walked away. "I want to go down to Bay Street and grab some lunch, okay? There's supposed to be a nice pub down there called The Prime Minister... or something like that... I think you would enjoy it."

Nick's eye caught sight of another couple walking toward him, but this couple had a sparkling blue glow about them and very familiar faces. "Hello, Josette. Hi, Grandpa Joe."

Grandpa Joe led Josette to the bench, and she sat down next to Nick. "This is a very focused soul that you have here, Nicholas. She told me all about her time with her little brother and asked me at least six times on our way here if you had any news for her."

Josette turned to Nick. "I am certain that I asked him many more times than that," she said instinctively turning on the charm. "And I can see where you got your demeanor, doctor. Your grandfather, there, reminds me so much of my own. A remarkable combination of a gruff and rugged man who wasn't afraid of rolling up his sleeves, a loving father, and an upstanding gentleman of the community."

Nick smiled at his grandfather, "He has always been my guide... long before he became my... guide."

Grandpa Joe gave Nick a nod of approval and leaned over to take Josette's hand into his bearlike mitts.

"It was a joy to meet you, young lady." Then he turned and started to walk away, "I will let you two be," he said with a quick wave to his grandson and faded away.

"You have much to say?" Josette said, barely able to contain her exuberance, as she turned to Nick.

Nick smiled and pulled out a packet of papers from his satchel. "Actually, I have found quite a bit on Liam. You will be happy to know that he made quite a life for himself after your passing."

Josette leaned back on the bench, pulled a small handkerchief from her bosom and dabbed the corners of her eyes. "I can't believe that my heart is racing like this, I don't even have one anymore... do I?"

"Not of your time, no."

"And I feel the butterflies as well," she said as her hand touched her stomach. "Tell me every detail, doctor,"

"First, I have something to show you," Nick opened the pages. The first page had a picture of a portrait painted in 1837, he showed it to Josette.

"Goodness me! That's my father! Why on Earth is he wearing a nautical uniform?" she exclaimed.

"Actually, this is Liam. He became quite an accomplished sailor because of you. This was painted in 1837 when he became Admiral of the Navy under President Andrew Jackson."

Josette gasped, "No!"

Nick began to read more, Josette moved closer so

she could look at the printed pages as well. "Lieutenant Edward McCall took command of the Enterprise during a battle in the War of 1812 and appointed Corporal Liam Loughton as second in command. From there he rose rapidly through the ranks of the Navy."

"My goodness… so, he… he had a good life."

Nick looked up from the papers and turned to Josette. "He had an amazing life! He personally knew six presidents! Unfortunately, there is a large gap in information after that. But he did have a family: a loving wife, at least two sons and nine grandchildren."

Josette was elated. To know that her little brother, Liam, was not only safe and sound but successful as well. Her view of the world became much brighter. "Is there more?"

Nick continued on another page, "He was a decorated war hero and skilled naval officer, Admiral Loughton was instrumental on growing and keeping the US Naval Fleet under the command of six different presidents. He retired in 1849, during the retirement ceremony, attended by President Zachary Taylor." Nick pulled out a newspaper clipping recounting the ceremony. "Admiral Loughton acknowledged that the importance of hard work and dedication were impressed on him at a very young age by *his beloved sister, Josette,* who passed away tragically when he was merely eight years old. But not before she had secured him a position as the cabin boy on a fine ship, giving him a lifelong love of the sea."

Josette began to weep with happiness.

Nick reached into the satchel one last time, "I have one last thing to show you."

Josette wiped away the tears and focused her attention. "Good Heavens! There is more?"

Nick showed her a photograph of a very prominent family that currently lived in Savannah.

She looked intently at the photo, pointed and looked at Nick. "My word! There's dad, mum, Liam, and myself! What is this?" she asked in confusion.

"This is a church photo of your great, great, great, great, great, great, grandnephew, Walter Liam Loughton, and his family; wife, Elizabeth: son, Liam: and daughter, Sophia Josette. They live here in Savannah. Your family tree lives on."

Josette, now, began to sob almost uncontrollably with tears of happiness streaming down her face.

Nick was not expecting that strong of a reaction. "Are you okay, Josette?"

The young woman stood up and faced Nick, "Thank you so very much, doctor. I cannot thank you enough for this."

Even in the morning light, Nick could see the pure golden white light that began to glow across the walk behind her.

"Josette," a voice called from the light.

Josette turned and saw her little brother standing

there as if pulled directly from the painting in Nick's hands. She ran to her brother, arms outstretched. "Liam! Dearest Liam!"

"It is time, sweet sister. Time to move on and be at peace," Liam said holding his sister in his arms as the golden white glow surrounded them. A wave of energy cascaded from the spot where they were standing, and they faded away.

Nick sat for a moment on the park bench and marveled at the wonders of the universe that he was now privileged to witness. After a moment, he took a deep breath, gathered his paperwork, and stood up. A hint of the coffee brewing in the nearby shop caught his attention. "Yeh, I could use a cappuccino," he said, smiling to himself.

Later, at the office, Nick went through the files of all those who had been considered opioid deaths. He specifically was looking for the file on Corporal McHugh. Once he found the file, he saw at once what he was looking for. The name of the officer that filled out the report... Officer Wayne Miller.

Nick leaned back in his chair and thought. "I can't believe that I missed that. It was right there in front of me."

Then he recalled the hypnosis session that he had

with Misty, he read through his notes, *"While I am on the phone with the police, just giving them our location, a squad car pulls up with its lights on and an officer comes over to us. He is very nice and consoling. He has everyone back away while he calls for an EMT and more police to secure the area."*

"She was just giving them the location… wait a minute," Nick noted, "Wayne arrived before a dispatch could have been made." He looked at the officers involved with the other reports. Five of them had been filled out by Wayne. Then, he noticed Wayne's badge number, Three Hundred Forty-Two. "Three. Four. Two. For God's sake, Nick, how did you miss that?" he chastised himself.

Grandpa Joe materialized next to the old telescope. "Because you were getting in too deep, son. You were blinded by your obsession and not treating this like anything else of importance in life… with balance and commitment."

"I hate to agree with you, but you're right. It's practically the first thing on every single report!"

"It's okay, Nicholas. You accept, you learn, and you move on. How is your friend, Wayne, doing?"

"Remarkably well," Nick concluded, "he doesn't remember anything."

"Hmm," Grandpa Joe thought, "I had an old army buddy of mine that had something like that. Bad fire fight that he was caught in. He was awarded a medal of valor for his bravery during the battle and though completely unharmed physically and emotionally, he couldn't tell you one thing that happened in that two-day period. He had saved the lives of sixteen other men, but he couldn't tell you how at all. It was all so traumatic that he just blacked out."

"Something like that, yeah, Grandpa Joe."

"Interesting... do you think that he will regain those memories at all?"

"No, not unless he goes under extensive hypnotherapy... but even then, it would have to be very specific."

"Well, that's a good thing. I couldn't imagine going through all that he had to have seen and done knowing that he wasn't in control when it happened."

"It's a blessing and a curse. He is always going to wonder what happened in that missing time. I just hope that he does well on the detective exam, so it gives him something completely different to focus on."

"That's sound advice, Nicholas. That is very good advice."

Nick nodded silently.

"So, during your fight with the demon... I take it that you found a way to weaken him? I mean, I see both you and Sarah made it out unharmed."

Nick got up from his desk and walked over to his grandfather, "We got lucky, got caught with our britches down, as you used to say. But, I think we put quite the hurt on him... but it wasn't even close enough to destroy him."

"So, he'll be back... with one hell of a chip on his shoulder, no doubt."

"No doubt... I must make sure that we are ready for him. Of course, the sooner we find him the better."

"Take the fight to him," Grandpa Joe inferred, "Always a sound strategy."

"Yeh, but I can't go up against him without a plan. I mean it, Grandpa Joe, we got ridiculously lucky up on Sarah's patio. It could have completely gone sideways on us at any moment."

"Well, I was thinking about that. Perhaps, you could use another set of hands," Grandpa Joe concluded.

Nick watched as his grandfather pointed his right finger and placed it on the eye piece end of the telescope. Slowly, he began to push it, swinging the main tube around.

"I've been practicing," he said lifting his left hand and stopping the telescope from spinning.

Nick's mouth dropped open in astonishment. "Yes. Yes, you certainly have!"

Grandpa Joe swung the telescope back to its normal position, "Well, it's not the ultimate goal of manipulating lottery balls... but I'm happy with my progress so far."

"Don't kid around like that! But yes, you should be proud," Nick lauded, "This is a leap into the realm of psycho or telekinesis."

"Psycha-tele what now?"

"Psychokinesis is the ability to have power over matter with one's mind. Technically, this would be more telekinesis, as you are moving objects. And considering that the mind/soul status in synonymous... this is huge!"

"Shucks, Nicholas. I just wanted to see if I could do it."

"But you believed that you could, Grandpa Joe, and you did. That was the key."

"Right, because 'belief is the most powerful force in the universe,' I know. I know."

"Clearly, it has some merit. After all, here you are moving objects at will."

"It's nothing."

"Either way, I'm glad you're here. I was thinking through some things that I wanted to bounce off you. When we made the Hat Man reveal himself and release Wayne, he said some things to us that may help us in the long run."

"Like?"

"He said that our dimension was infantile. What do you make of that?"

"As it sits now, I'm from a different dimension and that dimension has been around infinitely longer than the physical world. Sounds like he is from a different dimension altogether."

Nick went over to his notebook and looked. "According to the predominant theories of Quantum Physics, there are at least eleven dimensions that are mathematically provable. What if the Hat Man was from one of those other dimensions? More importantly, what if we had a way to send him back!"

"I would say that if you did have a way to send him back, that would pretty much take care of everything. But where exactly does one acquire a 'Send a Demon Packing Back to Its Own Dimension' device? Would that be another item in Sarah's collection?"

Nick visualized Volume Forty-Two in his mystical library and smiled. He actually *had* an answer. "No, but I have something that just might work from the ancient texts in my spirit library."

"Okay now, Nicholas, you've lost me again. I'm still wrapping my head around the whole telekinesis thing. A book will send him packing?"

"Not a book... a key."

"A key in a book..."

Nick laughed, "In the ancient writings of the Osirian Necronomicon, there is a passage that, when said correctly, is said to act like a key. It can open a portal to other dimensions."

Grandpa Joe waved his hand with a point of caution. "Wait a minute, now, how do you know that you would be sending him back to the correct dimension? Goodness, Nicholas, you don't want to release that monstrosity on some other poor unsuspecting world. That wouldn't be right at all."

"Fortunately, the writings take care of that... I just need to say the Hat Man's given name within the passage to send him back to the specific dimension that he came from."

"It's not *Hat Man*?"

"That's just what we have been calling him. But if I can get his actual name, the one that he was given, I just have to use it while reciting the portal incantation."

"Okay, then...so, then the question becomes, is there a baby names book for demons?"

Nick smiled, remembering that Sarah had taken a picture of every page of Il Dizionario dei Demoni come trasscritto dal Aurelius Augustinus delle Hippo. "Actually, I can get my hands on something really close that should do the trick."

Grandpa Joe grinned, "In Sarah's collection?"

"Well, in her laptop... I need to give Sarah a call, we *have* to get the name of that demon," Nick said picking up his phone. "And we need to get it fast."

"That's right. Take the fight to him... wait a minute," Grandpa Joe said snapping his fingers. "I found a way that I can be useful! I will start asking around to see if any of the folks on my side of the veil know where he is hiding out. Now that he isn't possessing your friend, he must be on the lamb and looking for a hideout."

Nick nodded. "That is a great idea!" he said while he waited for Sarah to pick up. "Just be careful, we don't know his full potential, we got lucky and caught him off guard. He said that he fed on fear, he didn't specify where that fear had to come from."

Grandpa Joe's eyes squinted a little and the corner of his lip curled upward. "I am in a state of universal harmony and abiding peace, son. Don't you worry about me," winked and faded away.

Nick smiled as he heard Sarah pick up. "Hey, I've been chatting with Grandpa Joe. You and I need to do some detective work in Saint Augustine's book... how soon can we get together?"

Sarah opened her laptop on her dining table and pulled up the photos that she had taken of Saint Augustine's book of demons. She had them on a split screen. Shortly after each page appeared the English translation come up on the right half of the screen.

Nick looked over her shoulder. "Any ideas where to start?"

"Let's do a search for what we already know about the Hat Man."

"I suppose, 'hell dimension' wouldn't narrow it down much."

"Probably not..."

Nick thought a moment, "I guess that feeds on

fear wouldn't help either."

"Not necessarily," Sarah countered, "There are several demons that like to make deals, give the illusion of a fair bet, just to take the person's soul. So, fear is actually a good start." She typed in *feeds on fear*.

The list dwindled down to one thousand eight hundred ninety-eight.

Nick ran his hand through his hair, "Well, it did cut the list down... what about *genius*?"

The list dropped significantly.

"Well, that narrows it down a bit... only one hundred forty-nine of them are described as geniuses," Sarah read.

Nick nodded, "That's good. That's good."

"Ok, what else can we use to narrow down our search?"

"Oh, author! He said he was an author. Let's try that!"

"Down to thirty-one."

"He mentioned that he missed his wings."

Sarah typed in the word *winged* and hit search. "Okay, we are down to twenty-three."

Nick nodded, clapped his hands together and rubbed them, "Okay. Okay. We are getting somewhere." He tried to remember what else the Hat Man said on Sarah's balcony. "Oh... what about smoke and cinder?"

Sarah searched for both. Nothing came up.

"Damn," Nick grumbled.

"Relax, Nick. We will figure this out."

He took a deep breath, "You're right. We will. Do you remember anything else that he said while he was rambling on?"

"Come to think of it, yes," she said as she put in the word *fangs* into the search screen.

Nothing changed.

"Ugh, still twenty-three." But then, he had an idea, "Wait, he said his fangs were powerful... what has a powerful bite?"

"A snake," Sarah said as she gave it a try.

Nothing.

Nick's eyes lit up with a spark of brilliance. He pointed to the keyboard, "Try *winged dog*."

The name "Caacrinolaas" appeared on the screen.

"Bingo," she said, "that's our demon." She read on, "Caacrinolaas: Also known as, Caasimola, Caasimolar, and Glasyalabolas is a High President of Hell. Commander of thirty-six infernal legions."

"Dear God..." Nick muttered.

"He is known to be an author, a genius, and is prone to murder and *inspire* murder. He was worshipped by the Sumerians in 3000 BC and held in contempt by the Israelites of the time. At the height of his power, he held the preferred the form of a winged dog with griffin claws to tear into his enemies."

"Well... it's been over five thousand years since this beast had a strong following... that must be why he is just appearing as a man."

"Thank goodness. I don't want to imagine what we would have to go through if he was at his full strength."

"Very true. But now, at least we have a name. Caacrinolaas. And now we can send this son of a bitch back to whatever hell dimension he is from."

CHAPTER
SEVENTEEN

Nick had his hands jammed into his suit pants. He paced back and forth on the steps as he waited for Sarah outside the museum. He had waited a long time for this exhibit to open and was very excited about sharing it with her. To him, it represented everything that the world around them was. Its vastness and its simplicity. Its seemingly orderly process and its chaos. He could barely contain his excitement.

Soon, Sarah approached, wearing a small black cocktail dress. His heart skipped a beat to see her so glamorous. She gave him a quick kiss on the cheek. "You look excited."

"I am," he replied, "I want to get to the exhibit early, so we can be in the front."

"I thought this was just an art unveiling?"

"It is, but it is so much more."

Sarah looked at him pensively. "This isn't performance art, is it? I mean, I'm all for going to see live theatre and the ballet, but I draw the line at people standing in kiddie pools having chocolate syrup poured over the top of them as a 'symbolic representation of social networking's suffocating nature on the individual' or some other thing."

"How do you really feel?" Nick smiled as he handed the tickets to the usher at the turnstile. "We're here for the Papillon Exhibit."

"Welcome," the ticket taker replied, "Just upstairs on the left-hand side in Gallery G."

Sarah took Nick by the arm as they walked into the museum. "Let me tell you a story from when I was about eight years old. As you can imagine, my father and I spent a lot of time travelling and looking at works of the great masters of art. One time, we went all the way to Chicago, to the Art Museum on Michigan Avenue."

"The Ferris Bueller Museum?"

Sarah shook her head, "Yes, but let me finish."

"Cool..." he said with a smirk.

"Shush... now, we walked in to one of the wings of the museum and saw rows and rows of armor and weaponry that was gilded and decorated all by hand from the fourteenth through seventeenth centuries.

Marvelous, hand-crafted masterpieces. My father looked at me and asked, 'Sarah, is this magnificent?' With wonder in my eyes I, of course, said, 'yes.' To which he agreed and asked, 'why?' I thought a moment and said, 'because it took a remarkable talent to make that,' to which he also agreed."

"I can see that," Nick said as they made their way up to the second floor of the museum, following the signs to the opening of the exhibit.

"Then we walked into the wing the held the paintings of the masters. We marveled at the depth and scale of A Sunday on the Island of La Grande Jatte by Suratt."

"Ooo, the Ferris Bueller painting!"

Sarah rolled her eyes, "Shush. Let me finish."

Nick apologized.

"Anyway, I remember looking at a tear rolling down my father's cheek when I looked up at him. He was overcome with emotion as he asked, 'Sarah, is this remarkable?' and I replied that it was. 'Why?' he continued. I replied, 'Because of the dedication and time that it took,' to which he also agreed."

Nick and Sarah paused a moment standing next to the statue called Bird Girl by Sylvia Shaw Judson as they waited for the rope to drop.

"Then we walked into what was called The Modern Art wing. My father stopped in front of a canvas that was about five feet by seven feet, it was painted entirely purple. In fact, that was the name of the piece, <u>Purple</u>. My father looked at me, took a deep breath and asked me, 'Now, Sarah, is this art?' I thought for a moment, surely, this was a trick question. I mean, we had just looked at truly remarkable, emotionally poignant and thought-inspiring masterworks... now he was asking me if what I was currently looking at was art?"

"Well, what did you say?"

"I said 'no,' and my father asked me, 'why?'... I nervously stammered, 'It's just a rectangle of purple... there's nothing about it that took talent of any kind... it's something that *I* could do in ten minutes... and I'm *eight*!"

Nick nodded his head, "Actually, I can see your point on that."

"Then my father leaned down and whispered in my ear, 'Just because a work might not speak to you, doesn't mean that it won't speak to someone else. Art is subjective. What may mean nothing to you, could make another fill with emotion or give them a sense of escape or wonder.' 'So, it is art,' I said triumphantly... to which my father laughed and patted me on my shoulder, 'Oh no, Sarah, this is garbage... but very, very expensive garbage, which someday, we may be lucky enough to sell... sometimes, there is no accounting for someone's taste.'"

The voice of the curator came over the speaker

system in the museum, "Ladies and gentlemen, welcome! Tonight, we are proud to invite you to see the unveiling of a truly remarkable piece of art in motion."

Sarah shot a look over at Nick.

He patted her on the arm, "Relax, it's *not* a kiddie pool filled with chocolate syrup!"

The curator continued, "For those of you joining us in our Gala room, please step forward and we will check you in. Enjoy the complimentary champagne and hors d'oeuvres while you have a chance to speak to the artist, Miguel Papillon.

It didn't take long before they were checked in and handed a glass of champagne.

The room was massive. There were two dozen tall boy tables draped to the floor in tablecloths for the guests to stand around. Some guests started milling around and wondering what was on the other side of the large black velvet curtain on the fair side of the room.

Sarah smiled and raised her glass, "This is a good start!"

Nick gently clinked their glasses together, "Agreed."

Sarah knew almost everyone there and quietly told Nick grand stories of their exploits. She pointed to one elderly lady in a bright red cocktail dress with a large gold and diamond broach on the upper left of her collar. "That's Minnie Holden, she was Miss Georgia, back in 1955, she outlived nine husbands and is one of my family's most prominent clients." She pointed to a man in his seventies and the young woman standing next to him, "That's Edward and June Hollister... June used to be his maid."

Nick smiled, "Eddie... you old dog," he murmured. He noticed the glowing blue figure of an elderly lady smiling broadly and standing right next to Mr. Hollister. In arm was a small Yorkie with its hair tied up with a bow exposing its eyes, in the other, she was fanning herself with hundred-dollar bills. He could hear the dog growling at the couple. "Mrs. Hollister... the first Mrs. Hollister... she was the one who had the money didn't she? And she had a dog... a yorkie?"

Sarah's eyes widened, "Yes... how did you know that?"

"Just a hunch," Nick said taking a sip of his champagne.

The curator walked in front of the gala crowd and stepped up to the lone microphone by the curtain. "Thank you everyone, thank you. Tonight, we are proud to present to you an exhibit that is a work in progress. The acclaimed artist, Miguel Papillon, has granted our museum the opportunity of a lifetime by installing this exhibit here in Savannah, Georgia!"

The crowd applauded.

"But you aren't here to listen to me! Let's get our guest of honor out here! Let me present to you, the man of the evening, the winner of the Golden Fern for Outstanding Artistic Vision, my friend... Miguel Papillon!"

The curtain lifted slightly and out stepped a modest man in his mid to late forties. His thick glasses and disheveled painter's pants belied the genius underneath. He cautiously stepped up to the microphone, bobbing his head slowly in appreciation of the reception. "Thank you, thank you," he said with an occasional wave to the crowd. "I am very excited to bring this installation to the city of Savannah. I hope it is something that you will enjoy over the next five years as it slowly progresses into its ultimate form. That's right, every time that you come to see the exhibit, it will be different..."

Nick was so engrossed in the presentation that he was unphased by the shimmering blue light behind him. He didn't notice a thing until he felt a tapping on his shoulder.   He turned to look and saw it was Grandpa Joe.

"Nicholas, we found him. Well, my old army sergeant, here, did. Grew up in the swamps of Louisiana and the best damned tracker that I have ever known," Grandpa Joe pointed next to him to a short broad-shouldered man with a two-day beard and a toothpick stuck in the right corner of his mouth. "Nicholas, this here is Sergeant Johnny Morrow."

"Pleasure to meet you, boy," the old Cajun said,

sticking his hand out to shake Nick's hand. Nick instinctively responded and his hand went right through Johnny's. "Egh, sorry, there, kid, old habits."

"It's good to meet you, sir."

"I ain't no sir. I was a sergeant... I worked for a living!" Johnny turned to Nick's grandfather laughing, "Thought you said this kid was smart?"

The artist continued to prattle, "... five years from now, what you see before you, will not be anything like what you see before you tonight... with the flip of a switch, the catastrophic events will slowly and painfully occur..."

Nick looked at Grandpa Joe and Johnny. "That's great, we can get after him tomorrow."

"Look, Nicholas," Grandpa Joe added, "Johnny has to get back to his granddaughter in New Orleans. He did me a favor by coming her to help me find this creature, but we gotta get going... I don't know how much time we are going to have. He may move his lair at any time. We need to strike tonight."

"... with the passing of each week, slowly the message of the installation will become more and more poignant..."

Nick was disappointed, he had been looking forward to this exhibit opening for months... but he understood. There were much bigger things in play. He turned to Sarah, "Hey..."

"Hey?"

"We've got to go."

Sarah looked puzzled, "Go? I thought you wanted to see this?"

"Grandpa Joe and his old army buddy have found the Hat Man. They say he could move at any time. We have to go... now. Gather as much Templar Oil as you can and the Whitechapel Mirror. I have to get my satchel from the office. Can you pick me up there, say in ninety minutes?"

"My God, you're serious... this is going down tonight?"

Nick gritted his teeth. "We may not get another chance."

Sarah chugged the rest of her champagne and set the glass on the table. "Let's do this."

As they quickly left the room, they could here Miguel finish his introduction, "And now, without further ado... I present... Armageddon!"

The sky was cloudy that evening, Nick crouched in the shadows as he waited impatiently for Sarah to get back, while Grandpa Joe stood behind the large oak tree out of site of the old historic mansion.

"At least it's cloudy out, Nicholas, that will make it harder for you and Sarah to be seen," Grandpa Joe concluded, "I'm on a completely different plain of existence, I may glow to you, but to the Hat Man, I'm just another spirit... he won't pay any attention to me."

The wind gently moved through the Spanish moss that hung down from the branches of the large oak trees around them. Nick's heart was pounding from the adrenaline coursing through his veins. He looked at his watch, "Where is she?" His mind raced through the plan, preparing him for the battle that would soon be upon them.

"We got that beast cornered, son. Don't you worry, Johnny used almost every contact that he could leverage to track him down. He's in there."

Nick sighed with relief as he saw Sarah come running over to them from around the back side of the building that housed the fiend.

She crouched down, "The whole building is encircled with Templar Oil. I even hit the windowsills on the first floor as well for extra measure. If anything; it should keep the Hat Man contained, we already know that it burns him... hopefully, it will hold him until we can get rid of him."

"You two go take care of business in there, I will make sure that if he slips out, I will find out where he goes," Grandpa Joe added, "Don't you worry, Nicholas. You have everything you need?"

Nick looked in his satchel and did a quick inventory. "Okay then. Notebook... check. Two more vials of Templar Oil... check. The Whitechapel Mirror...

check. Look's good here."

"And I still have two bottles of oil left as well," Sarah added tapping her pockets on each side.

"Alright then, go get this son of a bitch, Nicholas," Grandpa Joe directed.

Nick and Sarah waited for an approaching car to pass, then they headed toward the back entrance of the mansion.

Nick reached over the top of the gate and unlatched the hook. He opened the gate as slowly as he could, desperately trying to avoid any noise but the rusty hinges weren't completely cooperating with him.

The Hat Man was a creature of supernatural power, legendary in fact, and as such was stronger, could move faster than they ever could, and had the power to possess people; an ability that they had personally witnessed with what had happened to Wayne. It was an ability that the demon had honed over the centuries. It would take everything they that they had studied, every weapon they had, *plus* the element of surprise if they were going to be victorious.

They made their way through the high grass of the overgrown area behind the abandoned mansion and up the staircase to the wrought iron landing outside the door of the servant's kitchen. Nick checked the lock... it was open... clearly, the fiend was not concerned with corporeal enemies, as he wasn't remotely concerned with locking doors.

Once inside, they found the air damp and musty. Nick's mind flashed, this was an incredibly strong memory. The smell of the old building had triggered it, but he couldn't quite place from where.

The cloudy night that had helped them hide outside, worked against them now as it was pitch black inside. Sarah pulled out a small blue filtered penlight and shone it onto the ceiling to light their way toward the large door of the decaying parlor where the demon was residing.

Nick stood on the hinged side of the door, while Sarah stepped across to the handled side, their hearts pounded. If the Hat Man escaped tonight, not only would they most likely be killed in the process, but it was certain that he would go on killing for centuries or even eons more.

Nick reached into his pouch, pulled out his notebook, and opened it as he leaned on the wall. A bead of sweat trailed down his temple. He looked up at Sarah.

She was holding the Whitechapel Mirror in one hand. An artifact, which, if the stories were true would temporarily paralyze the creature.

"Timing on this is everything, one mistake..."

"I know, Nick... I know," she whispered, pulling out a vial of oil from the pocket of her jacket with her other hand.

He had never seen her so determined. She looked

at him with fire in her eyes. "Let's finish this," she stated, flicking her thumb upward to open the vial and handing it to Nick.

Nick found the passage from the Necronomicon that he had transcribed into his leather notebook. Then, he quickly and quietly went over the order. "You open the door. I will throw the vial of oil down in front of us. I will go in and you enter behind me. You need to hold the mirror over my shoulder facing the demon that should stun it long enough for us to open the portal, stay *behind* me.   I will finish reading the passage... and we will send this thing back to his dimension forever."

She nodded. They were ready.

Nick closed his eyes. He could hear his pulse pounding in his ears over the sounds of the creature inside the room. It was now or never.

Nick turned his head and gave a sharp nod to Sarah.

As planned, Sarah swiftly turned the handle of the door and pushed it open.

Nick kicked the door open the rest of the way and threw down a semi-circle of holy oil across the floor between them and the demon forming a mystical barrier that blocked the door.

Sarah followed immediately behind, holding the cross over Nick's shoulder as he began to read the passage from his notebook... they had caught the demon by surprise.

The black visage of the beast writhed in agony as Sarah held the mirror toward it. It seemed the lore had panned out; the creature could not bear to see itself in the visage and was pinioned to the spot.

Nick continued reading as the portal began to appear next to the creature. The room filled with cobalt sparks shooting from one object to another and a mystical cyclone began to swirl through the room.

Nick and Sarah held their ground. Once he finished the passage, there was a blinding flash of blue light and a sound shattering boom from the power of the dimensional gateway being ripped open.

Sarah closed her eyes in time, but Nick was caught off guard. He went to shield his eyes from the light, but when he did, he knocked the Whitechapel Mirror from her hand, it hit the floor just on the other side of the oil barrier shattering the mirror portion, leaving only the old crucifix intact.

The moment it hit the floor the creature, no longer a prisoner to the artifact, was able to roam around the room freely. In an instant, it shot from one side of the room to the other. It went to the window to initiate its escape.

The Hat Man looked back over his shoulder with a toothy smirk as his long bonelike fingers flicked the latch and raised the window up. He began to step outside when his foot hit the Templar Oil barrier that Sarah had placed just moments earlier.

The beast winced in pain, it burned and crackled with a small flame. Enraged, the fiend wheeled around on his assailants and let out a horrifying roar of frustration.

Nick knew that the portal would only stay open for a little while, if they could *not* get the creature into it before it closed, they would most certainly be his latest, but not his last, victims.

The unholy creature shot back and forth around the room avoiding the power of the dimensional gateway. It knew that if they crossed over the barrier of the holy oil, he could easily overpower them. "I have a proposition for you," the Hat Man hissed, "surrender to me now and I will make your deaths quick, perhaps... even painless."

Sarah slowly slipped down behind Nick trying to reach for what was left of the Whitechapel Mirror. She cautiously stretched her hand out toward it while keeping an eye on the beast.

Nick, suddenly remembered his nightmares, pulled Sarah back, and he reached for the artifact.

The creature shot up to them and grabbed Nick by the wrist the moment his hand crossed the line of oil between them. He yanked Nick across the barrier causing Nick's satchel to fall to the floor, spilling some of its contents out into the open. "A noble attempt at chivalry, fool, but chivalry... is dead," he jeered at Nick as he kicked the iron cross across the floor.

Sarah tried to reach for him.

"Sarah, no!" Nick shouted, knowing that it could easily slaughter them both if he crossed the barrier.

The creature stood in front Sarah, his hand around Nick's neck. His confidence was growing. "Hmmm... perhaps I could allow you both to run... I do love the thrill of the chase... it is... delicious," he taunted as his grip tightened on Nick.

The wind in the room was blowing items all around the room now. Sarah had to duck as Nick's notebook flew by her. It even caused a vial of Templar Oil to roll back behind the desk.

"If you hurt him, I swear, I... swear."

"I swear! I swear!" the Hat Man mocked. "I swear... that you will both die!" he cackled. "Do you have an inkling of what I am, you little pinch prick? Of how many souls I have taken over the centuries? You all do *my* bidding. I am the incarnation of carnal thought. I *live* inside each and every one of you!"

The demon was so close to her that she could smell the stench of death and rot wafting from it. It was as if the thousands of souls that the creature had taken over the years were festering within him. "We will not let you escape."

The demon pointed at the broken fragments of the mirror on the floor in front of her and squeezed Nick's neck a little more. He stared directly into Sarah's eyes. "I would thoroughly love to observe how you plan to make that protestation come to fruition," he grinned secure of an inevitable victory.

Nick gasped for air as he tried desperately to hit at the Hat Man. He struck at him with everything that he had in him multiple times, but the demon simply looked at him and smiled with ironic pity.

Nick looked down over the beast's shoulder. His eyes locked on to a strange sight. The vial of Templar Oil that had rolled behind the desk was floating in the air... not flying... floating. Suddenly, there was a large, weathered hand shimmering with an opal-blue hue grabbing the Hat Man on the shoulder.

"I believe that you are counting your chickens a little early, bub," Grandpa Joe said as he threw a vial of Templar Oil in the face of the monster.

The Hat Man shrieked in pain. Writhing in agony, he dropped Nick to the floor, and shoved Grandpa Joe flinging him against the wall.

Nick looked up to see the skin on the creature's face sizzle and burn in the flames.

During the commotion, Sarah grabbed the broken Whitechapel Mirror, doused it in Templar Oil and slid it on the floor toward Nick.

Nick grabbed the mirror and plunged the pointed handle into the chest of the Hat Man. The Hat Man threw Nick across the room as his chest burst into flames. Nick hit the back of his head against the bookcase, causing multiple shelves of old books to tumble upon him as he fell to the floor.

Sarah rush over to Nick while the Hat Man grasped desperately at the mirror, roaring in pain. But every time his hands would touch the relic, the oil burned him. He let out another series of blood curdling cries.

"Nicholas, the portal is closing!" Grandpa Joe pointed out through the cacophony of chaos in the room.

Nick, his eyes still blurry from the knock to his head, tried to convey to Sarah what his grandfather was saying. "Sarah... the portal!"

Sarah looked up and saw the portal dwindling behind the Hat Man. She leapt to her feet and ran at him in a rage. "Smile you son of a bitch!" she screamed as she jumped feet first in the air, kicking the Hat Man square in the chest, and driving the rest of the mirror into the demon's torso.

The Hat Man burst into flames as the Templar Oil coursed through him, he tumbled backwards and fell through the portal. Another series of loud, blinding flashes and he was gone. They had done it. The nightmare was over. They had defeated the demon. They had avenged Misty and saved countless others.

The swirling winds began to subside, and the blue static charges dissipated. Soon, the room returned to a basic and general mess with papers slowly flittering to the ground.

Nick got to his feet rubbing the back of his head. He walked over to Sarah and kissed her. "Really? Quoting Sheriff Brody from Jaws?"

Sarah smiled, "Shut up... It's a classic," and kissed him back.

Nick turned and saw Grandpa Joe getting to his feet.   "How did you know we were in trouble?" Nick asked him.

"Reach into your wallet, son," Grandpa Joe coaxed.

Nick looked puzzled but took out his wallet.

"You still have that silver dollar that I gave you, right? Do you remember what I said to you about that coin?" Nick's grandfather asked as he walked up to him.

Nick pulled out the coin and looked at it, his thoughts flashed back to their last evening together, he remembered the words at that moment as clearly as he had heard them so many years ago, *"I'm not losing it, Nicholas. I'm entrusting it to you. You hold on to that dollar there and I will always be with you."* Nick's eyes teared up; he felt like a kid again.

Sarah looked up at Nick. "I am assuming that we owe Grandpa Joe for that assist. Or is there another otherworldly associate that you know that can levitate vials of Templar Oil hanging around you?"

Grandpa Joe laughed and leaned in to talk into Sarah's ear, "The honor, little lady, was all mine."

Sarah's eyes shot open. "Oh my God! I hear him...

he said, 'the honor, little lady, was all mine' I heard him!'" she relayed to Nick, who looked with endearment at the two most important people in his life meeting for the first time.

Then Grandpa Joe leaned in and whispered something in her ear that Nick couldn't hear.

Sarah turned and smiled in the direction of Nick's grandfather.

The moment was interrupted by the sound of sirens approaching, Grandpa Joe turned to Nick. "I best be on my way... and you two should be as well. I think our little light show here has received a little more attention than we expected. Time to go, Nicholas!" And with that, Grandpa Joe faded away.

The sirens drew closer. "That's our cue," Nick said as he and Sarah headed to the door. He saw his notebook on the floor. Quickly, he grabbed it, "But I better not leave this behind!"

"Or this!" Sarah nodded and bent down to grab the satchel.

They left the old mansion, the same way that they came in, making it across the street and into the park to see the old mansion quickly surrounded by the police.

A crowd of onlookers grew in the square trying to see all the action. Nick and Sarah casually made their way past the mob and walked toward Sarah's car.

She unlocked the trunk, and they began to stow

their equipment in the back.

Closing the trunk, Nick saw a bright opal blue glow next to them.

Grandpa Joe held Misty's arm as the exhausted spirit of the girl looked with anticipation at Nick. "Is it true?" she asked, "Is it over?"

Nick confirmed, "The Hat Man is gone. Sadly, I don't know how I am going to be able to clear your name in regard to everyone thinking that you committed suicide though."

Misty smiled and wiped a tear from her eye. "It's okay, I can deal with it, it may take me some time though."

Nick looked over at Grandpa Joe then back to Misty, "It's alright. We are here for you. The main component that was holding you here has been eliminated... now, it is just a question of making peace with yourself."

Misty nodded. "I can do that. I know I can."

"Thatta girl," Grandpa Joe said, patting Misty on her arm. "A wise young man once told me that if you are self-possessed, you cannot *be* possessed. We have to get you back to being the best you that you can be."

Nick agreed, "A wise young man who learned from his *very* wise grandfather."

Grandpa Joe smiled and began to fade away, "Let's go, Misty. These two have been through a lot tonight."

Sarah looked at her watch, "Hmm, the ice cream

shop is still open," she said flashing her best puppy dog eyes. "My treat?"

Nick laughed and took her by the hand, "That sounds fantastic!"

CHAPTER
EIGHTEEN

It had been three months since the battle with the Hat Man. The leaves on the trees were falling and there was a crispness to the morning air that signaled that Savannah's cooler season had arrived.

Life was moving forward in ways that Nick never thought possible. He had moved out of his apartment on Broughton Street and had moved into Sarah's palatial penthouse condo on the East end of River Street. They would routinely watch the sunrise from the expansive balcony with press pot coffee and bagels before heading off to work.

Sadly, for Kevin, he was *not* invited by Sarah to move in.

Even though it had become abundantly clear that

Sarah didn't need to work for a living, since the events that had transpired, she felt more obligated than ever to make sure the family antique shop stayed on top as one of the best collections in the business. Of course, there was the side business, that she maintained as well. Not only in honor of her late and not-quite-as-crazy-as-everyone-had-thought Aunt Mary but one never knew when one might need that one specialized artifact... in case some other hideous creature rose up to terrorize and cause carnage.

It was hard work cataloguing all the mystical artifacts, but somehow, she made it look easy.

Nick still rode his bike to work every morning; the autumn colors and cool morning made it an enjoyable one. The SCAD students were starting a new year of classes, the tourists were enjoying the open container laws of the historic district. "Nothing like having a Bloody Mary and a good morning stroll," he heard a man say to his wife as he rode by them.

Nick made it to his office and hopped off his bike, took off his helmet, and locked both to the metal pipe that came out of the side of the building. He was filled with excitement about the prospects of the day.

"Good morning, Dr. Williams," Lisa greeted her employer in her cheerful manner as he walked in.

"Good morning to you as well, Lisa." Nick headed to the elevator and stopped. He turned and glanced at Lisa, who was pretending to be busy at her desk. He laughed a little bit and then took the stairs.

Lisa smiled with satisfaction, knowing that all her pestering over the last five months had finally paid off.

Nick entered his office on the third floor and his phone began to ring. Nick put his coat by the door, walked over to this desk, and picked up the phone, "Hey there, Wayne."

"Hey buddy! I did it! I made detective!" Wayne cheered.

Nick couldn't help but smile at the good news for his friend. "That's fantastic, I knew you could do it."

"It was all thanks to you and your help on the psych portion, I'm sure of it. I mean, observation, cataloguing, penal codes... that stuff was a breeze, but getting into the criminals' head... I couldn't have done it without you."

"I was happy to help. Hey, and you don't have to tell me if you don't want to, but any word from the doctor?"

"Actually, yeah... I have to go in for a few more tests, but it looks like I have hypoglycemia."

"Wow... well that explains the blackouts then, eh?"

"Sure does, man. Sure does. I'm just happy that it will be all behind me soon."

"That is really great news. It was a rough year for you."

"You're telling me! Anyway, I'm looking forward to the big night this weekend! Looks like we both have something awesome to celebrate!"

Nick opened his desk drawer and looked inside briefly. "It sure does."

"Alright, we will see you at eight-thirty."

"We?"

Wayne laughed, "Yeh... I'm back with Heather. She's been so supportive during all of this. Can't believe that I was going to let her walk away. Did you know that her family has like five generations of military in it? One of her cousins is even in the FBI Field Office here in Georgia. It's cool if she comes along, right?"

"Of course! The more the merrier."

"Great, man, catch you later," Wayne said hanging up the phone.

Nick ended the call and looked back in the drawer that he had just pulled out. He took a deep breath and felt the butterflies in his stomach. He and Sarah had the most unlikely of meetings, but he couldn't imagine his life without her.

A bright and sparkling opal blue glow bathed the room. It was Grandpa Joe and Governor Gwinnett.

Nick looked at his watch, "I thought that our appointment was at ten?" he asked.

"Oh, it was, it was, Nicholas. It's just that Button, here, had a breakthrough of sorts," Grandpa Joe explained.

"And I just couldn't wait to share it with you, my good man!" Button said as he tapped his cane on the floor with eagerness.

Nick when to his session chair and sat down. He motioned Governor Gwinnett to do the same on the couch, to which Button obliged.

"I'll leave you to be. Catch you later, Nicholas," Grandpa Joe said as he faded away.

"That's fantastic news, Button," Nick started, "what was this breakthrough?"

Gwinnet leaned forward and spoke with a resolve that Nick had not seen in his many meetings with the former Governor. "If I were to retain my animosity toward Lachlan, then I could never be free. He would have power over me... possess me, if you would."

"Go on," Nick encouraged.

"How could I possibly consider myself and my consciousness complete, if I have given over a large part of it to someone else in a futile effort?"

Nick smiled; it was obvious that Button *had* made a breakthrough... but was it enough?

Button continued, "Therefore, for some time now, I have resolved to release that hostility which has bound me to this plane. That, along with my acceptance for my actions against poor George, has made me complete."

Nick stood up and walked to the center of the room. "If that is so, Button, then why are you still here?

If you were complete and at peace, then why have you not joined your lovely wife?"

Button was crestfallen. He knew that Nick was right. If his conscience and conscious were clear, he should have been freed.

Nick looked at Button. "You are a God-fearing man are you not, Governor?"

"As much as any man could be," Button said firmly.

"Then would not your beliefs require you not only to accept your past actions, but atone for them as well?"

"Of course!" And as if a bolt of lightning had struck the statesman. He jumped off the couch and fell to one knee. Leaning his head against his cane, Button began to pray. "Dearest Heavenly Father, I am but a man. My flaws and imperfections are of my own making, and I accept them. It has taken me over two hundred and forty years to do so, but I have, I know it... I believe it. I also accept your everlasting judgment and wisdom regarding these and all matters. Your will be done."

A golden white light began to form around the Founding Father, Nick knew that Button had reached a state of enlightenment... in fact he had in that moment, accepted his shortcomings. It was his beliefs that were holding him back, punishing himself when it was not his place to reserve judgement. It took over two hundred and forty years for him to open himself up to it, but he had.

The light grew and Button got to his feet. He smiled at Nick then looked upward as a sense of completeness filled him. "My Dearest Ann, I am coming home," he said as the light enveloped him, and he disappeared.

The wave of energy filled the office from where Button once stood. Nick smiled secure in his accomplishment and loosened his tie.

"Not a bad start to the day," he thought to himself. "First, Wayne's good news, now this." He looked at the mirror in his office then he reached up and took off his tie. He rolled it up and put it in the drawer of his desk, while taking out a small box, which he put in his jacket pocket. Nick undid the top two buttons of his shirt, looked back into the mirror, and moved his head from side to side. "That's better... much better."

"You're looking much more relaxed, Nicholas," Grandpa Joe said reappearing in the room. "So, tomorrow is the big day, huh?"

Nick turned and smiled, "Tomorrow's the big day. Everyone is going to be there."

"And you asked her father for her hand?"

Nick nodded, "Of course."

"Good, it is the right thing to do. It may seem old fashioned, but it shows her family right away that you know that marrying her also means marrying her family.... wait... he did give you his blessing, didn't he?"

Nick laughed, "Yes, Grandpa Joe. He seemed very excited to have a doctor in the family."

"Wonderful! You got the package from your mother? The one I told you to ask for?"

"Yes, sir. It arrived last week."

"Still eight-thirty, right?"

"Yes, why? Are you worried about being late?"

"Do we have to go over the whole 'outside of space and time' thing again, son?" Grandpa Joe laughed.

Nick rolled his eyes, "Right, you are never late or early, you are..."

"...always where I need to be *when* I need to be there," they finished together.

"See," Grandpa Joe smiled broadly, "Always been a quick study."

The next evening, Nick and Sarah waved at Anthony as they walked into the foyer heading toward the elevator.

"Big gathering tonight, eh?" the doorman asked.

"Oh, just some family and friends coming over for a rooftop cook out. You should come up after your shift."

Nick gave Anthony a wink as he and Sarah got into the elevator. He had already informed him of the surprises in store for Sarah. Anthony would collect the presents from the guests when they arrived and bring them upstairs at the end of his shift. When she was overwhelmed with gifts from her friends, that was when Nick would propose. "Yeah, Anthony, make sure you swing by... when is your shift over again... eight-thirty-ish?"

Anthony smiled, "Why, yes, Doctor Williams, it is."

The elevator doors began to close as Sarah said, "Then it is settled! See you then!"

Nick and Sarah had only a few hours to get ready for the gathering. Judging by the number of RSVPs, it was going to be a very large and fun crowd. Sarah made her way into the kitchen and began the final preparations.

Nick made his way toward the patio terrace to make sure the beer was cold and there was plenty of Jack Daniel's available for her father's beverage of choice... two fingers of Jack, one of water on the rocks. He called it a 'true gentleman's drink.'

The Georgia football game was being televised as well. Everyone knew that at halftime, Nick was going to pop the question. Now, he just hoped that everyone had kept the secret... and that the home team was winning enough that all would be in a jovial mood... especially Mr. Beaumont.

About an hour before the rest of the guests were to arrive, a small group of ladies showed up to make everything perfect. Mabel and the girls, as they referred to themselves, were all friends of Sarah's mother, so when they walked in, it was as though the party had already begun. They finished plating all the platters and brought over multiple bottles of their own special beverage to drink.

"You do know that we have plenty of wine that you can have, right?" Sarah asked.

"Oh, my heavens, no," Mabel, the matron of the group spoke out proudly as she handed Sarah a glass, "This is 'Get the Party Started' juice... it's very special."

Sarah looked at what was painted on the glass and then back to the ladies in the kitchen, "Savannah Sluts?"

They all laughed enthusiastically and replied in unison, with the occasion giggle, "Southern Ladies Up to Something!"

"Does my mother know about this behavior of yours?" Sarah said, trying to be serious, but failing badly.

Another lady in the kitchen piped in, "Darlin', who do you think gave us the acronym! Now drink up!"

Sarah raised her glass and toasted, "To the Savannah...Sluts!"

The ladies all cheered.

Sarah took a sip of the fruitiest, most sugar and alcohol laden beverage that she had ever tasted. "Good, Lord!" she gasped.

"Smooth as a summer breeze and able to knock your britches off in two glasses!"

They all laughed again.

"Seriously, what's in this?" Sarah asked.

"Oh, just some strawberry wine…" Mabel started.

"and cognac!"

"and strawberry moonshine!"

"and more cognac!"

"Oh… and eight tablespoons of Sweet Savannah Orange Blossom Honey," Mabel finished.

Sarah laughed, "You all are going to be blind drunk by the end of the night."

"Well, that will be a new one for us," Mabel said piping the centers of the deviled eggs. "Usually, we are pretty well lit up by the time the party starts!"

"That's right," another lady chimed in, "This isn't our first rodeo, sweetheart."

Sarah shook her head as she put her glass down, "Well, thank you for your help tonight, ladies."

"Oh, child, we are happy to help out! Save us a couple of your mama's world famous fall off the bone ribs though!" Mabel giggled as she took another sip of her party juice.

It wasn't long before the guests started to arrive. Nick did his best tending the grill and keeping an eye on the game. Soon after, he joined Sarah in hosting duties and milled around making sure his guests were having a great time.

Mr. Beaumont, Kevin, and Bryon monopolized the bar seats. Somehow, they kept each other's drinks full and appetizer plates heaping without ever taking their eyes off of the game. Sarah's mother spent most of her time in the kitchen with her friends. Wayne and Heather looked incredibly happy; she was obviously a stabilizing influence on him. And most importantly, Sarah's dad was in great spirits, the 'dawgs' were ahead by twenty-one points near the end of the second quarter.

Nick watched and began to feel the nerves build as he knew what was coming soon. Out of the corner of his eye, he saw Grandpa Joe against the railing and looking out onto the river. Nick grabbed a bottle of beer and walked over to stand next to him.

"She is a beaut' of an old river, eh Nick?" his grandfather said as his grandson walked up next to him.

"Yes, it is, sir, it is a beautiful river."

Grandpa Joe patted Nick on the shoulder, "You ready for this, son? It's a big step. Is she the right one?"

Nick took a swig from his beer. He looked over at Sarah, who was glowing in the light of her hosting duties. He smiled at how everything seemed to be coming together. "Yeh, I'm ready. It is most definitely the right step." Nick looked at his watch. It was almost eight-thirty. Anthony would be bringing the presents at any moment. "Holy Smokes! I'll be right back," he said quickly making his way toward the front door.

He looked through the peep hole and opened the door just as Anthony stepped off the elevator.

It was half-time, so Mr. Beaumont and the football crowd started milling around. Kevin made a beeline for the bathroom, while Bryon went over to the dessert table for more Chatham Artillery Punch. Mr. Beaumont turned and raised his glass of Jack on the Rocks to Nick, then went into the kitchen to gather his wife and the other Southern Ladies in attendance.

Once everyone was gathered on the balcony, Nick and Anthony came around the corner with all the presents. The crowd started singing, "Happy Birthday."

It all took Sarah completely by surprise, which was the point. Nick could see the happiness in her eyes as her mother and the rest of the Southern Ladies gathered around her to present her with her very own wine glass at the end of the song.

Her mother hailed, "Welcome to the Club! Remember, fill it once a day and you will always be happy!"

"...fill it three times a day and you will *really* be happy!" Mabel added.

Nick made his way over to the railing by the outdoor sofa where Sarah and her parents were sitting and stood next to Grandpa Joe. Soon, Sarah was busy opening all the presents from her family and friends. Each one had a special meaning behind it and Sarah cherished the sentiments behind them all. She opened the small box that her father gave her to see a pair of diamond earrings that were owned at one time by Ms. Molly Brown.

"Sarah's eyes widened, "The Unsinkable?"

Mr. Beaumont grinned, "Is there another?"

"Open ours next!" Kevin and Bryon called.

Sarah looked at the presents in front of her, not knowing which one was theirs. Then her eyes spotted what was clearly a hockey stick wrapped, rather sloppily, in gift wrap. She picked it up and smiled apprehensively. "This one?"

The boys nodded, "Open it! Open it!"

The crowd chuckled and murmured.

"Are you sure? I mean... what could it be?" Sarah played along.

"Just open it!" Kevin begged.

Sarah unwrapped the present and sure enough, it was just as she suspected. "A... hockey stick," she said feigning a smile.

The crowd laughed.

"Wait. Wait. Wait," Kevin continued as he walked up to Sarah and her presents. "There's more. Look," he said pointing to the handle.

Sarah looked over the handle of the hockey stick expecting to find an autograph or something perhaps noting a Stanley Cup Championship... but there was nothing. She looked up at Kevin confused.

"No, no... there," he pointed, "on the end."

Sarah turned the stick and saw a small silver cap and latch on the end.

"It's a giant flask! Careful! It's full!"

The rooftop erupted again in laughter.

"We figured that you might need it, you know, spending as much time as you are with Nick nowadays," Bryon jabbed.

"Lord knows, we sure do! Why do you think the bartenders at Martini's know us so well!" Kevin added to even more laughter.

She opened the rest of her presents, from board games to antique broaches, and silk shirts to sofa pillows. She picked up the last box and looked at the card. It was from Anthony, the doorman. Her heart melted, "Anthony, you didn't have to get me anything. You helped plan this surprise tonight, didn't you?"

Anthony humbled nodded, "It was really all Doctor Williams' idea. I just played my part. Life's a stage after all."

Sarah smiled broadly and began to open the present. Inside the box wrapped in red silk was a leather-bound book. She read, "The Complete Works of William Shakespeare." Sarah looked up at the old doorman, "You know that I collect antique books too?"

Anthony shrugged his shoulders, "One tends to pick up on certain clues after seeing someone go through their lives for seven years."

"Thank you, so very much," she said holding the box to her chest. "And thank you to everyone for this wonderful surprise party!"

The crowd cheered once again, with laughter and merriment.

It was now or never. "Well, here we go," Nick said, excusing himself from Grandpa Joe.

"Go get 'em, kid," his grandfather encouraged, "After all, we all gotta die of somethin'."

Nick made his was over to Sarah and coaxed her toward the opening in the middle of the crowd. Putting his arm around her waist, he called out, "Everyone, can I have your attention for a moment. Sarah and I wanted to thank all of you for being here tonight. We both believe in the importance of family and friends. So, it makes tonight that much more wonderful that you are all here."

Sarah smiled and raised her glass, "To family and friends!"

"To family and friends!" the crowd toasted back.

Nick continued, "I know that by now, all of you have heard about how Sarah and I met."

Kevin called out from the bar, "Heard she made quite the impact!"

A large portion of guests in the crowd started to giggle and laugh, while the others groaned.

Kevin slowly slid down behind the bar, grabbing another beer, "Tough crowd."

"Yes, yes, she did. And she still does, every single day." Nick set his beer down and turned to Sarah. "You have shown me so much about myself. So much that I didn't know that was in me. You are my balance, my dearest friend, and my little magnolia…" Nick got down on one knee next to Sarah and the crowd started to cheer.

Tears of joy began to roll down Sarah's cheeks as the crowd continued cheering.

Nick turned to the group to hush them, "Guys… she hasn't said 'yes' yet!"

The group laughed but quieted down.

He looked up at Sarah and presented her with the engagement ring that Grandpa Joe had presented to his grandmother. "Sarah, will…"

"Yes!" she shouted with joy, flinging her arms around him as he stood up next to her.

They held each other and kissed in an embrace that felt like both an eternity and no time at all. In that moment, Nick understood the feeling that Grandpa Joe must have 'being outside of time and space.' To him, nothing existed in the universe except the two of them locked in that embrace.

He placed the ring on Sarah's finger and the roof top party erupted again in cheers and applause.

Grandpa Joe was clapping and cheering louder than anyone else on the rooftop patio, but only his grandson could hear him.

The party continued until almost midnight, most importantly for Mr. Beaumont, his *Dawgs* had won quite handily. Kevin and Bryon made great friends with the Southern Ladies in the kitchen and parlayed their new friendships into two large bags of Tupperware containers full of food from the evening. Wayne and Heather made sure to make plans with Nick and Sarah for the next weekend.

"Heather's family has a quiet little boat house over on Tybee Island. It will be great to just get away... without having to be completely isolated," Wayne informed them.

"Definitely," Heather added, "I have to have my Wi-Fi!"

Sarah and Nick looked forward to the quiet weekend of fishing and relaxation.

One by one the partiers started to leave. The Southern Ladies had everything cleaned up, leftovers boxed and labeled and in their respective places in the freezer or refrigerator. Soon, it was just Grandpa Joe, Nick and Sarah leaning on the railing and looking out into the night sky.

Sarah turned to Nick, "I'm kind of sad."

"What? Why?"

"I wish that your Grandpa Joe could have been here tonight."

Nick smiled guiltily.

"He's standing right next to me, isn't he," she said

playfully pushing him.

Grandpa Joe leaned over to Sarah and talked into her ear, "Welcome to the family, little lady."

Nick smiled and lifted Sarah's hand. The princess cut diamond sparkled in the moonlight. "This was my grandmother's ring."

Grandpa Joe put his arm around her, "And now, it's yours. You two make for a fine couple. A fine couple, indeed!"

Sarah closed her eyes, her heart fluttered as she heard his kind words, and she felt a chill wrap around her. "So, this is what it is going to be like for the rest of our lives, Doctor Williams? Always having a spiritual bodyguard watching us?"

Nick laughed, "No, he's not here all the time. He exists outside of time and space." Nick reached into his wallet and pulled out the old Peace Dollar that his grandfather gave him as a child. "He gave me this as a little boy, it helps keep us connected."

Sarah looked down at her spectacular engagement ring. "And now, I am connected too." It was comforting to have such acceptance in one's life, it was also rare, and she knew it. "Thank you, Grandpa Joe," she smiled.

Grandpa Joe took a step back and took Sarah's hand and placed it in Nick's. The chill faded next to the sensation of his massive paws wrapping around their combined hands.

She looked at Nick and Nick nodded with reassurance. She looked up and through the beams of moonlight, she could faintly make out the image of Nick's grandfather standing before them.

He leaned in again, "Now, little lady, I need you to promise me that you will keep an eye on him. He has a tendency to go *Ahab* now and then. Keep him balanced."

Sarah took a deep breath, "I will, I promise."

"Good, that's all I will needed to hear," Grandpa Joe replied, squeezing their clasped hands a little tighter, then Grandpa Joe faded away.

Nick and Sarah made their way inside from the patio. Nick stopped by the sliding door, and she made her way to the bedroom.

"I hope that my family and friends weren't too much for you tonight," Sarah called as she walked into the bedroom.

"Not at all," he called back while he shut and locked the patio doors. "They are a blast! Can't wait to see what happens at Thanksgiving when my mom and dad come down to visit... I don't think the General will know what to do with the SLUTS."

"Should be a wonderful time," she replied getting changed into something more comfortable, "We are still going to watch a creepy movie, right?"

Nick walked into the kitchen; it was spotless. It was obvious that it wasn't the Southern Ladies' first party. "You bet, and I have a great one picked out too! You want some popcorn?"

"What good is a creepy movie without popcorn?" Sarah called back.

Nick chuckled and threw a bag of popcorn into the microwave. "Three minutes!" he called back to her. "You want a soda or a beer?"

"Umm... beer!"

Nick smiled. How lucky was he to get a woman like this? Then he popped off his shoes and loosened his tie.

Sarah came out of the bedroom wearing her long flannel nightshirt from Victoria's, she had her hair up in a ponytail, and grabbed the micro-fleece blanket. She loved it, because it was so soft and cozy.

"Wow," he said looking at his fiancé. The only real light in the room was coming from the fireplace and the dimmed light in the kitchen. Sarah took his breath away.

Sarah blushed, "Oh c'mon, now... you've seen me in... well far less than this before."

Nick smiled, "Yeh, but now, you are my fiancé!" He walked to the front door and opened it. He smiled to himself, "Life could not be going better."

Then, he tied his tie around the doorknob, closed it, locked the door and set the alarm. "You better be paying attention, Grandpa Joe," he chuckled to himself.

Sarah jumped onto the couch and opened the

blanket. "So, what monstrous piece of cinematic horror are we going to watch tonight?"

Nick made his way back to the kitchen and poured the popcorn into a bowl. "I have chosen one of the scariest movies of all time!"

"The Shining?"

"Nope," he said as he grabbed some napkins, the bowl of popcorn and beers.

"Bram Stoker's Dracula?"

"No, but Keanu Reeves was surprisingly terrifying in that movie," he replied bringing everything to the coffee table.

Sarah leaned forward to give Nick a kiss, "Texas Chainsaw Massacre?"

"Nope," he said giving her a quick kiss and turning on the television. "Tonight's feature is so shocking, so brutal, so horrific that it caused a number of people to cover their eyes and even walk out during the film!"

"Rosemary's Baby!"

Nick laughed as he sat down on the couch and snuggled close to his new fiancé under the blanket. "Rosemary's Baby might as well be an episode of The Antiques Road Show compared to tonight's creeptastic feature… the 1995 cult classic, Showgirls!

OTHER WORKS
BY THE AUTHOR

(Non-Fiction/Educational)
Einstein, Quantum Theory, and the Pursuit of the
Paranormal: How Science & Belief Relate to Human
Consciousness & Paranormal Investigation

The Psychic Paradox: The Elusive Balance
Between Belief & Skepticism

(Fiction/Paranormal Adventure)
Ushabti: Eternal Servants of the God King

Made in the USA
Columbia, SC
10 September 2024

41487303R00173